I0551909

Typewriter Pub, an imprint of Blvnp Incorporated
A Nevada Corporation
1887 Whitney Mesa DR #2002
Henderson, NV 89014
www.typewriterpub.com/info@typewriterpub.com

ISBN: 978-1-64434-080-6

DISCLAIMER
This book is a work of fiction. The characters, incidents, and dialogue are drawn from the author's imagination and are not to be construed as real. While references might be made to actual historical events or existing locations, the names, characters, places, and incidents are either products of the author's imagination or are used fictitiously, and any resemblance to actual persons living or dead, business establishments, events or locales is entirely coincidental.

PSYCHO BILLIONAIRE

KASHMIRA KAMAT

PSYCHO BILLIONAIRE

KASHMIRA KAMAT

To my grandma, Madhuri,
and my late grandpa, Chandrakant Satam,
for encouraging me to keep writing.

PART ONE

CHAPTER ONE

KIARA

The first time I ever saw him was during a long rainy night. The clock ticked 11 PM, which was cutting close to the restaurant closing time. Since it was a weekday, the restaurant barely had any customers.

I worked at a small Chinese restaurant called *Sea Dragon,* where we served the best chicken dumplings and roast egg rolls in town—at least that's what the restaurant was popular for, and people loved visiting here all the time.

My coworker, Kathy, had left early tonight because she had a date. She had requested me to cover for her, begging me with her puppy eyes, and I eventually gave in since Kathy usually did favors for me too.

Thus, I was left me alone with Diego who seemed to be mopping a puddle of Coke that a kid had spilled a few minutes back off the floor. He gave me a tired smile, a smile that indicated the impending doom of Friday, knowing full well that it was going to be hella crowded. We barely had time to breathe on a weekend.

We were almost done cleaning all the tables when suddenly, Sam, the chef walked out of the kitchen frantically. Worry was written all over his face. He had never seemed so agitated before, so this was clearly something serious.

"What's wrong, Sam?" I inquired.

"It's my daughter," he replied. "My wife was telling me on the phone that Lily is being rushed to the hospital because she's running a high fever. I . . . I need to go."

"You can't!" Diego interrupted. "It's still an hour before closing. What if there's another customer?" He threw me a look.

"Can't you guys just manage for one hour? Please." Sam's pleading eyes turned towards me. "I need to be with my daughter."

I nodded. "We will manage." I placed my hand on his back, giving it a reassuring pat. "You can go."

"What? Are you nuts?" Diego shrieked. "If Manager Jeff finds out, we are going to get our asses handed back to us. And we could get fired!"

"Jeff doesn't need to know," I said. "It's just one hour. No one's going to walk in at this time"

Diego sighed and resumed his work. His face was going red. It looked like he was going to burst a vein or two. Sam packed his stuff and stormed out of the door, thanking me for the millionth time.

I watched from the window as he settled into his old Honda Civic and pulled out of the parking lot.

Fifteen minutes after Sam left, the little restaurant bell dinged, indicating there was a customer. I knew that if it was just one person or perhaps a couple, I could manage, but in walked three men in suits and occupied a table near the window. One of them was Asian, the other was a lanky redhead, and the third, by the window, looked younger than the two.

I approached their table with a smile, and they probably noticed I didn't have a menu card in my hand.

"Gentlemen, actually we closed early tonight because the chef had to leave due to an emergency. We wouldn't be able to serve anything at the moment," I said. "I apologize."

"Maybe you haven't noticed, but the weather's bad outside, and there aren't many restaurants in this area, and most of them are

3

closed," the attractive Asian explained. "Isn't there anything you can serve us?"

"Chicken fried rice and Wonton soup," I suggested. "That's the best I can make."

The group of men agreed to the suggestion. Feeling motivated to become the evening's chef for once; I rushed back into the kitchen, tied the apron around my waist, and began dicing the veggies.

Diego was nowhere in sight, probably sulking in the staff room at the back, having wanted nothing to do with my little adventure of serving the customers in the restaurant without a chef. He clearly did not trust my cooking skills.

I, for one, had always been observant of what Sam cooked and had tried his recipes at home a few times, and it had turned out good. Although I just knew a few things off the menu, it was enough to serve someone during desperate times like these.

A few minutes later, I served them their dinner. "Enjoy your meal," I said and resumed my work.

I noticed another man seated alone a few booths down. Diego had served him coffee and turned the *"Open"* sign to *"Closed"*

I could feel a pair of eyes boring into my back as I wiped the counter with a rag. I turned to look, and the young man from the trio was staring at me. He smiled, so I smiled back at him and looked away.

Something about his attitude gave me the creeps. I didn't dress sexy because I appreciated predators staring at my ass. It was part of my job. They told me putting on makeup usually earned a lot of tips, and yes, my coworkers were right. I knew it was appealing to some men to see women serving around dressed in a Chinese *Qipao*, and I received more compliments for it, but some men were downright pervy. That was what bothered me about this job.

4

The three men seemed to be enjoying the meal, and when it was time to pay, one of the men pushed his American Express card towards me, along with numerous hundred dollar bills.

"You're pretty good at cooking for someone who doesn't work as a chef," the dark-haired man said.

"Thanks," I said with a smile and then noticed the tip he had given me.

Four hundred dollars as tip? Either he hadn't noticed how much he'd given me or he was totally insane. The two men stared at him incredulously, and my jaw was probably on the floor too.

"It's for you. Don't be so surprised," he added.

"Are you sure?"

"Of course," he said.

A few seconds later, I gained my composure, and I knew that my face had lit up by then.

"Thank you so much, sir. I really appreciate it."

I was desperate, alright. I had bills to pay, my father's debts to clear, and a whole bag filled with responsibilities. It didn't help that my salary wasn't much, so the tips helped me a lot.

I pushed the money in my pocket and went as far as to see the customers out of the door as a polite gesture for their generosity.

After the coffee-drinking customer had paid and walked out, Diego and I were left to close the restaurant. He stayed at the cash counter to settle the bills while I took the trash out of the back door.

The storm had come to a halt. I placed some leftover fish and water for the stray cat that I had been feeding for over the past few months and started to make my way back inside the restaurant when a strong hand reached for the doorknob first and slammed the door shut.

I looked up to see who it was. The darkness made it quite difficult, but a flash of lightning allowed me to see that it was the same man as before. The man who'd generously tipped me.

I fidgeted. "Do you need anything?"

He straightened his blazer jacket and turned to look at his watch and smiled at me. "I can give you an extra two hundred," he suggested, smiling coyly. "What do you say?"

"I don't understand."

He sighed, took my hand in his, and placed it on the crotch of his pants, rubbing on it slightly, and groaned.

"I have my car parked just around the parking lot. We'll make it quick."

I snatched my hand out of his grasp, feeling disgusted. "I'm not a whore."

"Oh c'mon. I saw how you were smiling at me," he said as if that explained anything.

"I smile at all my customers. It doesn't mean anything." My voice was shaky by now.

"Just a quick fuck. You can do some exceptions for extra tips, right?"

I reached for my pocket and thrust the dollar bills in his face. "Here. I don't need your money. Now, move out of my way."

I should have known he was one of those creepy men who lured women by showing them the power of money. I shouldn't even have accepted such a hefty tip.

Stupid. Stupid. Stupid.

He let go of the door handle, so I opened the door and started walking in when he grabbed me out of nowhere, slammed the door, and locked it behind him. Next, he grabbed me and pushed me against the wall, ripping the top button off the dress.

I struggled, screaming for someone to help me when he covered my mouth with his palm. I heard my own muffled cries over the sound of thunder. I tried to knee his groin, and I may have scratched his cheek because it was now bleeding.

I smacked him, and he smacked me hard in return, muttering, *"stupid bitch"* under his breath. I was resisting so hard, but

I felt like I was going to lose the fight. I had this gut feeling that something bad was going to happen.

I realized this was the end; an ugly one where I would probably end up sexually assaulted and dead somewhere near the dumpster. They said you should never beg for mercy at the person causing an assault because begging usually fed their fantasy and made their experience even more fun, but I wasn't even in the state to think of all that.

I continued to repeat the words *"please"*. My dress was tattered and dirty from struggling on the ground. He had my wrists pinned down. His knee was nudging between my thighs as his hand made its way towards my panties when suddenly, he stopped.

I was brawling, trying to pull myself to a sitting position, covering myself and I dared to look towards him to see what had stopped the assault.

A man was standing in the alley. I couldn't see his face properly, but at that moment, I knew that he was my knight in shining armor.

CHAPTER TWO

The thunder rumbled through the clouds as he charged forward and threw one hard punch towards the man who was straddling me. I remained crouched on the ground as the scene unfolded before me. The stranger continued to pummel the assaulter.

The man tried to hit the stranger but missed every time. It seemed like he was no match for the person who was trying to save me. By the stranger's smooth moves, I had the impression that he knew some kind of kung-fu or karate or some other self-defense techniques.

I heard another bone-cracking punch, and the stranger literally pounded his head on the wall until the man's eyes rolled back and his body slid down towards the ground unconsciously.

I wondered if he was dead, and a part of me wished he was. I watched the stranger's eyes land on me, his confident strides approaching as I crouched on the ground.

He raised his hand towards me. "Can you stand up?"

I tried to pull myself into a standing position but winced. The man didn't wait; he put his right arm around my shoulders and the other under my knees as he carried me in his arms and walked through the kitchen backdoor and into the restaurant.

He placed me on the island counter and pulled out his cell phone.

"I'm going to call the police and an ambulance," he informed me. "Can you explain everything that happened?"

I bit my bottom lip. "I can't be admitted to a hospital. I'm fine."

I couldn't afford being admitted there. I didn't have the money.

"Let me get this straight. You were almost raped a moment ago. You're obviously hurt, but you don't want to get a medical checkup? Do I want to know the reason why?"

"It's personal," I explained.

He sighed, muttered something under his breath and said, "I have a first-aid kit in my car. I'll go get it. Do you think you can wait for me here until then?"

I reached for the corner of his shirt. "Don't leave me alone."

And for the first time, I noticed his stormy blue eyes, almost like gems looking at me with something like sympathy.

"The man's lying out there, cold. He's unconscious; I made sure of it. I'll be back in less than one minute. I promise."

I nodded reluctantly. As promised, the stranger was back beside me in a flash. He placed a small first-aid kit on the table and covered my shoulders with his jacket. I had been so caught up in the moment that I didn't even realize that my dress was almost torn in the front, and my bra was practically visible. I pulled the jacket close to me and zipped it up.

He brought a clean bowl of water, soaked a rag in it, and cleaned the wound on my knees and the bruise around my neck. He cleaned the wounds with precision like he had done this a lot of times before.

"This is going to hurt a little," he warned me before applying an ointment over the area. The bleeding had stopped so he covered it with a Band-Aid.

While he was busy treating my wounds, I had a good look at him. He had dark raven hair with wavy texture and eyes the color

9

of gunmetal blue. He was really tall and well-built with defined cheekbones and a chiseled jawline. His face was serious like he never smiled or joked very often.

Then it struck me. He was the same customer who had been served coffee by Diego. I wondered how he had found us. If he hadn't been there, I didn't even want to think what would have been the situation. I had short glimpses of a yellow tape strung in the alley, with my body stashed somewhere, naked.

I shuddered at the thought, and the man must have noticed it because he placed his hand on my shoulder. "Hey, it's okay now. You're safe with me."

Tears streamed down my face without me even realizing it. "Thank you so much for what you did back there. If you hadn't found me, I don't know what could have—"

He placed his finger on my lips. "Hush now. It's over. I will make sure that bastard goes to jail for this. We can't undo what's already been done, but what you can do right now is forget about this incident and move forward."

I nodded in agreement. I had always despised men—my father was one reason why, along with some of my failed relationships. I knew that men wanted only one thing from any woman, and that love did not exist. I hadn't met one man in my life who hadn't tried to get his hand under my skirt. But right now, even when I'd been open, the stranger hadn't even looked that way, so I guessed there were some exceptions.

I turned alert when I heard a car pull up into the parking lot, and I sat up straighter. A man walked in. He was also attractive and tall, but maybe just a few inches shorter than the knight. He had chestnut-brown hair, and eyes the color of dark chocolate.

When he looked at me, he passed me a nervous smile. "I'm Dr. Vincent, and I'm . . ."

"Well, you're not technically a doctor yet," the stranger interrupted. "A medical student would be a more suitable term."

Vincent threw him a look. "Well, he says that and yet calls me even when he's got something as mild as a headache."

I glanced towards the stranger. He had promised no doctors.

"Relax. Think of Vincent as a family doctor. He won't betray any information that you may not want to disclose, so rest assured your privacy is safe."

Dr. Vincent was a nice man; he smiled a few times, unlike the stranger who didn't seem to take jokes that well, the doctor made me feel comfortable which was what made me open up and tell him everything that had happened.

"What's your name?" Dr. Vincent asked me after a thorough checkup.

"Kiara," I responded.

"Kiara, it seems like your wounds aren't deep, so you should be fine in a few days. I suggest you take some medicines that I'm going to prescribe you. Do you live around here?"

"Yes, just a few blocks away."

"Good," Dr. Vincent said and then pointed at the stranger. "He's going to drop you home tonight."

"Thank you," I said, looking at both of them.

"You're welcome," Dr. Vincent said and then checked his watch. "It's getting late. Jasper, you should take her back home."

So the knight in shining armor's name was Jasper.

The doctor left, and we waited until the police came in and arrested the man lying in the alley. I had bruise marks on my body that proved it was an assault, but as a formality, they told me I had to come down to the station to give a proper statement, and I told them I would since I had no other choice.

Jasper assured them that he would make sure I was okay and that he would bring me to the station himself. When the police and the medics left, Jasper insisted that he drive me home. I didn't protest and let him guide me to his car, which was some sleek sports model.

11

I slid into the passenger seat and practically melted into the soft leather. I sneaked a glance towards him. I could tell from the way he was dressed up and the glimmering Rolex on his wrist that he was a rich man.

Ten minutes later, he was parked outside my house—a rundown one-story home with creaking floorboards, a permanent leak in the ceiling, and an old quilt for a curtain.

The neighborhood wasn't exactly *Beverly Hills* either and was infested mostly by druggies, gangbangers, and prostitutes. Not a very friendly place to live in. I could almost imagine some of the neighbors peeking out of their windows to see why a posh car was parked outside our driveway. Jasper's car stood out in this neighborhood like a sore thumb.

Jasper glanced at the old house then back at me, his gaze unwavering.

"Is this where you live?" he asked me, and I noticed how polite his tone was. It wasn't the usual mocking tone that some people used with me when they saw where I lived.

"Yes," I said. "Not exactly Buckingham Palace, is it?"

Jasper laughed. That was the first time I ever saw him laugh like that since we met. Casually, he raised his arm towards me and brushed the hair away from my face, and his fingers reached for my hand where he caressed my wrist. I knew at once that he had seen the marks that I thought I had carefully hidden.

"These marks on your wrist, they don't seem like they have been inflicted by that bastard in the alley. They look old," he pointed out. "You want to talk about it?"

I glanced out of the window. When I didn't say a word, he continued. "How old are you?"

"Twenty-three," I answered.

"You're legally old enough to leave this goddamn place. Why are you still here?"

"Because my mom needs me," I responded.

Jasper nodded and reached for his glove compartment. He retrieved a silver card out of a rectangular box and handed it to me. "If you ever find yourself in a similar situation, if you need help, do not hesitate to call me, Ms. Reeves."

"Thank you for everything that you've done for me today." I was genuinely touched by his gesture of going out of his way to make me feel alright. "And it's alright if you call me Kiara."

"Goodnight, Kiara." I liked how my name sounded on his lips. He gave each syllable a meaning, making it sound beautiful.

Like the true gentleman that he was, he waited until I walked to my door, and only after I stepped inside, did his car drive away.

He had addressed me as Ms. Reeves just a while ago before I told him that it was fine to use my first name. During any of our previous conversations, I couldn't recall telling him my last name, so how had he known? I tried to think hard, but it didn't make sense. Maybe my mind was foggy after today's incident, I probably slipped my full name without realizing it, and Jasper seemed like someone smart enough to remember the smallest of details.

"Who was that man, Kiara?" Mom asked me as I unzipped out of the jacket and realized I hadn't returned it back to him. "And what the hell happened to your face?"

I sneaked a glance towards the small table by the kitchen. Mom placed a reassuring hand on my shoulder. "If you're looking for your daddy, he isn't home. Don't worry."

I sighed, my feelings suddenly elevated. "I'm going upstairs to my room."

I didn't want to stress Mom by talking about what went down today. She was already going through enough.

I went back to my room upstairs and filled the entire tub with warm water. I was careful with the jacket Jasper had given me. I hung it inside my closet before stripping off the already ruined *Qipao* and sank into the tub. My entire body ached as I made

13

contact with the water, but it helped me soothe and forget all the vile things that had occurred today.

I walked out of the steaming bathroom a few minutes later, blow-dried my hair, and lay down on the bed. Exhaustion claimed my body as I drifted off, but then I had a dream. More like a nightmare. I was yet again in the alley, fighting off the man. It all played out like a videotape, and this time Jasper wasn't there to help me. I tossed and turned in my bed until my eyes flew open, and I realized where I was.

Safe. In my room.

Acting on reflex, I walked to my old closet and pulled out Jasper's jacket. I slept that night, snugging it close to myself.

It smelled exactly like him; an intoxicating scent of his perfume and a hint of his body scent. I buried my face into it and anyone would have pegged my behavior as creepy, but I didn't care. His jacket made me feel safe, and it helped me sleep peacefully that night.

CHAPTER THREE

I returned to work two days later and explained to the restaurant manager my injuries. Jeff was shocked and was polite enough to ask me if I still wanted a few days off. I declined his offer because I needed the extra money I made through tips.

Since my green dress was torn, I had to wear my red one, which was even more daring. Jeff also informed me that a tall, handsome man had come to the restaurant one night and asked about me. My heart did a quick somersault since I knew who it was.

When Kathy found out what had happened, she enveloped me in a hug and apologized for leaving Diego and me alone that night. She seemed genuinely embarrassed, and I didn't want to make her feel any guiltier, so I told her it wasn't her fault and that she wouldn't have known something like that would happen.

"Kiara, can you take the order for table number five?" Diego asked me, his hands full with serving plates.

"Sure thing," I said, picking up the iPad. I glanced at the table and was shocked to see who it was . . .

Jasper.

I stood glued to the spot near the kitchen area, drinking him in. Unlike the other day, Jasper was dressed in casuals—dark navy polo t-shirt over khaki trousers with a five o'clock shadow on his jaw. He looked otherworldly, totally impeccable. He was looking around, and then he called Kathy. I saw him speak to her. She nodded her head and made her way towards me.

Kathy was grinning by the time she walked into the kitchen and grasped my hand.

"Who's that hot guy? And how does he know your name?"

I could feel my cheeks catching fire. "He's the man who saved me that day," I said proudly.

"He's so gorgeous, Kiara. He's too damn perfect!" I could already feel her mouth drooling. "And he's asking for you. Don't waste your time standing here and just go." She literally pushed me towards the floor.

I stumbled and walked into the dining area. Jasper noticed me at once and passed me his infectious smile.

"Welcome back, sir," I greeted him. "Would you like to order something?"

He chuckled. "That's the thing, Kiara Reeves, I'm not here to order anything. In fact, I'm far from hungry. I just want to talk to you." He placed his elbow on the table.

He wanted to talk to me?

Before I could answer that question, he asked, "What time do you get off work?"

"About an hour from now," I answered.

Jasper nodded and flipped open the menu card. "I'll wait. And while I wait, I'll order for some Chow Mein."

True to his words, he waited. I noticed his electrifying blue eyes watching me, unabashed. It wasn't the first time I had caught a man staring; I had experienced that a lot of times, but I could distinguish between lustful *let-me-fuck-you-for-one-night* looks, and stares that were plainly looking at me with admiring eyes. His seemed to fall into the latter category.

From behind the kitchen counter, I watched him eat the noodles with chopsticks. His hands looked beautiful, long-fingered and graceful. I could imagine what those hands could do to—

Snap out of it, Kiara. Since when did you start acting like a hormonal teenager?

Besides, to have Jasper's hands over me, would be like a dream come true; a man as perfect and sophisticated as him would not date women like me. Women like me only got men like my father.

Drunk. Wasted. Women beaters.

The thought made me melancholic. When I was done with my shift for the day, I noticed Jasper wasn't seated in the booth anymore. I realized he had gotten bored of waiting and had left eventually, leaving behind a good amount of tip for me.

My heart sank with disappointment. I wanted to talk to him. I hadn't even gotten the opportunity to thank him properly when he had gone out of his way to visit this restaurant just to make sure I was alright.

And I hadn't even returned his jacket yet.

My car was still at the mechanic's shop, so I either took the local bus or walked to and fro from work. Today, it was extra breezy. I stepped out of the restaurant, and as the cool air assaulted my face, I noticed a shadow waiting in the dark.

I stepped back for a second until I saw who it was. Jasper stepped forward. "It's me. I thought I'd wait outside for you."

I tried to hand him back the money he left as a tip. "It's a lot. I can't accept that."

"It's your tip. Keep it," he said with a warm smile, his hands lingering on mine for an extra second.

"Last time I accepted a tip, it didn't work out that well for me."

"Trust me, I'm not that guy," Jasper said. "I won't hurt you."

I trusted him.

I shook my head. "You've done enough for me already. And your jacket, I still have it."

"You can keep that as well. I'm sure it helps you sleep better at night."

I giggled; first, at how funny he was, and second, that he practically hit the bull's-eye.

I decided to tease him back, "How did you know that I sleep with it?"

"For one, I was right outside your window these past couple of days," he admitted. "Next time, you better keep the blinds closed. You never know what types of stalkers are lurking in the dark, or perhaps even a psychopath."

I laughed again. He grinned. I didn't even remember the last time I had laughed with someone. He was a hilarious guy.

"You look beautiful when you smile," Jasper complimented.

I pushed a loose strand of hair behind my ear shyly. "I haven't seen you here before. Do you live around here?"

"I live in the next town. It's a twenty-minute drive from your restaurant," he answered as he dug his hands in his pockets. "So why didn't you call me?"

I was taken aback by that question. "I . . . uh, I wanted to. I'm really sorry. I should have called you before, then you wouldn't have to come here all the way just to make sure I was alright."

"Oh no. Did you think I came here for you? I was actually craving for some Chinese food."

"That's funny because I'm sure I heard you say you came to talk to me. So, what did you want to talk about?"

Jasper sighed. "If you don't mind me asking, are you dating someone?"

My heart skipped a beat. That was quite an unusual question. "Yes."

I swear I watched his features register disappointment. "Oh," he said.

"Chris Hemsworth, that's who I'm dating. He just doesn't know about it yet. Neither does his wife," I joked. If he could tease me, then I was good at that game too. "I've had a crush on Thor for ages."

Jasper burst out laughing, and I saw relief crossed his handsome features. "Well, I'm not that bad-looking, am I? I just don't have that much muscle and blond hair. I guess I'm lacking in those areas."

I nodded. "Not really. You're fine. I guess I can make do with dark hair and blue eyes."

His brows arched up.

What the hell was wrong with me? I was openly flirting with him. I had never been the flirty type.

I realized that I was a different person altogether with Jasper. He made me feel free, made me laugh and blush, and most of all, he made me forget my screwed-up life even if it was just for a while.

"Let's get to know each other by being friends," Jasper suggested. "Deal?"

"Sure. It's a deal," I said. I liked how he didn't hold back on anything that was on his mind; he was so different from the men that I had dated in the past. Those men were difficult to read, and even worse when it came to conversations. Jasper was at a very different level, he might as well be from another planet.

"Take care of yourself, Kiara," he said before heading towards his car.

"Wait," I called out, not wanting the conversation to end. He stopped short and turned. "I've wanted to ask you. That night in the alley, when . . ." My words were caught in my mouth, but I willed myself to continue, ". . . when that guy was trying to hurt me, how did you know I was there?"

"I had parked my car at the end of the street, near a rundown building, and I heard someone scream, so I thought I'd look, and I found you."

"What if there wasn't just one guy. What if there were three or five or more? They would have hurt you."

"I didn't think of that. It was an instinct to help someone in need."

19

"If it sounds cheesy, I still want to say it. You're nothing less than a superhero to me."

His lips broke into a smile. "I don't think I'm worthy of being a superhero."

"To me, you are," I insisted. "You saved me that day."

Jasper reached his hand out to me. "Show me your phone."

I stared at him for a moment, then rummaged my purse and retrieved the phone out of my pocket. He watched me carefully as I punched in the passcode and handed it over to him.

He typed away on my phone and gave it back to me. "There. If you need something, all you have to do is call your superhero. I saved his number in your phone."

I laughed. "Okay."

"How are you getting home?"

"I'll take the bus."

Jasper shook his head. "Come on. I'll drive you home. It's on my way."

"Are you sure?"

"Absolutely."

*   *   *

To say Jasper was a nice guy would be an understatement. He had this really charming and endearing quality about him that I wasn't able to describe.

A few nights back, I saw a darker side of him. I saw the way his blue eyes blazed as he pounded the guy and threw punches. It probably had something to do with men hurting women that ticked him off. He seemed like an old friend I never had.

Whenever I was within his close proximity, I felt my heart beat wildly, and it never happened before. Not with other men, at least. This was a new feeling.

This time, I didn't even need to give Jasper directions. He drove to my house like he hadn't driven there once but a lot of times before. He had a good memory. He stopped right outside my shabby driveway and pushed the gear into park. "So this is it."

"Thank you for the ride home," I said.

"If we are friends, you gotta stop saying thank you all the damn time," he said with a friendly smile.

I liked it when he smiled. It just made the butterflies in my stomach more aggressive.

"If not a thank you, then how about this?" As if possessed by a daring spirit, I unbuckled my seatbelt, leaned in, and pressed my lips gently to his. I kept my lips lingering there for just a second before pulling away.

What was this man making me do?

"That's something I approve." He stared forward, towards the empty road.

"Would you like to come inside?"

He seemed to be lost in his thoughts for a while and then nodded. "Okay."

I invited Jasper inside my home.

I felt a surge of excitement overcome me, the kind of feeling you have when you invite your high school crush over to your place. He parked the car and climbed out of it. I watched him curiously, eyeing the house before he followed behind me.

CHAPTER FOUR

Jasper looked really out of place when he walked into my home. The men I ever invited inside lived a similar, if not the same, lifestyle. Jasper's body language seemed relaxed, and he didn't seem the least bit bothered by the fact that the walls were peeling or that there was a leak in the ceiling. There was no judgment in his expressions whatsoever.

As I took Jasper's coat from him, I noticed the curiosity in his eyes as he looked around. The couch was worn out and patched up. The rug beneath was old, yet I made sure to clean it every chance I got.

Dad was usually seated in front of the TV, but he wasn't in view, so that meant he was out again, drinking and banging one of his chicks. He didn't care that there was a mounting debt under his name and the fact that more than half of my paycheck went into paying that debt. All that mattered to him was more money.

After high school, all my friends had left town for college. When I scrolled through their social media, I realized how much I had been missing; the type of normal life that they were having, a good job, and coming home to a nice partner.

What I had done instead was apply to a community college and stayed behind. I had sacrificed my future. I tried to tell myself that it was alright. It was all for my mom because I just couldn't leave her alone.

"Earth to Kiara!" Jasper snapped his fingers to bring me back to reality. He grinned. "What were you thinking?"

I shook my head. "It's nothing."

Mom walked into the foyer, her eyes darting between Jasper and me. She looked frail. She used to have beautiful voluminous hair like mine, but due to the years of mental torture she went through because of my father, she had started to look tired. There were dark bags under her eyes, and her once vibrant hazel eyes had lost its color.

I realized my mom was still staring at Jasper. I cleared my throat. "Mom, this is Jasper . . ."

I didn't even know his last name.

Jasper quickly raised his hand towards her for a handshake. "Jasper Lockhart, Ma'am. It's a pleasure to meet you. I'm a friend of Kiara's."

My mom looked at his hand and back to his face. Any normal person who knew me well would question how I had managed to be friends with someone like Jasper, who didn't even live in this neighborhood. She quickly wiped her hands on her apron and accepted the friendly handshake.

"Julie Reeves. Please call me Julie. I'm Kiara's mother." She glanced into the kitchen. "I just baked an apple pie for dessert. Why don't you join us, Jasper?"

"I would love to, but I really don't want to intrude. I was just dropping Kiara off from her work."

Mom seemed to be hell-bent on getting Jasper to join us. She waved her hand in dismissal. "The more, the merrier. Desserts are always better if they are shared. Come on now. It won't hurt to just have one slice. It's Kiara's favorite."

Jasper agreed and joined us at the table. Mom served him a generous slice of pie with a scoop of vanilla ice-cream. He tore a large piece of it and pushed it into his mouth. He pointed the fork in my mom's general direction.

23

"I've traveled a lot, and I've tried different varieties of pie, but I've never had such a delicious pie before. Trust me on this."

Mom beamed at him. "Oh, thank you. I'm glad you liked it." She quickly pushed another slice towards him.

We watched, mesmerized as Jasper devoured four slices of the pies, and that made Mom really happy. She loved it when someone truly appreciated her food.

And then out of nowhere, my mother decided to play the inquisition game that she enjoyed playing with any man that I ever brought home. She didn't seem to understand the basic concept of 'friends.' It was truly embarrassing since I wasn't sixteen anymore.

"Where do you live?" she inquired.

"I live in the outskirts of this town," Jasper said. He was pretty vague about the answer.

"What's your job like?" Mom further asked.

"I run a family business, the Lockhart Enterprise. It's something I inherited before my father passed away and decided to grow further."

I didn't miss the way my mother's eyes lit up as they met mine. I could see the message she was trying to send me through telepathy: *Kiara, you hit a goldmine!*

I sighed. My mother would never change.

"I'm sorry to hear that about your father," Mom said. "It must be difficult living by yourself," she added, her eyes flicking towards his left hand to check if he was wearing a wedding band around his finger.

"Not really. I've gotten used to it." Jasper's voice laced with nonchalance.

He hadn't mentioned his mother.

Mom quickly sneaked a glance towards me. I tried to keep a straight face. I wanted to ask her to let it go, but curiosity was a bitch.

Mom smiled. "Your mother must make delicious pies for you too."

24

I saw right through that statement. She wanted to see what he would answer.

"She used to, but not anymore."

I wanted to ask him why. Did his mother remarry? Or perhaps she died too and he couldn't speak about her because it made him emotional?

Before Mom could ask him any more questions, Jasper climbed to his feet, his plate clean. Glancing at the expensive watch on his wrist he said, "It's getting late. I should head home."

His expressions went dark, and something told me he wasn't exactly happy with the way the conversation had been going. I passed Mom a look of warning, and she stopped the inquisition at once.

An awkward silence went on for a while until Jasper thanked my mom for the pie, grabbed his coat, and made his way out of the house. I told him I'd call him. He just nodded as he slid behind the wheel, and I stood there until I watched the car disappear down the road.

As soon as I was inside the house, Mom bombarded me with another round of questions, "Where did you meet him? He seems rich. Where does he live? What kind of business does he own?"

"Mom! I don't know anything. We met at the restaurant, okay? He was a regular customer there."

"But why did he leave so suddenly?"

"You shouldn't have tried to pry into his personal life. Some people don't like to be asked private questions and he already seemed uncomfortable when you asked about his father. You should have stopped right there."

"But I . . ."

"I'm going to bed now, Mom. Night."

CHAPTER FIVE

Kathy was always stubborn and a pushover. If she wanted something, she made sure she got it. She had curly, flaming red hair, bright green eyes, and freckles over her nose. She reminded me a lot of the girl from *Brave*. Her smile was easy and magnetic—that was one reason she managed to get more tips than me in the restaurant even though she always argued I was better-looking than her.

My dad's loan sharks were here yesterday, asking him to pay up, and there was a lot of screaming and fighting. I had seen how one of their men had leered at me. Dad promised that he'd pay up within a week, but I didn't see that happening anytime soon, not when he was hell-bent on spending the money on gambling. He was under the impression that gambling could get him a ton of money that he could pay the loan sharks and solve our problem.

At that moment, I had packed my stuff and decided to leave the place. I didn't care if I had to live on the streets at that point; I wasn't going to be responsible for my father's miserable life.

Watching me pack, my mother had gotten teary-eyed and begged me not to leave. She said she would figure out about the money and that Dad would change eventually.

She was reciting the same old story again. Mom had been the only person who supported me growing up, and I respected her for that.

I hated how she manipulated me.

I hated how much I loved her.

And most of all, I hated how weak that made me.

When I asked Kathy if I could borrow some money, she told me she was financially tight—what with paying the rent and supporting her kid brother, it was hard to spare even a few bucks.

Instead, she had come up with an idea. Kathy worked part-time in a strip club during weekends, and that got her tons of money. She suggested I could do part-time for a few weeks as well.

The strip club was farther away from town. It was a high-class, posh strip club called, *Devil's Girl, the Gentlemen Club* which was accessible only to rich men who were bored with their wives and have far too much money to be spend on pretty girls.

That meant that bumping into townies and being recognized was an unlikely possibility. The deal wasn't so bad for fast money, but I didn't think I could dance on the pole half-naked with pervy old men leering at me. I had debated on the idea but eventually decided I could try for one night.

So here I was, dressed up in a silky cream camisole over lacy panties, making me the most overdressed compared to the other dancers. The neckline of the garment was deep, and that made my cleavage stand out even more, though I didn't have big ones.

I covered my chest with both of my hands, and the manager of the strip club laughed and said it just needed some getting used to. Once I got the taste of the money, I would also leave out the camisole and move freely. Heat rose up my cheeks as I wondered if I could do that. The other girls were professional strippers; they took off every bit of garment from their body on stage, but I was an exception; I was the only dancer who got to keep some clothes on. All I had to do was dance in a sexy way.

Backstage, inside the makeup room, I had second thoughts. I panicked when I saw the other girls prepping for the show and heard the sound of men cheering. Kathy applied a coat of harlot-red lipstick on my lips and then fixed my makeup.

When I looked in the mirror, I saw how different I looked.

The cream camisole made me look sexy as it hugged my curves. My legs were clad in fishnet stockings matched with high heels. My long dark hair cascaded down my shoulders. I looked every bit sexy; someone that men wouldn't keep their eyes off, someone that wives would specifically despise seeing in their respective neighborhoods.

I looked like the dirty little secret.

Tears began threatening to blur my vision. I looked towards the ceiling and willed the tears to go back where they came from as if my eyes could suck them in.

I grabbed a few Kleenex and dabbed at the corner of my eyes.

Kathy had suggested that dancing topless could get me more money, but I couldn't do that. My body was very private, and I didn't want to be there showing it off like that to just anyone. It was something only my boyfriend, or my future husband would see.

This wasn't the kind of life I wanted. All I had ever asked from life was a nice home and just enough money to survive on, but life threw me a curveball, and now I was stuck with this because of my father's bad decisions. My mom couldn't leave my dad, and I couldn't leave her.

I wiped at my tears and thought, *"Only this one time, I would help him, and then I would leave the house regardless."*

I felt a hand on my arm. It was Kathy. "Hey, what's wrong?"

She probably noticed I was getting emotional. "Nothing," I said.

"It's okay, Kiara. There's nothing to be ashamed about," she assured me. "We all need money at some point in our lives, and this is the fastest way. Trust me. You'll just feel awkward at first and then you'll get used to it. Ignore the men; just concentrate on your goal."

I nodded. She was right. I'd just have to ignore the people.

"If you're not comfortable after tonight, you can discontinue, alright? No pressure," she said with a smile.

"Thanks, Kathy," I said.

"No problem." She started fixing my hair again and pulled at my camisole, trying to show more of my cleavage.

"Kathy, don't!"

Kathy threw her hands up as if to say, *"Are you kidding me?"*

"Babe, you're going to dance with at least some clothes on, so cheer up. It will be fun, trust me. And your stage name is *"Barbie"*; just how I'm called *"Diamond"*. So never tell those perverts your real name, okay?"

"Okay," I said.

I wanted to believe her on the fun part, but as the time started to tick and my turn came closer, I began dreading the idea.

*   *   *

The stage was round, which resembled a polished tabletop and was wide enough to accommodate three girls. Plush sofa chairs surrounded the stage, as well as the other side of the club. The room was lit with neon lights, though the ones lighting up the stage had the brightest settings on to keep the focus on the dancers.

When I entered the stage, two girls were already dancing and twerking, clinging to the poles. There was one pole that wasn't taken, and I knew I had to be the one dancing there.

The club was packed; men clad in business suits were seated in every corner of the room. Waitresses were serving drinks around, and I noticed a bouncer leading a man out.

To say I was nervous would be an understatement.

I walked onto the stage, making sure I didn't trip in my high heels and began dancing at the pole. I tried to ignore men as

29

much as I could. I wasn't great at dancing as compared to the other girls who practically knew gymnastics as they swung upside down from the pole in a sexy dance. These were professionals, I was not. I had only learned dancing by watching videos.

Two minutes into the dance, someone in the crowd screamed at me to take off my cami. I stiffened. I was still wearing my undergarments so it wouldn't be that bad if I took it off, right?

The song *"Sexy Back"* by Justin Timberlake was blasting through the speakers. I tried to dance as naturally as I could. I noticed Kathy going all out with her dance. She looked sexy from every angle. No awkwardness whatsoever. She was smiling and having fun like dancing was what she was born for. One man stood up and sent a thick wad of cash flying towards her.

I continued to do my amateur dancing. Without thinking, I reached for the hem of my cami and took it off. I threw it at the audience and hoped I looked sexy doing it.

Maybe I started doing it right because someone from the audience cheered, and I heard someone yell, "Yeah baby!" I glanced at the club manager, standing on the other side of the stage. He gave me a smile of approval.

I continued to dance, and a few minutes later, another girl came up to me and told me to go backstage. Something was up. I picked up the lacy camisole and rushed backstage.

What had I done? Was I dancing wrong? Had they decided to fire me on the first night?

If that was the case, I was going to lose the opportunity to earn a ton of money, and then the loan sharks would be here.

When I walked into the backstage, the manager, Ronnie, was seated in a chair with a black stash bag on the floor. I saw the cash spilling out of the bag. He was counting it but his focus turned once he noticed me.

Ronnie was probably in his mid-thirties with spiky hair, tattoos covering his body, and a few piercings over his face.

He smiled at me. "You did a good job there, sweetheart, and guess what? You're in demand."

He handed me some cash which I took from him.

"This is your advance payment. If you keep this up, babe, you're gonna be rolling in money before you know it."

I looked at the cash. *Eight hundred dollars! What?!*

"So that's it? My job's done?" I asked him, relieved and already wanting to go home. If dancing for a few minutes was going to get me such a huge tip, then I may have to come back again.

But what Ronnie said next brought me back to reality.

"Oh no, honey. Someone from the VIP lounge saw you dancing there and made a request to send you in for a private dance. He was generous enough to make an extra payment to get you in the lounge," he explained. "You're lucky because you would only have to dance for a couple of men. They are here for a birthday party, so you better show them a good time. If you manage to entertain them, you'll probably walk out with one grand for a tip because these mofos are fuckin' rich."

"But Ronnie, I'm just a dancer. I don't want to strip and get naked," I protested.

Ronnie turned his cold gaze towards me. "Don't be such a spoilsport, Kiara. Tell you what, just take off your cami and bra. You can leave the panties on. You've got a nice sexy body; not really curvy or anything, but you're cute, and that's what they liked you for—being small and cute. Plus, they aren't allowed to touch you, they are just going to be sitting there watching. Just ignore it and think of the money you're gonna make by the end of the night."

Like leaving only the panties on made it any better.

I shook my head. "Ronnie, I can't."

But before I could protest any further, Ronnie had already walked out of the room and someone was fixing my makeup and hair while they doused me with expensive perfume and body lotion.

31

The smell was literally stuck to me like a second skin, and I was pretty sure it wouldn't come out for days.

I was asked to change into another lingerie—a red satin one with lace. The center of the bra had a bow on it.

Reluctantly, I wore the matching heels and made my way towards the VIP lounge, half expecting to see middle-aged men celebrating their fortieth or fiftieth birthday and hoping they weren't a creepy lot, but when I walked inside the dimly lit private lounge, I saw young men. In fact, they didn't seem much older than me. They seemed to be in their late twenties or early thirties, all dressed smartly in casual wear.

There were five of them exactly: a black male who was dressed in a blazer, an auburn-haired man, two blonds, and a dark-haired man sitting in the corner farther away from the small round stage.

A stripper was already dancing on one pole and literally baring her ass at the black male. He was getting the most attention, so I assumed it was his birthday party.

I walked carefully to the pole and began dancing. There was a slow song playing, *"Call Out My Name"* by The Weeknd. It was slow and sensuous, perfect for a slow sexy dance. I moved my hips seductively and danced with grace, taking my time to build up the atmosphere. The cash began rolling in, like a fountain of money. The auburn-haired man leered at me with interest. There were tears at the corner of my eyes, but I had to put up with this.

I touched the hem of my cami to take it off when an arm reached out and stopped me. It was one of the seated men. I hadn't even noticed him walk towards the stage until he grasped my wrist.

I flinched. They weren't allowed to touch the dancers. *Weren't they aware of that?*

The light was dim, so it was hard to see who it was at first, but then it was clear as day.

Same dark hair, blue eyes, and roughish handsome exterior.

"Oh come on, Lockhart. Get your ass off the stage!"

CHAPTER SIX

JASPER

Strip Clubs. They weren't something that really excited me. Why sit in one dim room and watch some pretty ass dance on stage when you can take one home and fuck her senseless?

I didn't believe in stripteases unless I got the real deal. Doing a birthday after party was Spike's idea; that bastard was always horny. He was into watching girls take off their clothes and dance erotically on poles.

I had told my so-called friends that I was leaving after the birthday party, but they wouldn't listen to a word I said and forced me inside the limo. It was a Cadillac Escalade; good choice for a limo. I'd give him that much.

The limo had leather seats that I melted into as soon as I settled down. The floors were carpeted, and the windows tinted. It was every bit classy. The right side corner also had a bar that served some drinks and snacks which was entirely self-service, but there were great choices for liquor.

There was nothing to complain about, although I couldn't have much for drinks tonight because I had to wake up early the next morning. I had a plane to catch for a business conference in London. The boys knew that and agreed I could leave after spending some time with them at the strip club.

We entered a gentlemen's club called *Devil's Girl*, a club that had a reputation for being the best posh strip club in town. Entry was only allowed to wealthy men; someone like me.

Spike and Lucas were regulars here with membership cards. Since I wasn't into this kind of shit, I never signed up for it and only visited when the boys made plans.

The moment I stepped into the VIP lounge of the club, we were served some drinks which I declined. I was seated on the other side of the stage. I watched as Tom received a phone call which he didn't answer, making the phone ring over and over again. He grimaced, excused himself, and exited the lounge. I knew who that call was from. It was Tom's wife, Penny, who suspected him of cheating.

If she only knew that he wasn't just cheating on her with another woman but also screwing around every chance he got, she would flip

And then there was Dylan, auburn-haired, sharp-tongued, a Wall Street genius, and a banker. He couldn't keep one girlfriend for an entire month without severely bruising her, and that's one reason why he had to visit these clubs: to make himself feel better, to give himself the illusion that these women wanted him for the money, which could be true to a fault. But once any woman got to actually know him, they'd know what a sly bastard he was.

Lucas, the one who we call the blond cat of our group, was the only sane person in my circle of friends. He was smart, intelligent, a millionaire, and also a skilled magician. He was so good that he sometimes did shows in Vegas. The only out-of-the-ordinary thing that Lucas had was how he kept his partners collared. He was into the BDSM lifestyle, and his partner, Amy, surely didn't mind that sort of life.

And then there was me. Not any different from these bastards and yet I thought of myself as someone who was better than my friends. Superior in every order.

Dylan slid into the seat beside me, and the silver *Rado* on his wrist glimmered. He probably saw that I had noticed because he said, "Bought it yesterday for eight grand, gold plated."

I smiled, trying so hard to keep my anger at bay. "Looks dapper on you."

He had been waving his hand the entire day just so someone would notice and comment on it, but I was seriously tired of having his left hand in my face all the fucking time, so I had to give in.

"Right?" He scratched the little stubble over his chin. "Cecilia said it looked elegant and that I should buy this kind of watches often."

Right, Cecilia would also agree to jump off a cliff after a few beatings. I didn't understand why she would even put up with such a pompous asshole. Sometimes when I looked at Dylan and his smug expressions, I have these mental images of me bludgeoning his brains until he didn't have any gray matter left, but I continued to smile, acting civil as always.

A blonde with huge breasts walked in and began showing her ass in Tom's face, which I'm sure he was enjoying immensely. The other men seemed to be enjoying the show as well, except me.

I had different tastes. I wasn't turned on by fake meat. I liked slim and curvy women, someone who could fit right in my lap like a delicate doll.

As if fate had read my mind, a brunette walked into the lounge. She seemed wobbly on her feet, and I imagined her to be a new recruit. Tom elbowed me, bringing my attention to him.

"I saw her when we walked into the club. She was dancing outside. I asked Ronnie if he could send her in, and he agreed. Good for us because, boy, that ass looks fine."

Tom was already panting like a rabid dog.

I turned my attention back to the girl. She wasn't that tall if the heels were removed. Her skin looked pale under the illuminating lights, and her hair, which was grazing her waist, was

36

long and dark brown. She has average-sized tits and a sweet round ass that could fit my palm.

She was definitely my type. She was wearing a camisole, the neckline a V that shows off her natural tits. I realized she wasn't looking at any men unless she had to, and when she turned, I felt like the air was knocked out of my body.

I sat closer to see if I was wrong, but I wasn't. Dancing on the Weeknd's slow song was Kiara. There was no mistaking her. She grabbed the pole and moved her body up and down in a slow dance. I felt a spurt of rage burn through me.

What the hell was she doing in a fucking strip club?

They were all eye-fucking her like dogs in heat. I was pretty sure Tom would try to persuade her to give him her personal information after the show was over.

I had to stop this. They shouldn't sit here and eye my girl like that. My legs had a mind of its own as I left my seat and climbed the narrow stage. Before I knew it, I was dragging Kiara towards the lounge exit.

She better have a bloody good reason to be dancing in front of all these men and for riling up these strange feelings inside me.

CHAPTER SEVEN

KIARA

The last person I thought I'd see here was Jasper. At first, I thought I was hallucinating. Maybe this man wasn't Jasper but someone else and I had imagined it to be him—my knight in shining armor.

He had been on my mind since the last two weeks. He was nice enough to give me his number but never made an effort to contact me after that day he had paid my house a visit.

I assumed Jasper didn't want to be my friend anymore, and yet here he was again, glowering down at me. He moved with a confident swagger; like that of a cat. He was dressed in a long trench coat. His t-shirt hugged his toned body, and the jeans fit him to perfection. The coat had his initials embroidered on it: 'JL'. The outfit matched his black boots. He looked like a dark fallen angel created to lure innocent women into committing grave sins.

"Care to explain what the hell was going on there?" he growled, his eyes watching me like a hawk. I didn't miss the way his eyes dropped down to my heels and slowly moved up my body.

I flinched from the tone of his voice. "I was just working here as an exotic dancer."

Jasper's eyes widened in surprise. "Exotic dancer? So, you were going to take off your remaining clothes and slow dance naked on the pole in front of a bunch of my friends?!"

"I didn't know you were with them!" I said in my defense as if that explained anything at all.

Jasper gave out a bitter laugh. "You think if it weren't me or my friends, it makes dancing naked on the pole any better? Is that what you're telling me?"

My lower lip trembled. *Why was he acting like such an asshole?*

"Answer me, Kiara," he urged me to go on.

"I . . . I didn't have a choice!" I replied.

"What happened to the waitress job?" he asked me, almost too calmly, but I could read his expressions. He was beyond irate.

"I had only considered stripping as part-time, and it wasn't like I was really planning on going naked."

He motioned his hand towards my barely-there clothing. "You're practically already naked. There's nothing left to the imagination to be very honest. For fuck's sake, cover yourself, Kiara!" Jasper said through gritted teeth. He took off his coat and pushed it into my arms forcefully. "Wear this right now," he commanded.

The way Jasper said it forced me to slip my arms inside his coat. I stood there, both of us staring at each other. I could smell his musky perfume on me now. Tears teetered my vision. Jasper didn't have any right to say any of this. He wasn't my boyfriend or my father! How could he be so harsh?

"Why do you even care?" I asked before I could even stop myself.

"I do. I care if you're going to be working in a strip club baring your ass out for other men to see. Do you understand me?"

"I'm not even your girlfriend," I whispered to myself.

"What did you say?"

"I don't know why you're angry or acting like a damn alpha, because the last time I checked, you never texted me or came to visit the restaurant in two weeks. And now you barge into the club, watch me getting undressed for your friends, and demand answers. How's that fair?"

He got hold of my chin and forced me to make eye contact. "I was trying to stay away from you for your own good."

I didn't know what he meant by that. His fingers grazed my cheek, "You don't understand, Jasper. I need the money. I had no other choice."

"You could have asked me. I told you to call me if you needed help."

"I can't take your money!"

"Yes, you can and you will. Damn your pride. That's what friends do; they help each other," Jasper said. "Text me your bank account details, and I'll have some money transferred."

I shrugged. "But I can't repay the money soon. I need time."

Jasper sighed. "I don't need you to repay me at all."

"I can't do that!"

But Jasper wasn't listening to another word—he ignored every word I said.

"Now, you will tell Ronnie that there's a problem and that you won't be able to work here anymore. Okay?"

"What excuse do I give him?"

"Tell him your boyfriend doesn't like it."

I laughed. "But you're not my boyfriend, Jasper."

A small wicked smile played on his lips. He leaned into my ear, and in a silky voice he said, "We could change that if you want."

Jasper was just so unpredictable. I had never met a man like him before. He could be soft and gentle at times, flirty and attractive the next, and then you wouldn't even notice he was showing you his dark side. He was the type that sent a chill down my spine—so very possessive and intimidating that you start to wonder if he was even the same person.

Jasper buttoned the trench coat all the way up. It was ironic because now, not even a bit of my skin was exposed. If I had left the coat open, I might have ended up looking like a posh hooker. The coat went past my knees.

I recited the same excuse Jasper insisted I should to Ronnie, and he insisted that he wanted to see my boyfriend. He obviously thought I was making excuses for bailing on my job tonight.

I led him out of the club, and true to his word, Jasper stood by the club entrance waiting for us. A cab was parked near the curb on standby.

I saw Ronnie's expressions change when he saw Jasper. It seemed like they knew each other.

Jasper opened the passenger side of the cab and told me to sit inside while he had a chat with Ronnie. I did as I was told because I realized that arguing with Jasper didn't get me anywhere, especially when he was not in a good mood.

I slid the window down, but I wasn't within earshot. I tried to listen to bits of the conversation, but all I could see was Ronnie trying to avoid eye contact and Jasper towering over him while speaking. I managed to hear the last part.

"If you call her again, Ron, and if you try to push her into stripping for you again, I swear to you, I'll burn down this entire place. That's a promise. You already know I make good on my promises."

I watched Ronnie nod his head and apologize. Jasper said something to him again, and then Ronnie stormed back inside the club. Jasper walked back to the taxi and settled in beside me.

"Your friends are inside the club," I reminded him.

"I didn't really care about coming here in the first place, but I'm glad I decided to tag along today."

I took his hand in mine and squeezed it. "You keep helping me every time, Jasper. I don't even know how to thank you."

"Don't, Kiara." Jasper turned to face me, taking both my hands in his. "I'm not really a good guy."

41

I shook my head. "You're the first person who's ever cared to look out for me, and it means more than I can tell."

Jasper wasn't listening. His attention was somewhere else. He touched the button of the trench coat I was wearing and unbuttoned the top one, followed by the few below that. He opened the coat all the way down to my bare stomach but made no attempt at removing the coat off my shoulders. He continued to stare at me, his eyes heavy with what I assumed was desire.

I felt my cheeks warm, and my stomach began flipping.

Even with him being as bold as unbuttoning the coat and staring at me, I didn't feel uncomfortable; just the contrary. I squeezed my thighs together as I felt heat pool between my legs.

"Forgive me for interrupting you, Kiara," he said in a low husky voice. "I want to confess to you what I've been thinking since I saw you on that stage today."

"What were you thinking?"

"That you look like a goddess out of a mythical book," he said, flicking his gaze towards the front of the taxi where the driver was. Jasper pulled down the partition screen for privacy. "That lingerie looks perfect on you."

"Thanks." I was becoming giddy. I wanted him to kiss me and put his hands all over me; just do anything to help free me of this need that was building up inside me.

He traced his finger on my bottom lip. "Do you know why I was so angry earlier?"

"Why?" I felt like I was losing myself in those smoldering blue eyes.

"It wasn't because of you. I loved what I saw, but I hated that those other men were looking at you too. It just made me so fucking mad," he explained, now caressing my jaw. His fingers dipped further down towards my collarbone.

"I . . . I understand," I managed to say.

"No, you don't, *precious*. You don't understand a damn thing," he said, smiling, and I loved how he called me precious.

"I'm saying I wanted to climb up there on the stage, tear your clothes off, and fuck you right in front of all those men who were looking at you to show them that you were *mine*."

I was rendered speechless by his boldness. He continued, "And I'm sorry for having these thoughts, but I can't control what I think, and I didn't mean to be rude to you earlier."

"I don't know what to say."

Jasper slid his arm around my waist and pulled me closer until I was sitting partly in his lap. He leaned in and drew my mouth to his almost too urgently like he had been waiting patiently for this moment.

He kissed me slowly at first, his tongue seeking entrance into my mouth. I opened up just a bit, and we kissed deeply; his tongue coiled around mine deliciously, and his fingers slid beneath the cami and traced the skin just below the swell of my breasts. His fingers traced my nipples over the dress.

My skin was burning with urgency. I moaned, raking my fingers through his soft curly locks. Jasper palmed my breast and squeezed it gently.

"Jasper!" I whispered. I sneaked a glance at the driver. "He'll see us."

Jasper shook his head. "He can't. I put the screen up, sweetheart." He claimed my lips again, this time with a fiercer passion, pulling me closer to his chest. I could feel his manhood pressing against me, but suddenly, his fingers stopped the caress, leaving me wanting more.

Why did he stop?

He pressed a chaste kiss on my lips and placed me back on the seat beside him; both of us panting from the passionate kiss. "Your house is here," he whispered, "I'll text you, okay?"

I nodded, although there was a heaviness in my heart that I couldn't describe. I didn't want to leave him. He was literally a woman's wet dream.

Jasper looked at me, his eyes mysterious beneath those long lashes as the shadow of the moonlight lingered on his handsome face.

"Can you promise me something, Kiara?"

"What is it?"

"Don't ever go to that club again, baby. I don't like it. You're not like those other women; you're special," he said, taking my hand in his as he kissed my knuckles softly like a true gentleman. "And if you need help with anything at all, I'm always here for you. Okay?"

"Thanks. I feel better just knowing you'd do that for me," I said sincerely as I reached for my purse to pay the taxi fare, but Jasper waved my hand away. I wouldn't listen to a word because he had already done enough for me, so much that I was almost ashamed that I was so helpless. This time I didn't let him pay no matter how much he tried to convince me to let it go.

He chuckled and muttered at how stubborn I was. "Goodnight, Kiara."

I stepped out of the cab and then stopped, remembering something. "Your coat?"

"Don't worry about it."

"I have your blazer jacket with me from the other day, and now I'm taking your coat. Looks like I'm going to have to make a new wardrobe for your jackets."

Jasper chuckled. "You can keep it, sweetheart. Make a collection out of it. I don't mind."

"Night, Jasper."

*   *   *

Mom was already peeking out the window when I entered the house. It was past midnight, and I didn't think she would be even up at this hour. I was pretty sure she had witnessed the little

44

conversation outside without having any idea what we were talking about.

And she proved me right by saying, "I don't trust that boy, Kiara."

She hadn't asked me what I had been doing out so late, why I was wearing an excessive amount of makeup, or why I was dressed like I had just spent a few hours in a rich guy's penthouse because it didn't matter as long as I brought home money. I knew she cared about me, but it didn't matter where money was concerned.

"Why would you say that?"

"There seems to be something off about him, some type of darkness that I can't explain. He is . . . " she trailed off. "He just doesn't seem normal."

"You asked me how I met him. Two weeks ago, I was closing the restaurant when I went out the back door to throw the trash, and a man tried to assault me. Jasper saved me from something awful happening, Mom. He's a good man, and I don't doubt that," I said. I could feel my entire body twisting with the memory of that day and how I'd have been ruined if he hadn't been there on time.

"I just want you to be careful, honey," she said calmly. "He seemed nice that day when he visited our home, but as soon as we asked him a few questions, he was evasive."

"Maybe he doesn't like to discuss his personal life. Maybe he's just too shy or doesn't easily open up to strangers. That doesn't explain anything."

I settled down on the couch as Mom handed me a cup of hot cocoa. Her eyes watched me curiously. "Do you like him?"

"I like him a lot, Mom," I confessed. "More than I should, and I want to find out where this relationship is going exactly. I never felt this way for another man before. Is it weird that I've started to like him in such a short time?"

Mom shook her head. "It's not weird, darling. It's natural to like someone who looks out for you, who cares for you, and you know what's strange? I used to feel the same way about your father," she admitted, staring into the distance. I knew where she was going with this. "He was so nice back then. I was totally in love and then I got pregnant, and we got married. My little illusion of a happy life was shattered."

Mom looked sad, and I knew the story after that. Mom had made the wrong decision. She married a snake—an abusive, alcoholic cheater.

The silence in the room continued. We were both comfortable with it, leaving ourselves to our thoughts.

She was the first to speak, "Whatever you decide, just think with your brain, because sometimes, the heart makes the wrong decisions."

I nodded. She had always given me that advice.

"Jasper seems like he's from a very influential family," she continued. "And it's really strange he's interested in you."

"So, you're saying I should be rich for Jasper to actually like me? That social status matters in these cases?"

"There's always one thing that men want, and most of the time, they treat women as a goal. As soon as Jasper gets what he wants, maybe he wouldn't want you anymore. He would get away with it, honey, because he is from a wealthy family, and you'd have to spend the rest of your life dedicated to a baby that you hadn't planned for. And then one day, he'd fight in court for the baby's custody while he marries a woman of the same social status. Do you understand what I'm saying, Kiara? You'll only be reduced to a keep."

My vision was blurred with tears. *How could my mother be so harsh? Didn't she think she was crushing my feelings?*

"I don't want to upset you, darling. I'm just telling the truth. Look at the way he dresses, I can smell the scent of his expensive perfume from a mile away, and those shoes? I don't know much about fashion, but it seems like he had them custom-made and shipped from foreign countries," she explained, "I don't see why he would be interested in anyone who lives in this trash neighborhood."

"That's enough, Mom! I get your point," I snapped angrily and didn't wait for her to say anything as I climbed up the stairs to my bedroom.

I heard her call me, but I closed the bedroom door behind me. I didn't want to listen anymore to her advice. I peeled the coat off my body and checked the name tag.

Armani.

I threw the coat on the floor angrily and climbed into bed. I hated feeling like this so much, and I hated that my mom could be right. I mean, who was I kidding? Jasper surely had a ton of money. I knew that the day I had met him. The type of cars he drove was a dead giveaway, and yet I still foolishly checked the name tag of his coat.

I tried to not think of it that way because it hurt to think Jasper would be like one of those guys who were nice at first, and once they got what they wanted, they just let the girl put the pieces back together. This wasn't high school anymore, and Jasper was a responsible adult. Mom was being ridiculous. We were just friends.

But friends don't kiss like that.

I thought about our kiss in the car and how passionate it had been. He kissed me like his life had depended on it. Just thinking about it made me feel happy, and I couldn't deny how I felt for him too.

Whenever I was in Jasper's presence, I had butterflies take flight in my stomach, and I had never felt that way before. I decided to ignore Mom's words and face the situation as it came at me.

My phone vibrated beside me. I glanced at the screen, and a smile tugged at my lips knowing who it was.

Jasper was texting me.

CHAPTER EIGHT

Jasper: Were you sleeping?

Me: Not really. You?

Jasper: Just thinking of a certain someone.

Me:I'm jealous of that person.

Jasper: Oh, you don't have a reason to be jealous, baby. If you have to know, I was thinking of you.

Jasper: Happy?

Me: Very. ☺ So whassup?

Jasper: I was wondering . . .

Jasper typed, and then his typing stalled. I kept staring at the screen for so long, it was crazy. He was keeping me hanging on purpose.

Me: What is it?

I saw the three dots appear at the end of the chat, indicating that Jasper was typing.

Jasper: I was wondering if you're free next weekend so I could take you out for dinner and a movie or anything else that you like.

I kept staring at the screen. He was asking me out on a date! A real date!

Jasper: Hey, Kiara?

I realized I hadn't responded for a couple of seconds, and maybe he started to wonder why I wasn't responding when I was online.

Me: Yeah, that sounds nice. I'd love to go.
Jasper: Perfect! Wear the same red lingerie you wore today.

I laughed. What was with this guy? He could be serious one minute and be flipping funny the next. I decided to tease him back.

Me: So, you want me to go out with you wearing only lingerie? Other men are going to look.

Jasper: I meant underneath a dress, sweetheart. ;) Don't get too cocky with me.

Me: Or what, Mr. Lockhart?

Jasper: I don't want to scare you.

I started to respond but stopped when I saw he was typing.

Jasper: But you will find out soon.
Me: Nothing you'll say will scare me, honey. Try me! ;)

Jasper: Will it scare you if I say that I want to rip your clothes to shreds and fuck you within an inch to your death? ;) You want that, baby?

I was probably too shocked to respond. I knew Jasper was a little eccentric; he could be sweet and gentlemanly but could speak in a way that made you wonder about his dark humor. I knew he was only joking, but that didn't stop the chill running down my spine, and didn't prepare me for what he was going to say next.

Jasper is typing . . .

My heart began beating faster.

Jasper: I plan on fucking you, then skinning you next and then adding your head to my ever-growing collection of heads in my basement.

When I didn't respond, he continued.

Jasper: Did I scare you enough, or do you want to hear more of my date ideas?

I didn't know what to say to that.
Jasper: Are you mad at me?
Kiara?
Oh, come on, baby!
I was just saying what Ted Bundy must have said to his dates. I'm totally kidding, love.

*   *   *

"Kiara!" Kathy snapped her fingers, and that brought me back to reality.

51

The glass was already filled with the soda to the brim and was spilling out of the cup.

"Oh. Um, I'm sorry. I was just . . ."

"Thinking of the tall, dark, and handsome guy? Yeah, I get it," she said, folding her arms across her chest. "Ron told me how your prince charming came in the VIP room and swooped you away and forbade you from working for him, which is a shame, considering the fact that you could have made a lot of money."

"I wasn't comfortable with that job anyway, Kathy!" I replied. "I don't have it inside me to strip it down in front of a bunch of strangers."

"Oh right, I forgot. You're Miss Perfect. Stripping is just for sluts like me. That's what you thought, right?"

"Oh, come on, Kathy. I never said that."

Jeff's head bobbed from the kitchen counter and glared at the two of us. "You two there, stop arguing and get to work!"

I began wiping off the excess drink that had spilled on the counter. Kathy huffed beside me, dropped what she was doing, and walked out of the restaurant.

I realized Kathy was hurt about me bailing on her that day even though I had promised to be an exotic dancer for only one night. Why that would even bother her was still beyond me.

Just when I was done cleaning the mess, my phone began vibrating in my apron pocket. I retrieved the phone and saw the words *"Mom"* flashing on it. I noticed that Jeff was busy flipping the burgers on a grill, so I made an excuse of using the bathroom and made my way inside one cubicle and shut the door.

"Mom?"

Mom was being hysterical on the other end, and I couldn't hear a thing. "Mom! I can't hear what you're saying. Just calm down first."

She said something else, and then there was a loud shriek followed by a bang. "What's happening there? Mom?" The phone suddenly went dead on the other end.

I burst out of the bathroom and made my way to the lockers. I stuffed everything inside my bag, not even bothering to change out of my work clothes. I went to the kitchen to find Jeff and told him that my mother was in trouble, and that I needed to be there with her. Surprisingly, Jeff didn't protest as he let me go. I suspected it was because he had seen the agitation on my face.

I hailed down a cab, and told the driver to drive as fast as he could. The man was reluctant at first but then managed to navigate out of the traffic with ease. I reached home in about fifteen minutes.

When I stepped out of the cab, I saw the lights in my house were switched on, and I could hear my father's loud voice booming through the door.

Afraid, I took a step back and almost hightailed back to the restaurant. But I couldn't leave, not when my dad was here causing a commotion. The door was likely left open, so I didn't bother to knock.

When I entered the living area, it was littered with beer cans, and the stale smell of smoke permeated the air. I had to press my hand on my mouth to stop myself from gagging.

My mother lay on the kitchen floor, sobbing, while my dad threw a string of curses at her. He was still bellowing when I walked in. His gaze rested to me. His lips curled in an ugly sneer.

"Princess is home," he slurred. "I expected you to be back home earlier, sweetheart, but that's fine, as long as you have what I want."

I just stood there, shaking with fear. It was like all those childhood memories came flooding back. Mom had just given him our monthly savings last month, and now he was back again to ask for more. He had asked for forgiveness, and Mom said that Dad was trying, but here we are, back to square one.

A vicious drop of alcohol, and he would forget all the promises that he had made. Not that I expected him to magically become a good father and a husband.

53

Why couldn't he just walk away from our lives? Why couldn't he just leave us the heck alone?

Everyone in this town knew Sean Reeves's many shenanigans, how he would spend every single penny of our hard-earned money in drinking and clubs, how he would get into trouble with the wrong people in those places and get arrested, yet Mom would still be there to bail him out.

All that was needed was his sorry excuse of an apology, some croc tears, and voilà, he had the woman back in his arms. The entire town saw how he'd abused his wife and neglected his child all those miserable years. My mom could've walked away when she had the chance, but I was starting to wonder if she was really blind—either that or Dad possessed a magic wand that I wasn't aware of.

And me, I had been stupid enough to hold on to the few nice childhood memories that I had of him. He took me to parks, to movies, or the zoo, and then things escalated. Our life was enveloped by the dark cloud of my father's addiction with him being the storyteller of our doomed fate.

This time I was going to stand my ground.

This time I wouldn't let him take the money.

His dark eyes, much like my own, watched me. He dug his hands in his pockets. "You already know what I'm here for, sweetie. Now stop wasting my time, and give me the money."

I started to move towards Mom to help her up, but he pushed me back and placed his filthy boot to her thigh.

"Didn't you hear what I said? I'm sure you made some good tips at the fancy restaurant you work at." He raised his hand towards me, palm up.

"Hand it over like the sweet little girl that you are. Don't make Daddy hurt your Mommy. Come on, be a good girl now."

He spoke to me like I was still five.

"Let Mom go, and I will give you the money," I said.

I heard Mom sob loudly, and she looked at me through her tear-stricken eyes. "Baby, just leave," she whispered.

I went upstairs to my room and pulled out all my savings from the little savings box in my wardrobe. I didn't want to give him any more money, but I had run out of choices. I couldn't refuse him when he had my mother under his boot. He had every power to hurt her if I didn't give him what he wanted.

When I reached the landing, the two were tangled in a wrestling match on the floor. Mom had a swollen eye. Dad had caught her by the roots of her hair and was dragging her off his body while she continued to hit him with failed attempts because Dad was stronger.

"Stop it! Stop it, both of you!" I shrieked at them. "I have your money. Take it and get out of my home!"

He practically smacked Mom away from his body with such a force that she collided with a wooden chair. He snatched the money out of my hands as I rushed to help Mom.

He counted the money and pocketed it. Dad's furious gaze leveled with mine. "Is this some kind of a joke? Where is the rest of my fucking cash? This isn't enough."

"That's all I've got!"

"I will be back tomorrow to collect the remaining cash. I don't care how you get it. Do you understand?" he said, and started making his way out of the door. "If I don't get it by tomorrow evening, I'll walk away from your life, Julie. Mark my words. Your husband will be better off with a whore than a sorry excuse of a wife and a good-for-nothing daughter."

That was hilarious, coming from someone like him, and even funnier was how it broke my mother's heart. Even though she was beaten and her clothes torn, she said, "No, Sean, please . . ."

He reached the bottom step, and I knew I'd see him again tomorrow; hurting us, hitting Mom like he had done today. The cycle of torment was never-ending.

Every fiber in my body was filled with *rage*. It was such a powerful emotion. My mind blurred, and I saw red. All I could think of was being done with this situation. We didn't need him in our lives. I didn't think twice before I reached for two empty beer bottles and smashed them into his head.

When I came back to my senses, it was already too late.

His body lay still on the ground—a thick pool of blood spreading around his head.

"Daddy?" I tried to wake him up.

I didn't mean to kill him.

"Dad?"

I silenced him for life.

I could hear my mom screaming, and even though my father had tormented us all our lives, she was crouched there beside him, sobbing.

"Sean, wake up, please."

My mother was a piece of work, wasn't she? She still loved him in her own twisted way.

"What have I done?" I whispered to myself.

Just as the reality of the situation sunk in, Mom's eyes became vacant as she climbed to her feet. She gathered the money scattered on the floor. She then disappeared into the kitchen, and I heard some shuffling. She walked out with more money. Her expressions were unreadable as she handed me the envelope containing the money.

"I never let your father take all our savings; I saved up quite a lot." It turned out she was smarter than she had led me to believe. "Take the money and leave, Kiara."

"Where would I go?" I cried.

"Away from here," she said.

"But Dad . . ."

"He's dead." The pain was quite evident in her voice. "It was an accident. Okay, honey?" She took my hand in hers. "It was a simple act of self-defense. It wasn't your fault."

56

I could see the pain in her eyes as she hugged me fiercely. "I will sort it out, baby. Until then, you need to hide. When things go back to normal, you can come back home."

"I can't leave you alone!"

"Don't worry about me! Frankie will help me out," she assured me.

Frankie was my mother's old friend who stopped by every once in a while. At first I had suspected him of having an affair with Mom, but that was beside the case. They were just friends, though I knew Frankie had feelings for her and cared deeply about us—something that my father should have done.

I didn't think it was a good idea to flee the scene, but Mom insisted that I should leave, and that she would take care of the situation. I wasn't left with any other choice but to pack some stuff.

That night, I took shelter in a dull, grimy motel just a few kilometers away from home. I had decided to stay low for a few days until I figured out what to do next. I survived on cheap hot dogs and packets of chips for two days. The money wasn't going to sustain me even for a week. I couldn't even go to my previous job. My phone had over a dozen missed calls and texts from Kathy and Jeff. The last text was from Jasper.

A gust of cool breeze assaulted my face as cars zoomed by. The eerie silence was filled with the roar of the wind. I had walked a long way, and now I had no idea where I was.

When I found a little joggers park, I settled down on the bench under a tree.

> *Kathy: Hey Ki, I know I've acted like a total bitch. I'm really sorry bae (>.<) Please forgive me. Let's go out for tacos tomorrow. My treat <3*

> *Kathy: Heyyy! Are you really that pissed? I've been calling you. Why didn't you answer your phone? Reply to me. Luv ya :-**

Jeff: Kiara, it's been two days and you haven't been to work. Are you sick? Call me asap.

Kathy: Babeeee, it's been four days! Why aren't you replying??? Jeff is going nuts. I'm worried.

Jasper: Hey. You haven't replied to my texts, and you don't answer my calls anymore. I was just joking the other day, you know how I am. I swear, it was just a joke. Miss you, sweetheart. Call me.

I wiped the tears that had trickled down my face as I read the texts. There were people who cared about me, and yet I felt so utterly lonely. I could ask Kathy if I could stay at her place, but I knew better than to call her. I didn't want to put her in any trouble since she wasn't doing that great financially, so asking for her help was not an option. I knew I couldn't go back home either, and that left me with only one other option.

But how could I contact Jasper and ask him for another favor? He had already done enough for me.

As if on cue, my phone started vibrating. It was an unknown number. I realized it must be the police who had successfully tracked down my number. I didn't have any other choice anymore.

I answered the call, "Hello."

There was a momentary silence on the other end. "Kiara?"

I recognized that deep husky voice. "Jasper?"

"Sweetheart, your mother told me everything." I could hear the hesitation laced with concern in his voice. "About your father."

That's when I couldn't control the floodgates that opened up deep inside me.

"Jasper," I choked a sob. "I'm so scared. I don't know what to do . . ."

"Let me help you, Kiara."

CHAPTER NINE

The guilt and shame from what I had done to my own father came back to me in spades. I half expected Jasper to never show up, thinking I wasn't worth all the trouble, but as always, he was here to help me.

When I walked out of the park, I noticed the black Aston Martin pull up by the curb. I approached the passenger side, and waited until the window rolled down and Jasper peered out.

"Hop in," he instructed.

I climbed into the car and sank into the soft leather seats, placing both hands in my lap. I repeatedly told myself that I couldn't be weak; I couldn't start crying, but the reality of the situation was so jarringly obvious in my mind. It wasn't changing no matter how guilty I felt.

I felt Jasper's hand slid under mine, his fingers interlocking mine gently. We stayed like that for a while. His thumb traced a pattern on the back of my hand which was soothing. I could feel him gazing at me.

"It's not your fault, Kiara. You did it to protect yourself," he said, his voice barely a whisper.

"I killed my father," I choked a sob, covering my face with my hands. "I can't forgive myself. The police, Jasper . . . What if they think it was planned? I don't want to spend my life in prison."

I knew I was bordering on the verge of hysteria, but the possibilities of getting caught and convicted were obvious, unless there was some miracle.

Jasper's arm went around my shoulder as he pulled me closer. "Shh . . .everything is going to be alright. I'm here now. I won't let anything happen to you," he assured me, kissing the top of my head. "It's a promise."

I believed him, and his encouraging words made me cry harder. Jasper was my solace and my knight in shining armor. Even though the pain seeped deep into my bones, I felt at ease somehow.

With Jasper by my side, I believed that everything was going to be alright. He let me cry until I had no more tears left. I breathed into his shirt, and a few minutes later, he let me lay back into the seat as he pushed the car into drive and maneuvered it onto the road.

I looked out of the window as houses and trees passed. Jasper gripped the wheel with one hand and held my hand with the other.

Exhausted, I didn't even realize that I dozed off. I slipped into a dream. In the dream, I was dressed in an orange jumpsuit with my wrists locked in shackles.

That was enough to pull me out of the dream. It seemed too real, I had to double-check my surroundings. I was still in Jasper's car. A soft opera song drifted from the stereo. It sounded lovely yet haunting.

My eyes traveled to the digital clock on the dashboard. The time read 9:45 PM, which meant I had slept for almost an hour.

When I glanced out the window, I realized that we'd crossed town.

Where was he taking me? I assumed we were just going to drive around and Jasper would help me find a solution to my problem.

"Where are we going?" I asked him.

Jasper passed me a smile. "You'll see."

61

"You're killing me with suspense," I said.

He brought my hand to his mouth and kissed the knuckles.

It was at that moment I knew.

I loved him.

Not just because he was kind and caring and that he rescued me from situations in the past, but because I felt so comfortable around him. Granted, Jasper was like a Rubik's cube. The things he said sometimes were hard to decipher, but I knew in my heart that I would do anything for this man without batting an eye.

After my mother's relationship with my father, and the few men that I had dated in the past, I thought love didn't exist. I never felt like my heart soared every time I looked at someone, nor did I feel like I was flying in a hot-air balloon as I did now.

When I was with Jasper, I almost forget to breathe. He made me forget all the difficult things in my life. It also made me worry.

Did Jasper even remotely feel the same about me?

He had hinted a few things in the past but never outright said he liked me or something along that line. If he didn't like me back, I was going to end up with an unrequited love. I knew it was very old-fashioned of me to gush and obsess over a man, but I just couldn't help myself where Jasper was concerned.

"We're almost here," Jasper's voice cut through my thoughts.

Mountains surrounded the area; a scenic view ahead. A colossal mansion loomed proudly ahead amid the lush trees. The car approached the metal gates that had the letter 'L' on either side of it.

Jasper reached out for a small remote control and pressed a button. The gates opened slowly. I drank in the spectacular scenery surrounding the equally impressive mansion which seemed modern yet had a gothic feel to it.

I knew Jasper was wealthy. My mom knew about it, only having met him once, but never in my wildest dreams had I thought he was so rich as to live in a place like this.

Jasper probably noticed my reaction to the house. "It's a modern Italianate mansion built by my great-grandfather in the 1800s," he explained proudly.

"It's a beautiful home."

"A home without a family isn't really a home, is it? It's just fancy house.," he said. "I'd love to turn it into a home one day when I already have a wife. So far, I live here alone with the house staff." His eyes twinkled with amusement. "When I was young, this house was filled with people. Now the silence is almost too suffocating."

"Oh," was all I could manage to say. This was such a beautiful home, and it deserved a big loving family with children playing in the garden, a loving woman cooking meals for her family, and a husband to love and provide.

But Jasper lived here alone.

How lonely could that be?

He drove around a large fountain dominating the center and parked in one of the vacant parking spaces. I wondered why he had brought me to his house out of all places.

As if he read my mind, he said, "It's not safe for you to go back to your house or any shady motels, so I assumed its best you stayed here for a while until we figure out what we can do about your situation."

I shook my head. "I don't want to intrude. It's your space. I can't just barge in and stay here for as long as I want."

Jasper placed his hand over mine. "You're definitely not intruding, and I would be more than happy to have company."

I smiled at that. Jasper was stubborn. It didn't seem like the topic of living in a motel was still open for discussion.

The mansion was at least three stories high with an innumerable number of large windows. I had only seen houses like this on TV that were owned by celebrities, and I couldn't believe that I was now about to live here for at least a few days. There was a beautiful courtyard, all set with a table.

"Are you just going to stand there and stare?" He chuckled. "Come on, it's even better inside."

The central foyer of the mansion was wide and spacious. The flooring was shiny white marble. The house was built decades ago, but with time, it seemed to have been renovated and modernized. Carpeted sweeping staircase glided from both sides, leading to the grand foyer upstairs.

We entered a large open space living area that seemed to be the size of a mini football field with a fireplace so huge, it could fit a bed inside. The crystal chandelier above matched the ivory walls.

Persian carpets, rich gold drapes, huge oil paintings . . . the house screamed opulence. Everything was so breathtakingly gorgeous, all down to the matching décor.

Jasper smiled beside me, probably enjoying my reaction to his space.

"There's also a mini home theatre that could accommodate a dozen people, a spacious library on the second floor, a gaming parlor which is one of my favorites, and a bar with my collection of vintage liquor."

"Does the home theatre have popcorn and a nacho machine?" I decided to tease him.

To my utter surprise, he nodded. "It does. It also has a soda vending machine, and a gumball machine."

"Do celebrities visit your home?" I queried.

"Not this mansion because it's so far away from the city, but they visit my other homes."

"How many other houses do you even have?"

Jasper chuckled, leading the way. "Not to brag, but since you asked, I have a penthouse on Fifth Avenue, another mansion in Beverly Hills, the largest one in Aspen which is my favorite, an old family mansion on Lockhart's island, then there are apartments in

64

London, Switzerland, France, and Dubai . . ." He paused. "You want me to go on?"

"There are more?" I stared at him incredulously. "And you have an island after your name?"

He just smiled as an answer.

"Any place in the house that you wouldn't want me to wander into?"

"The bar where I keep the vintage liquor. You touch one of those bottles, and you've made an enemy," he said good-naturedly.

I was speechless. My entire house would fit into the foyer of this mansion. A middle-aged lady, probably in her late forties stood at the foot of the stairs. She was dressed elegantly in a beige shirt and a black skirt. Her brown hair was tucked in a neat bun, and she had the most beautiful grey-green eyes I had ever seen. She smiled warmly at me as she saw us approach.

"Kiara, this is Margret. She's the housekeeper who's been with this family for as long as I remember." With that remark, the two smiled at each other. "And Margret, this is Kiara, the beautiful damsel in distress I told you about."

I laughed. "Did he just describe me as a damsel in distress?"

"The same way that I'm a knight in shining armor. That's a good pair, you know." He passed me his devilish grin.

I couldn't miss the subtle hints he dropped in from time to time. Margret smiled in silence at the exchange.

"Get some rest, Kiara, and I will see you in a while for supper."

I nodded and thanked him again. When we were done with the basic introduction, a tall young man, somewhere between his thirties materialized. An apprehensive look was plastered over his face, but I still managed to pass a nervous smile. Without a word, he lifted my baggage. Margret decided to introduce him.

"This is the assistant housekeeper, Morgan. Should you require anything, he will be at your service. If not, you can always call me, and I will assist you."

"Thank you," I said.

Morgan was a man of few words. He didn't spare me another glance as he took my bag and began climbing the stairs.

"You're always welcome. I assume you must be tired. I'll have the bath ready for you upstairs in the guest room if you could follow me, Miss Kiara."

*   *   *

The guest room was a spacious bedroom on the second story. A white wooden canopy bed was at the center with plush cushions and a soft feather-like comforter. I had always dreamed of having a bed like this to sleep in. It also had a large white dresser with an oval mirror and a wardrobe. My feet melted above the soft white carpet.

Margret opened the built-in wardrobe full of outfits hanging from it. Beautiful gowns, cocktail party dresses, and casuals were neatly arranged inside, along with formals that hung at the top.

I was mesmerized by it. I opened the last door to find a wide collection of footwear on at least five different shelves.

"If the clothes are not to your liking, I can arrange to get them replaced for something more suitable to your taste."

"I actually brought some of my clothes from home." I pointed at the small bag lying on the floor until I realized it was missing. "Whose wardrobe is this?" I asked.

I could have sworn I had seen Morgan bring my bag into this room, so why wasn't it here?

"Mr. Lockhart has a cousin living in London who visits every once in a while. Camilla uses this room, and this closet belongs to her."

"I can't use her things"

66

Margret waved her hand in dismissal. "Trust me, dear, she wouldn't mind. Camilla has a kind heart and besides, she had once used an entire wardrobe of outfits for a month. She doesn't make a habit of using it twice. She likes a change. It will go to charity anyway."

It made me feel a bit better, although I couldn't miss the meaning behind that last line that *I* was perhaps charity.

"What about my bag?"

"Which bag, honey?"

"The one that had my clothes in it," I said.

"Oh, you wouldn't need that anymore," she said with a smile, and before I could question her with what exactly that meant, she left the room, closing the door on her way out.

I wondered if Morgan left it in another room. I sighed and decided to have a nice warm bath. I smelled like mud and cheap motel soap. My hair was dry, untamed, and in urgent need of some conditioner.

The adjacent bathroom was just as luxurious and spacious with smooth Italian granite flooring, a vintage porcelain bathtub at the far end of the bathroom, and a golden French Louis chair by the mini dresser.

My gaze traveled to the long cabinet. I opened it to find different varieties of bodywash bottles, soaps and shampoos lined up on three shelves, along with lotions, moisturizers, and other stuff. The fragrance drove me insane.

I realized how lucky Jasper's cousin Camilla was to have this luxury as a part of her daily life. I soaked into the steaming tub and took the opportunity to rub every inch of my body to remove the grime.

Once Jasper found a way to solve my problem, I wouldn't be having the pleasure of experiencing such a relaxing bath anymore. I thought of Mom and how life had been unfair to her.

One thought led to another, and I ended up thinking of Dad. I remembered every small detail of the night I hit him. Hot

67

tears trickled down my face, and I allowed myself to cry in silent mourning.

CHAPTER TEN

After the best sleep of my life, I woke up at exactly 8 AM the next morning and was summoned downstairs to join Jasper for breakfast.

I dressed casually in a t-shirt and jeans and was surprised at how perfectly Camilla's clothes fit me. I descended the stairs slowly, and it wasn't hard to spot the dining area. Jasper was seated at the head of the table, and when he saw me walk in, he passed me his usual warm smile.

"How are you feeling, Kiara?" he asked me.

"Much better, all thanks to you," I said, taking a seat right beside him.

"Is the new room to your liking?" he inquired.

I laughed. "What's not to like? I feel like I've met a fairy godmother who flicked a magic wand and changed my life completely."

Still smiling, Jasper nodded. "Well, I wouldn't go as far as to call myself a fairy godmother, although I think it is a gentleman's duty to help and support a woman in her difficult times."

"You're very modest and kind," I admitted.

I thought I heard him mutter, *"I'm far from it"* when Morgan walked inside the room, pushing a trolley filled with cakes and assortments.

"What do we have for breakfast today?" Jasper asked the butler.

Morgan recited the elaborate menu which was a little too much for a table that only consisted of two people (unless Jasper ate like a monster). A petite maid approached the table and served portions of food. My plate was towered with pancakes oozing with maple syrup, a side dish of strawberry shortcake, toast with blueberries and fresh strawberries, and sunny-side omelet with hash browns. There was even orange juice and coffee.

Jasper probably realized that his little breakfast had rendered me speechless because he said, "Please help yourself."

I dug into the food like a hungry lion caged up in the Sahara Desert for months. I think I had forgotten who was watching me for a second because I literally devoured everything. I noticed from the corner of my eye that an uncanny smile played on his face.

The few minutes after that were filled with sounds of the silver clanking with the cutlery. Jasper was raising a glass of juice to his lips when he received a phone call. He excused himself, leaving the room, and a minute later, he returned to his seat. There were lines of worry crossing his handsome features.

"There's some news," he declared.

"What is it?" I asked.

"You shouldn't have fled the scene after . . ." he trailed off. A bit later, he continued, "The police were investigating, and they think it wasn't an accident . . . that you killed your father on purpose."

The fork slipped right out of my hands. I lost my appetite all of a sudden. I started to feel nauseous. "Do you believe that, Jasper?"

His gaze was locked on mine as if he suspected me of deliberately murdering my father. I went on, "I didn't kill him," I said in a hushed whisper. "Please trust me. It was an accident."

"I trust you, Kiara, but I have some inside sources informing me that the police suspect you of foul play. My suggestion right now would be for you to continue staying here with me and let me handle this my way. If you are taken into custody, I daresay it would only end up in chaos."

My mind had already gone blank. The police wanted me for questioning, and I was doing a great job by hiding like a coward.

"If you're willing to listen, I will advise you about how we can go about the situation."

"I'm all ears."

"I know you're not going to like this, but it's best you cut all contact with your friends and family for a while. Let the police investigate. Your mother will tell them that you weren't even in town when it actually happened. I'll pose as your alibi should the need arise, and even if something were to go wrong, I have the best attorneys in the country. No one will be able to lay a finger on you. You have my word."

"That means I would be a freeloader," I said nervously. "I know we are friends, but I can't let you pay for everything. I can't keep asking you for favors, I feel awful."

Jasper took a quick drink of his coffee. "I have a proposal for you if you're willing to consider."

"What kind of proposal?"

"In exchange for everything—that includes my protection of you, a roof over your head and the billionaire lifestyle—you agree to be my companion for social gatherings and other charity functions. You see, I need a presentable woman beside me at all times, and you're a beautiful woman who also happens to be my friend. So, it's safe to assume that you wouldn't be quite troubled by the offer."

I sat back and tried to process the information. He specifically used the word "companion" and threw in words like "social gatherings" and "charity functions," but why did I have a feeling that Jasper was sugarcoating his proposal to make it seem rather acceptable?

"I'm probably misunderstanding this. You want me to get dolled up and attend functions in exchange for me living in your house?" I asked.

Jasper nodded. "Since you were eager to be of help, I think it would be a fair trade."

"Am I going to be your mistress?" I decided to stop beating around the bush and get straight to the point.

Jasper laughed, the sound a deep rumble. "That's a very old-fashioned word. Companion is better suited for this arrangement."

Heat rose to my cheeks. He couldn't possibly be suggesting what I thought he was suggesting, right?

"That includes sex as well?" I asked frankly. My heart started beating faster as he prolonged his answer, slowly sipping his coffee again.

"Not if you don't want to, but I'd like that as well," he admitted boldly. "Trust me, once you have me in your bed, you'd want to keep me there."

His overconfidence made me blush. I might as well hallucinate about Jasper putting a ring on my finger. Perhaps, this could be a dream. Next thing I knew, I would wake up in one of those dirty motels I had lived in during the last few days and realize that this had all been a figment of my imagination.

I loved him.

Unconditionally and irrevocably. Jasper had done so much for me without asking for anything in return, and now he was giving me a chance to return the favor.

My mind was preoccupied with a dozen questions. Was the arrangement really alright? Or was I finally losing the last bit of self-respect that I had by agreeing to be his *mistress*? Oh no, scratch that, his *companion*? Did that mean I would be his one and only?

Think about it, Kiara.

I'd get to live in a mansion where I wouldn't even have to lift a finger for anything; material things I had always wished for. I'd get a taste of a life I never even thought of in my wildest dreams, but the most important of all was the fact that I was going to do it all for Jasper. He was asking me to do this. Surely, he wouldn't ask if he didn't like me even a little bit, right?

"Kiara." His soft voice almost startled me. "You're thinking too much again. We're both adults who happen to be single, and are great friends. We're perhaps a perfect match. I thought it would be a great opportunity for us to get to know each other better, if nothing else."

"What if the police recognize me in one of your parties and ask you about me?"

"As I said, I'll pose as an alibi and tell them you were with me when it happened. That's not something for you to worry about. I have the necessary people and the means to get that done. Rest assured."

"I'd like to ask something else if it's alright."

"Ask away, love,"

"If I agree to it, Jasper, will you remain faithful to me as a partner?"

"Of course. I don't really enjoy playing doubles," he said, but I couldn't read his expressions. "And I'd expect the same loyalty from you."

"May I have a little time to think please?"

"Yes, you may. Although I'd like it if you hurry up because I have a few events lined up, and I'd be more than glad to have you on my arm by then." He passed me that dazzling smile.

"I'll tell you my answer by tomorrow," I said, taking a bite of the lemon tart.

"Tomorrow is fine," he agreed.

The conversation stirred to another topic, and I wondered if Jasper had done that on purpose to ease my tension about his proposal. I knew it had worked because I was smiling and laughing by the end of breakfast.

"May I have your phone, Kiara?" Jasper asked me, raising his hand towards me, palm up.

"Sure."

He took the device, flipped it, and removed the battery and the sim card.

I passed him a questioning look. "Why did you do that?"

"We will get you a new phone. In case you're questioned by the police, you can say you misplaced your old phone. You don't need your colleagues and friends calling you and asking you questions and complicating things further. We will wait until the investigation simmers down."

He then passed the contents to Morgan. "Get rid of it."

Jasper wanted to take proper measures in ensuring my safety, and that explained why I had to stop using my phone. It was possible that the police could track me down with it and that would cause unnecessary hassle.

"I'm going to Hong Kong for a business conference for three days. I suppose that would be enough time for you to think about my proposal."

Three days were more than enough, and I had already made my decision, but I gave him a nod. If I agreed to his proposal now, I was afraid I'd sound too eager.

He gave me his heart-melting smile, kissed the top of my forehead, and in his seductive voice, he whispered, "I'll be waiting for your answer."

With that, Jasper sauntered out of the dining room in confident strides.

CHAPTER ELEVEN

For three days straight, I almost had nothing to do. The Lockhart mansion was part of a large estate with acres and acres of land.

When I walked outside into the courtyard, I could hear the soft lapping of the lake waters. It was soothing and peaceful. There was a small cabin on the other side of the lake amid the pine trees with a barn and a stable. I wondered if the cabin belonged to Jasper, and made a mental note to ask him to let me see it someday.

I changed into a lemon-colored loose blouse over faded jeans and white sneakers, something casual for a walk in the woods. I spent thirty minutes just enjoying nature and the whooshing of the leaves from the trees. The cool summer breeze blew on my face and whipped my hair. The sun was setting, leaving the sky an orange hue, shielding itself behind the mountains. It was like a beautiful painting in vivid colors.

I basked in the beauty of nature, walking deeper into the woods, dodging the branches of trees that were jutting out and hopping off fallen tree trunks. I checked the time and realized I still had about an hour before dinner. My thoughts shifted to Jasper and wondered how nice it would be to take a walk here with him. It would be downright romantic. He was supposed to be here yesterday, but it seemed like work had held him up again. I couldn't blame him. Jasper was a busy man, after all.

As I walked further, my sneaker hit a twig or something, and I toppled over and fell flat on the muddy ground. Dirt caked my top and my jeans. I groaned as I climbed to my feet, brushing off the leaves and the matted soil. I kicked what I thought was a twig, and something shiny went flying from the ground.

I quickly kneeled on the ground and picked up the shimmering object. Sure enough, it was a silver ring, embedded with a red stone of some kind. I wondered if the ring was real or the fake kind that you find in thrift stores. It looked quite real.

I didn't know if it was instinct when I clawed my fingers into the dirt and like a dog trying to hide his bone, continued to dig the soft dirt further. I dug deeper and it kind of reminded me of how I used to dig in the sand when I played at the beach when I was eight. There was nothing else I could find.

Absolutely nothing.

What did I expect? I watched too much CSI and crime documentaries to think I could find a human body. Silly me.

I pushed the ring into my denim pockets and decided to ask Jasper about it myself.

*   *   *

I was bored around the house with nothing to do on my hands, so I helped the head chef, Lola, prepare breakfast in the morning. We were baking banana bread. Lola mentioned that it was Jasper's favorite.

My thoughts drifted to my mother, and I wondered if she was doing alright. Before leaving for his trip, Jasper assured me that he had spoken to Mom and told her how I had to maintain a low profile until things simmered down a little. I just missed her so much. I wanted to talk to her at least once.

The thoughts were clouding my mind when suddenly, I felt a pair of hands cover my eyes. The familiar scent of the cologne assaulted my nose. I touched the hand.

"Jasper, you're back!" I said gleefully, my heart filled with warmth.

I was still giggling, and my hand was still in his firm grasp as I spun around to face him.

I froze.

Leaning against the granite counter, dressed in blue denim and a white Ralph Lauren t-shirt, was a man a few inches taller than Jasper. I recognized the man as the doctor who treated me that fateful night I was almost raped.

Dr. Vincent grinned. "Wrong answer."

I smiled. "What are you doing here?"

"I'm doing quite well, Kiara. Thanks for asking."

I laughed again. "I'm sorry. I was just surprised that's all."

He snagged an apple from the fruit bowl and took a large bite. "To answer your first question, I'm here because this is my house. I suppose I could ask you the same?"

His house? Jasper never mentioned of anyone else living with him.

And how was I supposed to answer his question without giving away too much information?

"I moved in here with Jasper," I said, keeping the words simple and my tone discreet.

Vincent's brows twitched upward. "So, you and Jasper are together?"

I gave a nod, and I thought I saw disappointment cross his features.

"Well, didn't think my brother was really relationship material, but I guess people change." He winked.

Jasper's brother?

I examined him closely. Vincent's hair was light brown, bordering to blond. The sunlight that streamed from the kitchen windows made him look almost like Goldilocks's long-lost cousin.

While Jasper always looked like he had walked off the Paris fashion week runway, Vincent had a simple boyish charm. He had brown eyes that looked almost topaz in the sunlight, kind of like whiskey. If you looked closer, their face structure was almost similar. It was clear they were brothers. I wondered how I wasn't able to make the connection then.

I shook my head. "Jasper never told me he has a brother."

Vincent chuckled. "Trust me, there are a lot of things that Jasper hasn't told you."

I tried to think if there was any hidden meaning behind those words. Vincent hopped down from the barstool. "Oh, how rude of me, my lady. I haven't made proper introductions. Vincent Lockhart, Lord of the Manor, although calling me Vince would suffice." He took my hand in his and kissed my knuckles. "How do you do?"

I had this image of a historical fiction romance, the Lord of the manor meeting the beautiful girl. I laughed.

I decided to play along. I did a little curtsy. "Pleased to make your acquaintance, Lord Vincent. I'm Kiara Reeves."

He offered me his arm. "Would you like to take a walk with me in the courtyard, Lady Kiara?"

"That would be wonderful, kind sir." I locked my arm in his as we walked out of the mansion towards the courtyard.

By the time we reached the gardens, I was laughing hysterically. Vincent was hilarious, and I kind of wished I had met him under different circumstances, one that did not include me needing a doctor for sexual assault.

We settled by the fountain, watching as the water spilled out of the cupid's arrow. The gushing sound of the water was almost music to the ears.

"Does that mean you would be living here too?" I asked.

Vincent shook his head. "Not really. I live just outside of the town, and sometimes I like to drop by to keep an eye out on my brother," he explained.

"Shouldn't it be the other way around since he's your older brother?" I teased him.

Vincent shrugged. "Well, he is the older one, but we seemed to have reversed roles since childhood. Jasper's always been the troublemaker while I was the perfect example of a boy scout."

"Oh, I'm sure."

"Enough about Jasper," Vincent said. "I'd like to know more about you and how exactly did your meeting with him transpire into something like this."

"Something like what?"

"A relationship," he said as a matter-of-factly. "Tell me how. I need the juicy details."

I smiled. That's the story I loved to recite. "Well, as you're already aware, we met under very unusual circumstances. A few days later, he came to see me in the restaurant that I worked at. He was nice, funny, and I liked him then." I sighed, recalling the painful events that followed after that. "Jasper's helped me in my most difficult times. He stood by me when no one else did, and I seriously owe him a great deal."

Vincent's scrutinizing stare was locked on me. "Is that why you are with him? Because you think you owe him?"

"No! Of course not. I'm with him because I want to be. I've never met someone like him. Jasper makes me feel so special, and he treats me right. He's . . . well, he's too perfect for words."

His eyes narrowed at me, and I couldn't read his expression. "You love him, don't you?"

"Is it that obvious?" I asked shyly.

Vincent chuckled. "As clear as day, my lady."

Time easily passed with Vincent. I realized the brothers were so distinct from each other. Jasper was more like a puzzle, the broody, mysterious type while Vincent was an open book. While I usually melted under Jasper's gaze, Vincent's approach was friendlier. They were different in their own way.

We walked back into the mansion at brunch. It was funny how easily we'd become friends in such a short time.

"Do you seek the darkness, Kiara?" Vincent asked me.

"I'm sorry, what?" I threw him a look.

Vincent laughed nervously. "Never mind." He took my hand in his again and kissed the knuckles. "Until next time, my lady. I look forward to our next secret rendezvous."

I laughed. "Likewise."

With Vincent long gone, his words continued to haunt me. *Do you seek the darkness, Kiara?*

CHAPTER TWELVE

JASPER

The last thing I expected when I drove through the mansion gates was to see Vincent's black chrome G-wagon parked in its designated area. Automatically, my blood started to boil.

What did he want now?

The plan was to be back in three days, but then I had received a call from my secretary who informed me I needed to attend to some business urgently. Three days turned to five, and now that I was finally home and wanted some answers from Kiara, my younger brother had decided to make an appearance.

I touched my forehead to the steering wheel and took deep, calming breaths. My fingers wound around the wheel tightly until they were white. I was four years senior to Vincent, and yet he seemed to always act like my older brother.

Vincent had always been Dad's favorite. No matter how better I did academically, how many trophies I got, or how I continued to show them that I was *better,* they never accepted me. Vincent had always been the best, but I surpassed him over the years. Vincent wasn't business-minded, and that gave me the upper hand. Father had no choice but to hand it all over to me.

The gift box lay on the passenger seat. I picked it up, composed myself, and started walking into the house.

What would Vince do anyway? Try to ward me off from making advances at Kiara? Would he tell me to fuck off like he usually did? He always did have the tendency to stick his condescending little nose where it didn't belong. If he so much as tried to meddle in my matters, I'd tell him where to put it.

I walked through the foyer and heard the sound of laughter coming from the music room on the right. I crept slowly to the door and stood behind to watch.

Kiara was seated at the piano, the one that I played during my bad days while Vince was settled right beside her. Their backs were facing me, but I could tell from the way she laughed that he had joked about something. He was teaching her Mozart's, *"Piano Sonata No. 11"*, which he usually played—and the only one he knew because the rest of his days were spent buried inside medical books. I was pretty sure the idiot played it just to impress girls, the way he was doing with Kiara.

The golden specks in his hair glowed under the sunlight, and he had the usual amused expression on his face. She said something, and he responded, taking her hand in his and showing her which keys to press. People hardly recognized us as brothers because we looked different.

And we were different in every sense of the word.

I leaned against the doorframe with my hands folded across my chest. I watched as Vincent brought his hand to Kiara's face and pushed a lock of hair behind her ear, a casual brush of his fingers but deliberate nonetheless.

He had the goddamn nerve to touch my girl and flirt with her.

I had this sudden urge to push him down under a flight of stairs or perhaps in front of a speeding car. The piece stopped playing, and I brought my palms together in a slow clap. "Marvelous!"

Both of them spun around to face me. Kiara's face lit up like Christmas lights while Vincent's face blanched and was as pale as the fucking white shirt he was wearing.

I approached the piano and ran my fingers on the keys. "You've outdone yourself playing it, Vince," I said, trying hard to keep myself from saying things that were actually on my mind. "You aren't perfect yet, but you can play well. I'm proud of you." I ground my teeth.

"Thanks," Vincent replied, avoiding eye contact. He knew how great I was at bullshitting.

Kiara was still mesmerized. "Do you play the piano as well, Jasper?"

I nodded. "Yes, I do. I took lessons when I was ten, and I continued to play it during my leisure hours even now. In fact, I was the one who taught Vincent that piece. Didn't I, lil' brother?"

He hated my guts whenever I spoke to him like he was a mere three-year-old.

Vince sighed. "Yeah, you did."

"That's so sweet," Kiara cooed as she placed her hand on mine. I could see the attraction she had for me in her eyes as clear as day. The admiration she had for me was growing each day.

I laughed. "He was such a sweet little boy, Kiara, always following me around like a little puppy."

Vincent had started to play with the loose threads of his jeans. His face showcased nonchalance. Kiara giggled, obviously thinking of this as a cute little childhood thing between brothers.

I turned to face Vincent, pinning him with a hard stare. "You've got to prepare for your exams, am I correct?"

"Vincent has exams?" Kiara seemed distressed. "Oh, if I knew earlier, I wouldn't have insisted on you teaching me the piano. I'm sorry I took your time, Vince."

Oh, so now Vincent had become Vince? How many days or hours did it take for this transition to happen?

"It's alright, Kiara. Sometimes I need a good break from my usual routine." He passed her his killer smile—the type that usually brought women to their knees before his gaze dropped to mine along with his smile.

I passed him my best *"Don't-you-dare-fuck-with-my-girl"* stare, and that immediately told him to take his leave.

"I'll see you around, Kiara," he said.

"See you," Kiara called out after him.

I claimed the vacant seat by the piano beside her.

She looked at me bashfully, her long lashes peering at me.

"You shouldn't tease him like that, Jasper."

I leaned into the sweet scent of peaches. "Oh, come on, sweetheart. It's a big brother's job to tease their younger siblings."

She laughed and reached for my tie, toying with it with her fingers. "How was your trip?"

"Not that great," I responded.

"Why not?" she asked innocently.

I gave her a quick peck on the lips. "Because you weren't there with me."

I knew I had said the right thing because her eyes sparkled with love and admiration for me. "Would you like me to teach you to play the piano?"

Her smile widened. "Of course."

"How about we perfect the same piece Vincent was showing you earlier?"

"That would be great," she responded eagerly.

I taught her how to play the piano and was quite surprised to see that Kiara was a fast learner. Once I showed her something, she would grasp it quickly, and that impressed me. I was right to have chosen her. She was the one. There was no doubt.

*   *   *

KIARA

Jasper taught me how to play the piano, and I liked how his long elegant fingers worked expertly on the instrument. After he had showed me a few times, he let me practice.

I made some mistakes, and we laughed about it. I didn't remember having this much fun before. It made me forget all the messed-up things in my life. I liked how his warm blue eyes watched me with delight. I was falling hard for this man, and it was almost too suffocating.

He leaned in, and I smelled the musky male scent of him that made me swoon a little. Before I knew what was happening, Jasper slid his hand under my thigh, and the other grasped my waist as he pulled me into his lap.

I gasped when his lips crashed against mine. The hand that held my waist went up to feel the curves of my body. His mouth was insistent on mine, parting my lips so his tongue could plunge deeper. I couldn't help the low moan that escaped my throat.

My hands brushed over his shirt front, and his fingers moved over my breasts. The blouse was silk, so I could feel the heat of his palm as it squeezed my right breast.

"Jasper . . ."

His mouth had stopped assaulting my lips and moved down to trail kisses along my jawline where I could feel the wetness of his tongue tasting me—ravishing me. He was like a madman obsessed with possessing me, like a beast unleashed.

The intensity of his mouth, along with the possessive touch of his hands, was a little too much, and I was becoming giddy from all of it. If kissing him was so exhilarating, I wondered what sex would be like with this man.

And just like that, I was jealous of every other woman that had him in bed before me.

Nothing about his touch was soft; it was all dominant and unabashed. That's what I liked about him—how unapologetic he was. I didn't think any woman would ever want his hands to stop doing what he was doing to me, and it made me realize just how

85

shameless I had become when I took his hand and dipped it inside my shirt. With other men, I couldn't fathom doing that, but with Jasper, I didn't feel awkward.

His fingers grazed my nipple and then pinched it. I made a gasping sound when both his hands cupped my breasts firmly. I saw his head lowering as he took one breast in his mouth and suckled the tip until I was moaning his name.

A smile played on his lips as he took control of my mouth, and that drowned all my moans. He chuckled, and I whispered, "Someone will see us."

Swiftly, Jasper was up on his feet, letting my legs wrap around his middle. He closed the door, took the lid prop of the piano, and pulled it down. He placed me on the edge of the closed piano and took my mouth in a deep kiss. My hand slid against the front of his pants; I could feel how hard he had become. He was thick and long, throbbing for me.

I heard him growl. When Jasper's fingers reached for the hem of my skirt, he pushed the skirts up to my waist. His expert fingers peeled my damp panties to my ankles, and I felt his thick fingers reach the folds between my thighs.

Before I knew it, I was spreading my legs wider. I was being completely shameless, and I hardly cared. Jasper chuckled under his breath and whispered in his sexy voice, "You are so wet for me, you dirty little whore."

My cheeks flushed. Of all things, I had never expected him to say that, but Jasper didn't seem like the kind of man who'd be a gentleman in bed. Maybe he got his kicks by name-calling.

I cried when his finger continued to rub against me. I arched my back as his fingers slid inside of me. I was lost in a frenzy of emotions and feelings. Jasper knew what he was doing, in fact, he was an expert in seduction. I didn't quite remember feeling this way with my previous boyfriend.

My eyes closed because it became a little too much. Being in love with a person and having him love me back—at least that's what I thought this was about. He probably missed me so much during the past few days that he couldn't stop himself from having his hands over me, and honestly, I didn't mind. It was clear that we felt the same about each other.

I was getting close to climaxing until I felt a sharp pain. I tried to sit up, but he held me tightly in place, and I clenched my teeth as the pain surged through me again. It took me a second to realize what had happened. Jasper had thrust inside me. I thought we were just messing around, but it turns out we weren't.

We were having sex. A little warning would have been great.

I went up on my elbows to see Jasper's expression laced with desire. Anyone would think we were making love, but we weren't.

He pulled out of me and drove into me so hard, my knees buckled. The pain overpowered the pleasure. I was going to tell him to slow down. I wanted to tell him that I needed some time to accommodate him, but my voice was lost in his growls of carnal desire. He continued to thrust inside me relentlessly until I felt his release.

When Jasper was done, he pulled my skirt down slowly, and I heard the sound of his zipper. He was still panting when he said, "That was lovely. We should do it again soon."

I remained sprawled on the piano as I heard his footsteps walking out of the room. The door of the music room closed behind him.

It was a while later that I realized I had been thoroughly used.

CHAPTER THIRTEEN

JASPER

I had mastered the act of calmness. Over the years, I became good at faking it. When I had seen Vincent and Kiara sitting together on that bench and Vincent smiling down at her, I saw red. I had the urge to claim what was mine.

It was just foreplay at first, and I had planned on leaving soon after, but when I saw her sweet little cunt and felt how tight she was, I lost my senses, and before I knew it, I was thrusting inside her. To top it off, I had been exceptionally careless, not having used protection and all.

I hated it when I couldn't think straight, and especially when I was unable to read minds. From the way Kiara had been giving me the cold shoulder, I realized I had done it wrong. I shouldn't have let my emotions get the best of me, but it just happened.

One thing led to another. Maybe she shouldn't wear those sexy silk blouses anymore. I screwed up. Now I had to make it right.

I was in my office, talking on the phone with a client, when Vincent stormed inside. He didn't seem quite in the mood, and I wondered if this was about the same issue we had gone through innumerable times. Vincent was dressed in a black Polo t-shirt over denim jeans and had his legs crossed in front of him, his eyes scanning the office.

My secretary, Molly, walked in with a tray and placed two cups of coffee on the table along with some assortments. She passed Vincent a quick smile and turned to face me as I hung up the phone.

"Sir, you have a meeting with Mr. Petrov in twenty minutes."

I flashed her my winning smile. "I remember, but please remind me again a few minutes before the meeting starts."

"Of course, sir," Molly responded and then turned to Vincent. "How are you doing, Mr. Lockhart? It's nice to see you in the office after a long time."

Vincent took a sip from his cup. "The coffee always brings me back here."

Molly giggled, obviously charmed by Vincent. We Lockharts were very good at pleasing women and getting them to do exactly what we wanted.

Molly was an average plain-Jane—dark hair, dark eyes, all the way down to the nerdy glasses that topped it off. Her boyfriend was an average Joe, working somewhere in retail at a minimum wage job.

Although I would have liked to have someone beautiful work alongside me, I had chosen Molly specifically because of her average looks. I didn't believe in office flings, more so due to the fact that I liked to concentrate on the work and make the company better rather than being completely distracted by a piece of ass.

Also, it seemed like Molly could detect danger from a mile away. She always had her eyes downcast. She was polite, did her job properly, and never wore anything inappropriate. Most of all, she didn't try to get my attention by dropping the entire pen holder just so I could get a peek inside her shirt. The last time a PA had tried that, I fired her ass before she could say, "sorry".

I dismissed Molly after giving a brief instruction to hold all my calls until lunch break. When she was out of the room, I turned my attention to Vincent. "To what do I owe this pleasure, Junior Lockhart?"

I knew how it pissed him off when anyone called him by that name. Vincent had always been "Junior Lockhart", our father was called "Senior Lockhart", while I was always the unwanted bastard who actually proved himself in the end.

"Are you playing her?" he asked me.

I knew he meant Kiara, but I decided to play innocent. "Molly? No way. She's not my type."

"I meant Kiara." His tone told me he knew I was bullshitting as always. "She seemed upset about something since this morning, but she refused to tell me what it is."

"Oh, is that why you're here? We could have discussed this at home; there wasn't any need for you to drive all the way to the office," I pointed out.

"That's not the only reason why I decided to visit, and you did not answer my question," Vincent said accusingly. A pause later, he continued, "This time you went too far, bringing a woman back to the mansion to live with you, and she doesn't seem like the type you used to . . ." he trailed off, unable to come up with the right word. "Kiara seems quite levelheaded and it would be a shame to see her get hurt because of your childish behavior."

"I don't need you to give me any pieces of advice about what I should do and shouldn't. Rather, I'd appreciate it if you mind your own fucking business."

Vincent nodded, picking up a glass paperweight and rolling it between his fingers. "I'm minding my own business, although I should let you know that if I have the slightest clue that you're in fact hurting her, I'll be forced to take matters into my own hands and that's when it won't be pretty. The tabloids are sharks, sniffing for any small amount of controversy they could get their hands on,

90

and I'd be glad to oblige. Trust me on this, Jasper, I have some really heavy evidence that could expose you."

"Are you threatening me?" I loved a challenge when I saw one.

Vincent chuckled. "That's one way to put it."

"What do you want?"

"I'll be clear so we understand each other better. Last time, when I voiced my desire to build a hospital, you refused to give me the required funds." He regarded me from over the rims of the cup. "Now, I don't need the funds. All I want is forty-five percent of the company revenues."

I grinned at him, seething inside. "I always thought you could be a stand-up comedian."

"I believe neurology is better suited for me," he said in good humor, enjoying every bit of my discomfort.

"Well, not to be rude, lil' brother, but forty-five percent revenues for contributing absolutely nothing seems quite unfair. As you already know, I manage all the operations of the company. The staff that I have right now are all trained and qualified. Everyone who works here earns their place. What can you offer the company?"

Vincent laughed. "Well, I'm a Lockhart."

I laughed back at the joke. "Not good enough. I built this company from the ruins; it is what it is today because of my hard work. Why would I—"

He slammed two pictures on the table. "These will go directly to Kiara and the media."

That's when I lost it. "You bastard!" I growled at him.

He smiled. "Funny coming from you." That smile vanished into a grim expression, one of a triumphant player who had played his chess pieces right.

He had me in check, that sonofabitch. "I know how much you like playing games, but I realized that Kiara seems more important to you than your previous toys. Forty percent final."

"Thirty-five," I said. "Don't push me."

Vincent hummed an unfamiliar tune. "Forty percent and I'll burn the pictures and all other evidence."

"Will that matter? It's probably saved in your laptop." Vincent smiled. "You know me quite well. Thirty-five will do, I guess."

Before he could walk out of the office, I called out to him, "Vincent, pack your bags. I don't want you in the mansion. By tomorrow, I expect you to be gone, and if you try to meddle in between my relationship with Kiara, consider the thirty-five down to five. I wouldn't even care much about the tabloids. Are we clear?"

"Crystal." Vincent had a wide smile on his face when he walked out of the office.

I gritted my teeth and brought all the stuff on the table tumbling down with a swipe of my hand. I took a few deep breaths and by the time Molly walked into the office, I had a smile plastered on my face. Murder was on my mind.

Rage was taking all over, and it would only be a matter of time before I snapped at someone and then they would see how ugly it could get. Nobody fucked with Jasper Lockhart, the only one who dared to was Vincent. Vincent knew those were the only threats he could pull. He couldn't go too far as he lacked power, and crossing the line would cost him.

Even though Vincent had already left, I could still smell the loss in the air, his megawatt smile was proof enough.

*   *   *

KIARA

After that day in the music room, Jasper acted like nothing happened. He hadn't forced himself on me. I willingly encouraged him, but I had thought our first time would be in bed and not on

92

the flat surface of a shiny black piano. I had fantasized about us together a lot of times, and every time in those fantasies, I imagined going on a date with him first and end up with me wearing the sexiest red lingerie before we make sweet love in bed. Slow and sensuous. Not raw and animalistic.

The thought continued to disturb me. It has been over a week since I came to the mansion, and I continued to feel detached from the world outside. Having no connection with my mother or Kathy, was disturbing enough that I started to wonder if Jasper actually had any feelings for me.

I knew it was wrong of me to be selfish. Jasper had done a lot of things for me, but I felt worthless. Every time I asked him about talking to Mom, he refused and said that it wouldn't do me any good. He said that once things had fallen back into place, he'd take me to her himself, and I believed him.

Within the little amount of time that I had been staying here, I became friends with Vincent. He was funny and nice sometimes I laughed so much with him that I forgot about everything that troubled me.

I looked forward to seeing him every evening. My thoughts were interrupted by the housekeeper, Morgan, who appeared busy with loading baggage into Vince's G-wagon.

"What's going on here?" I asked him.

Morgan sported his usual solemn expression. Sometimes, I wondered if he was a robot. "Master Vincent will be leaving today in the evening."

He was saying something else, but I tuned it out completely.

Vincent was leaving today?

I took off into the mansion and went to that one place I knew I could find him—the music room.

I stopped short at the door, watching him play a sad tune. My eyes were moist, and tears trickled down my face as I clapped slowly. He turned to face me and passed his dazzling smile. He climbed to his feet as I made my way towards him, and we stood in the center of the room, looking into each other's eyes. Not a word was exchanged between us.

Vincent cleared his throat and said, "I must be a good musician if I can make a girl all emotional."

My heart started to leap out of my throat. With a shaky voice, I asked, "You're leaving?"

His expression was almost apologetic. He glanced at the mansion and then turned to face me. "Yes, Milady, I am."

My lower lip quivered. We spent the last few evenings by the fountain, sharing stories and joking about. I was losing another friend, a close friend.

"Don't," I choked. "Don't go."

Vincent took my hands in his. I didn't pull away or protest. He reached out with the other and wiped a tear off my cheek. "I was always told to make decisions with my head, and never to follow my heart if I really wanted something, and I've always done that." He caressed my hand with his fingers. "This time, Kiara, I'm having a really hard time not following my heart."

"What does your heart say?" I asked.

"To stay here with you," he admitted.

"So stay," I whispered.

Vincent shook his head. He was hurting, I could see it. "I can't."

"Why not?"

"If I told you, would you leave Jasper and come with me?"

I remained silent, taken aback by that question. "I can't, Vincent. Jasper's done too much for me. I . . . I love him."

"You can't betray his trust?"

I nodded. He went on, "I understand. My situation is somewhat similar to yours. I owe Jasper a great deal for things that he has done for me as a brother. He's a bit eccentric, but I feel like he may be changing for you."

I was flabbergasted by his revelation. Could it really be true?

"Changing? How so?"

"Well, he was easily bored with dating a woman within a week's time, but you have managed to become important to him—important enough that he'd let you stay in this house. It seems like his world revolves around you, for which I'm quite happy and also sad."

Why are you sad?"

"Because it means I can't have you, Kiara," he said simply, brushing my hair away from my face. "I have a dream of building my own hospital one day."

I smiled at him despite my heart breaking. "That's wonderful."

"I want to help people, and in order for me to do so, I have to make some sacrifices, and that's the path I'm leading to right now."

I didn't understand what he meant, but I nodded. I could feel my heart shattering into a million pieces.

Unable to hold in, I sniffled. "Stay here, Vince." I was so pathetic now that I had resorted to begging. "You're my best friend. I'll be lonely."

Vincent's expression mirrored my own, but he wasn't crying. It seemed like he was breaking inside.

"I'm sorry," he murmured and then he leaned in and pressed his lips against mine in a chaste kiss—almost like a peck. "When I come back, you'll see a new man. You'll see a man that holds more authority. I won't ask you to wait for me, neither will I make any promises, but I want you to know that I'll be there for you if you need me."

He passed me a small note. "Here's my new number. Don't hesitate to call me should the need arise."

I placed his number in my pocket. "I will."

"When I leave this evening, I want to see a smile on your face. Okay?"

I nodded and he continued, "No matter what happens, I'll always be here for you."

That evening, I stayed in the balcony of my room and looked down into the courtyard. Vincent was standing by his car, talking to a servant. I couldn't go down to say goodbye for the last time. It was too painful, so I decided to watch from a distance.

As if sensing my gaze on him, Vincent glanced up and waved at me before he climbed inside the car.

I stood there until I saw the car drive away through the imposing metal gates of the mansion.

I flung into bed with my face buried in the cushion and cried.

CHAPTER FOURTEEN

About an hour before midnight, I sneaked into the kitchen downstairs to make myself a little snack. Having lived an underprivileged life the entire twenty-three years of my life, it made me value things so much more now that I was living in this mansion, especially food.

Every time I took a bite of the morsel, I remembered my Mom. When I wasn't reading a book or doing something else, I often wondered how my mother was coping with the loss of my father and if she secretly held me accountable for his death. Even though Dad didn't act like a normal father most of the time, it didn't change the fact that he was still my father.

I opened the stainless steel refrigerator's double doors and rummaged through it to look for some contents to make a quick snack.

"Are you hungry, dear?"

I almost jumped out of my skin. Margret smiled in understanding. "Sorry to scare you, Miss Kiara. I saw you walk into the kitchen and thought I should offer to assist you in anything that you may need."

"Well, I was a bit hungry and couldn't really sleep. I can manage. I really don't want to trouble you."

"Darling, it's my job." She walked towards the open refrigerator and pulled out some contents.

I settled down in a high chair pulled up against the island bar where she diced a tomato and an onion. She offered to pour me wine, and since wine was my weakness, it was hard to refuse.

The mini bar was stocked with bottles of wine. Margret told me that they were vintage and export quality, some of the finest. I told Margret that I didn't want to waste any expensive wine, but she insisted that I try, so I did. When she told me the price, I stifled a cough.

The sandwich she prepared was delicious. I didn't fail to rain her with compliments. We were talking about everything and nothing in particular when I decided to ask her something.

"How long have you been working for the Lockharts?" I asked her, taking the last sip of the red wine.

"A really long time," she said.

I nodded, deciding that it was a vague answer. "I was just curious about what happened to Jasper's mother. I'm sure you're aware of how hard it is to get him to talk. Sometimes he's in a great mood, but other times, I feel like I don't even know the person. I want to get to know him better but I understand that as a hardworking man, he has a lot of responsibilities," I continued. "He never spoke of his mother . . ."

Margret shrugged. "Yes, darling. Jasper has had a difficult childhood, but it's not really my place to say anything if he hasn't spoken to you about the matter—the same goes for his mother. I'm sure you understand, Miss Kiara."

"I understand." I smiled, despite the fact that I was disappointed to not have the little information that I was looking for. I had asked Vincent and he hadn't been quite helpful either.

"Margret, can I ask you for a favor?"

This was my only chance.

"What is it, darling?"

"Do you have a phone?" I asked her and then continued with my request, "I would like to call my mother. It would only take a minute. I promise."

Margret appeared tense, but nodded and handed me her cell phone. I quickly dialed my mother's number. It rang a few times, and I prayed it wouldn't hit the voicemail. Luckily, she picked up at the third ring.

"Mom?"

"Kiara, is that you?" I heard my mother's shrill voice on the other end.

I almost cried from hearing her voice for the first time in two weeks. "Mom, I missed you."

She told me she was doing okay, and that I shouldn't worry about her. When she asked me where I was living for the last week, I explained that I was staying with a friend, and that I would return once I figured out what to do.

She explained that the police had questioned her and that she managed to keep my name clear from the entire debacle. I was relieved to hear that. I promised her that I'd call her soon.

I had a broad smile on my face by the end of the call. I felt truly content with the information that she was alright.

"Thanks for letting me call her, Margret," I said sincerely, giving her hand a little squeeze.

She patted me. "You're welcome, Miss. Kiara."

"Please don't tell Jasper about it."

"I wouldn't tell Jasper. Please, don't worry," she assured me.

"What can't you tell me, Kiara?"

The both of us looked at each other and froze. From Margret's expression, it was pretty clear who had silently walked in on our conversation.

I spun around to find Jasper leaning against the door frame.

Was he standing here long enough to hear the entire conversation?

"It's nothing. I was just asking her for some advice."

Jasper's hair was tousled, but it ended up looking stylish. There was slight stubble against his jawline which gave him a mature look. His midnight-blue eyes stared at me intently.

Even in the dark, I could feel the intensity burning from them. His chest was completely bare; soft brown curls sprinkled over it. He appeared to be only wearing sweatpants below. I had never taken notice of him shirtless before. His shoulders were broad, biceps were defined, and he had a nice set of abs with a V-cut stomach. I could have been drooling.

"What advice?" he asked, his eyes darting from Margret to me.

"She just asked me what you normally preferred during lunch, and if she could try something from her recipe in the kitchen tomorrow. She wanted my advice regarding that. It was supposed to be a surprise," Margret explained and then smiled at me.

Nice save Margret!

Jasper looked at me as if to question if that was true. "Yes, that was it," I agreed.

His face broke into the usual smile, totally Disney Prince-worthy. "I'll pretend I didn't hear any of it."

"Thanks for your advice, Margret."

She winked at me. "Anytime, honey."

Jasper led me back upstairs silently, and all the while I kept thinking what would have happened if he had heard about the call. Would he be upset?

"Kiara, why don't you change into some other clothes? Let's go for a long drive," Jasper suggested, taking hold of my hand.

"A long drive? At this hour?"

"Yeah. It would be fun. I usually go for drives when I have to cool my head. You haven't been out of the mansion for over a week, so I think you'd like the change."

"Okay, that sounds good," I agreed, and stormed into my room to change out of the night suit. I threw on a casual t-shirt over denim and my favorite *Trussardi* sneakers.

100

These days, I have been living in luxury, wearing expensive Italian clothing and practically living a dream life. Sometimes when I wake up in the morning, I wonder if it was just a dream.

But this was a reality.

When I met him in the parking lot, he was already waiting for me inside a flashy red Lamborghini.

That's right. A freakin' Lamborghini.

I had never even seen one in real life before, let alone sat in it. I stared at the car in awe. Similarly, I had never been a car junkie, but one has to be blind as a bat not to appreciate this car.

I slid into the passenger side of the car. The windows weren't tinted like some of his other cars.

He regarded me for a minute and then smiled, probably because my jaw was already on the floor.

He chuckled. "Do you like it?"

I touched the plush leather seats and the fancy dashboard, "What's not to like? I mean it's a Lamborghini! I bet it cost you a fortune."

"Can't say I didn't when I had to spend five-hundred thousand dollars for it. It's a *Lamborghini Aventador SuperVeloce*."

The excitement in his eyes was that of a child bragging about their most expensive toy. "It has a seven-fifty screaming horsepower. Can you imagine? It's one of the best fucking cars." He then continued to talk about some more car-related things that I didn't quite understand, but I just nodded along because he was completely consumed by his obsession with it.

"My friends get orgasms just looking at this car, and they keep begging me to let them drive it even once, but I'd kill myself before I let any of those bastards have a lick at it. I never let Vince touch it either. You're the first one, Kiara. You're the only person I allowed to sit in this car."

I laughed. "Thank you for the honor, Mr. Lockhart. I feel lucky."

"All my life, I've been underestimated. My father, Vincent, and everyone else in my life. It doesn't matter now. If you want something really badly, you just take it."

Something about the way he said it with such confidence made me anxious.

He continued to stare at me for a minute, his expression not betraying any emotion. "Have you experienced the feeling that gives you a heart-pounding adrenaline rush?"

"What do you mean?"

"It's this really incredible feeling where you know that you can either live or die through it, but you are the one making those choices. You make one wrong move and it ends for you, like a gamble of life." His eyes were burning with exhilaration.

I would be joking if I wasn't a bit curious as well as scared. The look on his handsome face was anything but normal.

Before I could answer, he said, "Let me show it to you, Kiara."

I fastened the seat belt as he lifted up a latch. There was no gearbox. Instead, it was lined up with a lot of buttons, and truthfully, it looked quite confusing. I mean, he could tell me this car had wings and could fly, and I'd believe him.

Jasper appeared to be confident, so I trusted him to do the right thing in driving the beast. After lifting the latch, he pressed some buttons and pressed on the gas. The engine roared to life.

It wasn't a sound like any other. The car sounded like a hungry lion let loose in his kingdom—like the king of the jungle.

Jasper drove through the imposing gates of the Lockhart mansion and smoothly pulled it on the road. Once we were on the main road, he practically tore through the lane. The sound reverberated through the car, making my heart race faster. It was truly an experience; like I was riding the fastest rollercoaster in an amusement park. He drove pretty fast on the highway, I had to hold onto the handlebar just to be on the safer side.

"Isn't it just awesome?!" he exclaimed as he hit the gas harder.

"It is," I agreed.

We were screaming, laughing, and just having a good time. The car was fun. There was no doubt about it. An hour later of driving on the highway, he took a road interchange that led us back to the mansion. It was a semi-busy street with people blatantly staring at the car—some were even taking pictures and waving at us.

When we stopped at a traffic signal, another sports car in the next lane rolled down its windows and a middle-aged man complimented, "Cool ride." He was accompanied by another friend in the passenger seat.

Jasper smiled and waved back. "Thanks."

The car seemed sporty too, and it was making a rumbling sound similar to the Lamborghini. The man's mouth curled up in a sneer, and something about the whole situation was ringing sirens in my ears.

He said, "Mine isn't a Lambo, but I'm sure it can still beat your car any day."

Jasper laughed in a teasing, playful way—one would even think it was downright evil. "Wanna bet?"

I placed my hand over Jasper's. "We can't race here. It's a residential area," I reminded him.

I could already see the blazing hunger for racing in Jasper's eyes. As if he didn't hear me, Jasper responded, "Alright."

"We will race up to Willow's Mart, and that's about a few kilometers away," the man suggested. "The first man to reach there wins the race. If I win, your car is mine, but if you win, well, I'll give you whatever you want."

Jasper grinned, putting on his dashing smile in order and said, "Well, I don't really think you can give me what I want, but I'm not someone who backs out of a challenge."

He was taking the man for granted; like he just suggested a duel in a gameplay and not real road racing.

When the signal flashed green, the engines roared, and the cars sped forward like in a Formula One racing track.

"He's fucking delusional if he thinks he can beat me," Jasper said calmly. His palms clenched at the wheel tightly. The Lamborghini raced forward like a cheetah hunting its prey, and if I was enjoying the ride a few minutes ago, I was certainly terrified now.

Jasper pushed a button and pressed on the gas hard, he was literally speeding on a sixty-limit road.

"Jasper, slow down," I urged him.

The car zoomed forward, cutting through the streets like lightning. When there was a stop sign, Jasper drove off in the red signal, and I stared at him incredulously.

"You can't cut through the traffic signal!"

"Do *not* tell me what to do," he snapped at me.

I sat back in the car, feeling scared for my life.

The car weaved through the traffic almost too crazily in a zigzag. I felt like we were going to collide against an ongoing truck but he spun the wheel so hard, I screamed.

The other sports car that Jasper was competing against was lagging behind, but seemed like it would catch up in a moment. The two were battling side by side when Jasper pushed another button and the car rocketed.

Tears sprang in the corner of my eyes.

"Jasper, please slow down!"

You make one wrong move and its ends for you—like a gamble of life.

I understood the meaning of those words now. Jasper did this all the time, and he enjoyed the thrill of it as if it were a game.

A game of death.

He was recklessly driving now, taking fast turns, not stopping at red lights, and dodging cars. I could've sworn I heard a police car start up a siren, but Jasper didn't bother to stop. It was like he was possessed by a madman, and he was enjoying it. He was enjoying jeopardizing the lives of the other drivers on the road as well as ours.

I didn't know how many times I repeated the words, *Please stop the car*, but it was of no use. I closed my eyes tight and knew I'd die any second when the car came to a screeching halt.

I opened my eyes, and noticed that we were parked outside Willow's Mart.

There was no sign of the other racing car. Jasper looked bored, but there was a triumphant smile on his face. "They were supposed to be here by now. Guess, I'll declare myself the winner."

"You knew they couldn't beat you and yet you still decided to take the bait. For what purpose? You almost got us killed!" I shrieked at him.

"Almost. But we are not dead," he said it like it proved anything. "Wasn't it fun?" he asked, daring me to say otherwise. "Doesn't the fact that one wrong turn could get us killed in a car crash any second of any minute through the ride, thrill you?"

"You're just crazy. I want to go home," I declared.

"We are going home now, but first, we are going to wait for those idiots for a few more minutes."

I pursed my lips, knowing full well he wasn't going to like what I was going to say next. "Not yours. I meant my home."

His eyes widened. "You've got to be kidding me."

"You heard me. I want to go back to my mother."

"You can't go back there, and that's final," he barked.

I turned to look through the window as he pulled out of the parking lot. He fiddled with the radio station, stopping at the live news.

"A black sports car has collided into an ongoing truck just south of River Heights, a few kilometers away from the Willow's Mart. The driver, thirty-five-year-old Matt Boyer, and his brother, thirty-year-old Ed Boyer have

sustained serious injuries and have been rushed to the hospital. Police speculate it was due to rash driving."

CHAPTER FIFTEEN

The four walls of the mansion were now becoming suffocating to live in. As the days passed, I was starting to feel empty inside. I had a feeling like I was almost being used.

After the music room, the only time Jasper touched me was after the night we had narrowly avoided death. He walked into my room the next night and gifted me a stunning diamond necklace that he had gotten custom-made just for me from Tiffany's.

I didn't really care about the gift as much as his emotions if he had just told me I meant something to him. Jasper whispered sweet things into my ear but it felt almost rehearsed.

He was sitting on my bed, touching the hem of my dress with his fingers raking up my thigh. Jasper had given me something expensive, of course he'd expect me to give him what he wanted, and that's what mistresses do, right?

I automatically spread my legs, feeling obligated to do my duty to him. He kissed me tenderly, pouring every emotion into that kiss, making me think that he was actually in love with me.

I knew he wasn't. To Jasper, I was just someone he helped, fed, and sheltered—someone who was supposed to warm his bed.

And what did that make me?

A shameless slut.

My mother had been right. Women like me couldn't be anything more than a keep for someone with such a high social status. That's exactly what I was.

When I woke up in the morning and looked at myself in the mirror, I almost didn't recognize myself.

Who was this woman who was letting a man use her body just so she could get a good life? *The good life didn't matter,* I realized. It was my heart that was playing tricks.

Every time he was around, saying nice things to me and taking me out for dinner, my resolve of staying strong melted and all I saw was a bit of an unusual man who may fall in love with me if he gave this relationship a chance, and I wanted that so badly.

And so I let it happen.

Jasper ravished my body with his expert hands and mouth, and I can't say I didn't enjoy it. The empty look on his face was what bothered me and his inability to show me his emotions.

It wasn't lovemaking by a long shot, it was downright 'fucking'. I could tell the difference between the two. While I loved him, he didn't. It was just as simple as that. When we were both breathing hard and spent, instead of kissing my forehead or cuddling with me, he would zip his fly, run his fingers through his hair, and walk out of the bedroom as if it were a transaction—a luxurious life in exchange of sex.

It sickened me what I had become, and it wasn't even for the money. It was just for the man I thought would love me back.

Just a little.

*   *   *

I decided to put an end to it. I wanted to stop feeling so used and for that, I needed to get away from this mansion.

As if faith could read my mind, an opportunity arose in the disguise of a birthday party. Jasper's best friend, Lucas, was throwing a grand party at his house and Jasper had asked me to be his companion for the evening. It was an opportunity I would never pass.

Dressed in a long, beautiful evening gown, I descended the stairs. The dress was beige in color, studded with tiny golden flowers all over. The shoulders were strapless and the neck was a little deeper than what I'd usually wear, but it was feminine and sexy. I liked it right off the bat. I found a matching pair of glimmering, high heels and a clutch bag.

Jasper was waiting for me at the foot of the stairs, dressed in a navy tux, his dark hair ruffled back. He looked like a movie star. Jasper always wore the best outfits, everything that was in fashion and never an outfit repeated twice. He took his appearance very seriously.

As he watched me walk towards him, his gaze raked from top to bottom. His eyes shone with something that I wasn't yet familiar with.

Was it lust?

"Well?" I asked.

I gasped as he pulled me tightly into his arms. His hands that were on my waist dropped to my hips and he gave it a squeeze. His lips connected to my jaw as he trailed lazy kisses down my throat.

"You look nothing less than the rarest of gems," he whispered. "I could eat you right here."

"Hmmm . . ." I whimpered.

Just a few nice words from him and I was a puddle on the floor.

"Now, go back to your room and change into another dress—something that's not too revealing and doesn't stick to you like a second skin." He kissed my cheek, smiling.

I was puzzled. "I thought you liked the dress."

"I do, Kiara, but I won't appreciate other men looking at you and thinking of you in their bed, and that dress makes you look like a meal." He indicated towards the dress. "Go on now. Wear something else that's appropriate, and then, when we get home, you can change into this one just for me."

I bit my lips again, stopping myself from saying something that would upset him. I scurried upstairs towards my room and threw open the wardrobe. I picked out a less revealing dress this time, which was a long satin pink gown—plain but elegant and had a lovely butterfly brooch jewel.

I loved the previous dress more but knew Jasper didn't approve of me wearing it in public. Jasper had a possessive streak. I just didn't know how far it went until now.

*   *   *

Jasper explained that Lucas Johnson was his very longtime friend. They had met during high school and instantly hit it off. He also mentioned that Lucas was a prominent magician, and sometimes even performed shows in Vegas at his leisure.

When I had asked him about his other friends, he wasn't very keen on discussing them so I decided not to push him.

Lucas's home was a two-story Victorian mansion, vintage with a gothic architecture and quite smaller in comparison to Jasper's enormous one. The house was easily a modernized *Addams family* home.

I hated how Jasper paraded me around in the party like a gold medal, telling people that I was his girlfriend, although I knew that wasn't true. These people didn't even know me, didn't know who I was or where I came from, yet I could feel their judgmental eyes follow my every step. It was like they could see right through all the designer clothing.

I didn't belong here.

Jasper introduced me to his friends, Tom and Dylan. Spike, he mentioned, couldn't make it to the party, and was currently traveling somewhere in Southeast Asia due to his work.

Both men were dressed in impressive tailored suits and looked just as handsome, but of course, their attractiveness paled in comparison to Jasper's. He was completely at a different level and I couldn't stop thinking if I was the subject of envy for a dozen women.

The men had made polite talk and asked me the questions that Jasper and I had rehearsed a number of times. While Tom was being nice, Dylan had a strange look in his eyes that made me uncomfortable. He closely resembled a vulture, ready to tear its prey to shreds. The look in his eyes reminded me of the man in the alley that day.

I shuddered.

I tugged at Jasper's sleeve so he turned his attention to me. "Is it alright if I sit down somewhere?"

He rubbed my shoulders and looked at me lovingly. "Of course, precious." He led me to a table at the far corner where there were two beautiful ladies already seated. The women were laughing and sipping on wine, enjoying some delicious-looking appetizers.

When we approached the table, the blonde glanced up towards me.

"Ladies, would it be alright with you if my beautiful companion, Kiara, joins your table?" Jasper asked politely, giving them his best Oscar-winning smile that probably had women falling all over his feet.

"Sure, we'd love for you to introduce us to your girlfriend, Jasper," the blonde pointed out. Her smile was sweet and genuine compared to the ones I had been receiving throughout the evening.

It kind of made me jealous at how familiar they were acting with Jasper. I wondered if one of them was his ex, but then I was relieved to find out that they were both Dylan and Tom's partners respectively.

The blonde lady in a royal-blue dress was Dylan's girlfriend, Cecilia, and the brunette in the red gown was Tom's wife, Penny. After the fast introductions were over, Jasper was pulled away by one of his old clients and that left me to deal with the women alone.

At first, they eyed me curiously. Cecilia was the first to speak, "We never thought Jasper would get serious again with a woman. Everyone thought there wasn't any hope for him, you know after . . ."

"After?" I asked.

Realization registered on her face. She exchanged looks with Penny. "Oh, I'm sorry. It's not my place to say such things."

They knew about Jasper's past relationships.

"But one thing is for sure," Penny continued, smiling at me. "He's acting differently around you. The way he keeps stealing glances towards this table is proof enough that you have him where you need him to be. It's kinda cute."

"I second that," Cecilia said.

The girls giggled and I joined in on their good humor.

"Kiara, which college did you go to?" Penny asked me.

I didn't have any reason to lie about the college I had been attending, so I gave them a real name and they just nodded, probably wondering why I hadn't joined an Ivy League college. I was glad when their conversations changed track, and they started gossiping about someone I didn't know. The topic shifted gears once more and then they talked about sex which was the last topic I wanted to be a part of.

"Men will be men, you know. They aren't satisfied with just one woman. That's the sad reality," said Penny, taking a sip of her wine as her gaze followed someone.

I glanced in the same direction to see Tom laughing and talking to a tall woman. She whispered something in his ear and he touched her shoulder lightly—making one would think that the two were a couple. Penny caught me staring, and she flushed. She excused herself, and started walking towards her husband.

Cecelia clicked her tongue. "Poor Penny. Tom really can't keep his dick in his pants for one second. She's caught him cheating on her over a million times already. Dylan told me that."

"So why is she still with him?" I asked her, astonished.

112

"Because she loves him blind, and where would she go anyway? She's not like us, Kiara. Penny doesn't come from a wealthy background. If she divorces Tom and still manages to get her settlements, it just wouldn't be enough. Once you've gotten used to this lifestyle, you can't go back to how you used to be."

I nodded. If I was Penny, I knew my decision would have been different. There wouldn't be a million chances, once would be enough for me to pack and leave.

"Well, I can't say good things about Dylan either. I caught him cheating on me once, but it was just once, and I know it never happened after that," she said, and I placed my hand over hers.

It was like she was trying to feed herself some horse shit, because I had caught her "so-called" boyfriend steal glances at me more than once.

"You're really lucky compared to us, Kiara. Jasper is a nice man. He's polite and such a gentleman."

"He's a little different, isn't he?" I asked her, trying to dig for some juicy inside story.

Cecilia nodded. "A little. He's straightforward and that's what people like about him, plus he's quite the keeper."

It seemed like Jasper had paid this woman to give me a good report.

"He's a little demanding," I whispered.

"Demanding?" She appeared confused. "What do you mean?"

I could feel the blush creep into my cheeks. "About sex."

Cecilia laughed, waving her well-manicured nails at me. "Why is that something to worry about? It just means you're desirable to him. All men are demanding in bed. If you want to keep the man, you gotta do it, honey."

"It's not just that, Cecilia. I don't think Jasper loves me," I said, unable to hold it in any longer. I needed to talk to someone. My hands were shaking. "He just . . . well, he just wants my body."

There, I said it.

"No, darling, I don't think that's true." She squeezed the life out of my hand. "You're so beautiful and you seem so kind.

Jasper just doesn't speak about his feelings. I'm sure he loves you. If not, he wouldn't introduce you to us."

I wasn't convinced yet.

I nodded and downed the entire glass of the wine. Cecilia continued to hail down every waiter serving wine and gulped each wine glass with enthusiasm. By the end of the fifth, she was laughing nonstop and talking about something that didn't make sense.

A shadow fell upon me and that's when I looked up.

"May I have the honor of this dance?" Jasper's hand was raised towards me.

He placed his hand on my waist and circled my arms around his neck. It was a sensuous, slow dance. I waltzed across the dance floor, moving smoothly to the song in the background. He looked at me like I meant the world to him and yet there was still something missing entirely.

The DJ played a slow Ed Sheeran song. My head rested against his chest as we swayed to the music. In that moment, I knew I would never love anyone as much as I loved him. He had the ability to destroy me completely without intention.

I lifted my head up and our gazes locked. I wanted to see one last time if there was something in those beautiful blue eyes that conveyed his true feelings. His soul appeared to be empty just like his eyes. My heart broke into a million pieces.

I cupped his face in my palms. "Jasper."

"What is it?" he whispered.

"I love you," I confessed, and before he had time to say anything, I continued, "I don't expect you to love me back. I just want to know if you feel something even an ounce that I can hold onto."

I realized my hands were shaking as I waited for him to answer. His expression betrayed no emotion as he continued to stare at me in baffled silence.

His silence was the only answer I needed. It would have sufficed if he had remained silent, but what he said next nearly blew my mind away.

"I love fucking you in bed. Isn't that enough?"

I flushed, stunned beyond words. Out of all the answers I had predicted, this hadn't even crossed my mind. I told him that I loved him, and he blatantly said that he was only interested in one thing, nothing else. I wondered if this was the same man who had saved me from my worst fate time and time again.

I stepped back from his touch and started walking away. I heard him call out my name but I didn't glance back. The last thing I needed right now was for him to follow me. I tried to fight back the hot tears gliding down my cheeks. I had chalked up Jasper's behavior so far as him being childish, but this was the last straw.

Being wealthy, handsome, and a man who acquired everything, it was a no-brainer that he wanted me in bed and he successfully achieved that without batting an eye. It only happened in books or movies that a billionaire fell in love with a damsel in distress. In real life, none of that happened.

In real life; the damsel in distress was just reduced to someone he could use and discard.

I held onto the granite counters of the bathroom and cried until I had no tears left. It hurt so much. In the end, I was just a daft little idiot who assumed that after giving my body to him, I'd eventually have his heart. I hadn't asked him to love me back, had I?

All I wanted was for him to tell me if there could be anything in the future.

His bluntness had proven one thing.

I was going back home.

Back to my old life.

CHAPTER SIXTEEN

Throughout most of the evening, I maintained my distance from Jasper. I could tell that he wanted to talk to me, but I was doing my best to avoid him. I was looking for one chance to be out of his sight, so I could leave the mansion.

I decided that once I was out of here, I'd hail a cab and go straight home. After dinner, when Jasper wasn't in view, I sneaked into the courtyard of the mansion and looked for an exit that didn't draw too much attention.

I took the heels in my hands and started walking towards the main exit.

"You dropped something." The deep voice that came from behind me put a halt to my steps.

I glanced back to find a very attractive blond man standing a few feet away, holding what seemed like a shiny trinket. A closer inspection revealed that it was my earring.

"I think having just one earring dangling in your ear wouldn't be very attractive, although I'm pretty sure you can pull it off without much of an effort seeing how gorgeous you are," he complimented, grinning at me. His eyes were a striking shade of green that pierced right through me.

I took the earring from him. "Thanks," I said.

"Apologies, I didn't introduce myself. I'm Lucas Johnson. It happens to be my birthday today, but it's quite a shame that you're here and yet I can't place you very well and for that, I'm extremely sorry," he said, and his hand reached out for a handshake. "Have we met?"

"Happy birthday, Mr. Johnson," I said, accepting the handshake. "And to answer your question, it's a no. We haven't met before. I'm Kiara Reeves."

That name surely rang bells because his eyes lit up. "Of course, and please call me Lucas," he said, smiling, but his expression conveyed a level of discomfort. "You're Jasper's girl. Am I right?"

I just gave a nod, not knowing how else to react. His next sentence rendered me speechless. "If you were looking for a way out, I know the easiest around here."

His gaze darkened and I instantly knew what he meant. There were some people you met and instantly knew they couldn't be trusted, but there were others who you just knew to be someone on your side.

"Has he . . ." I stammered. "Has he always been different?"

Lucas didn't need to know who 'he' was referred to. It was quite apparent from his expression that he knew exactly what I was talking about.

"Different isn't exactly the word I'd use for him. My only advice to you, Kiara, will be to take this opportunity and leave."

"You're his friend, why would you suggest that?"

"Because I know him a lot more than anyone else ever will. He can be very selfish and persuasive when it comes down to something that he wants."

I pondered over what he said for a minute.

"I have a special magical act coming up tonight. I will ask you Kiara, to stay and enjoy the show."

"I would have loved to, but this is my only chance to get away from him. I can't let it go," I admitted.

My decision was final. From the corner of my eye, I watched as Jasper approached us. He was halfway through the well-manicured lawn, but still out of earshot.

117

I turned to Lucas and said, "I need your help."

*　　　*　　　*

Jasper and I were seated in a wide room, kind of like a mini auditorium. We were in the front seat along with Jasper's other group of friends—Dylan, Tom, Cecelia, and Penny. Everyone seemed excited about Lucas's show.

I leaned sideways to speak to Jasper, "How long has Lucas been doing these illusions?"

"A very long time. He's been doing it since his childhood," he says. "It's his passion, but as you're aware, the heir of a multimillion-dollar company simply cannot be selfish enough and decide to make a career out of a mere hobby," Jasper concluded.

"But that's not fair," I blurted out.

"That's how life is, Kiara. It's unfair," he agreed. "Lucas was also featured in the *Penn & Teller Show*. Can you believe it? Although he couldn't take the trophy home, he knew what he was doing."

The room plunged into pitch-black darkness. Jasper took my hand in his and caressed it softly. Not once did he apologize for what he had said after our dance. He was acting almost indifferent, like that particular scene didn't even happen.

The curtains slowly ascended, revealing a stage with numerous props and a cheerful young man in a black tailored suit.

He spoke into the microphone, "Good Evening, ladies and gentlemen, boys and girls. You may already be aware that the parties in this house are never complete without our host's performance. Tonight is no exception as we are going to see some of the most popular acts by our very talented illusionist. Please welcome Lucas Johnson."

The room filled with a round of applause and cheers as the lights dimmed and smoke erupted in the center of the stage. When the smoke dissipated, Lucas was already standing on his spot. A silver half cat mask revealed only his mouth.

Thirty minutes in, and I was already impressed by how good he was at this. He produced a white rabbit out of a hat, then a dove. He did some illusions with cards, including his sleight of hands. It was so clean and elegant. The audience was mesmerized.

The man in the suit named Ian spoke, "Now, ladies and gentlemen, we will see the last act of this show."

A huge black rectangular box was wheeled onto the stage by two very beautiful women wearing black clothing. They had the whole gothic look going on. One of those girls I recognized was Amy who Lucas had introduced me to.

The girl had a spiky haircut and had a collar around her neck. Jasper told me that Lucas was into the BDSM culture and Amy was his submissive—a *willing submissive*, he added. I had seen the way the two looked at each other like they were in love and understood each other like no one else could, and that was what mattered.

Lucas opened the door of the box, it was more like a tall cupboard, big enough to fit in a person. He then proceeded to show the empty box to the audience as it revolved on all sides.

"This act will need a lady from the audience. Who would like to volunteer? Any takers?" Ian asked. "Although, I won't guarantee you'll be back home in one piece, ladies."

Laugher filled the crowd.

"I wouldn't mind." That was Dylan who earned some more laughter from the audience, along with an elbow jerk from his girlfriend.

There were some hands raised from the audience for the volunteers. Penny was enthusiastically waving her hand. "Me! Pick me!"

My heart did a double somersault when Lucas passed a smile in my direction.

"Ohhh, looks like the magician wants to choose the subject himself," Ian said as Lucas stepped down from the stage and started walking towards us.

He held out his gloved hand towards me. I threw a sideways glance in Jasper's direction who nodded his approval. He seemed too ecstatic about this. Jasper loosened his hold on my hand and let go. I slipped my hand into Lucas' as he led me onto the stage.

"What is your name?" Ian asked me.

"Kiara Reeves," I said.

"Miss. Kiara, are you willing to take this risk?" Ian joked.

"Yes." I nodded.

"Miss Kiara, it would be best if you ask permission from your boyfriend because Lucas will teleport you to an isolated island somewhere. However, there's also a high possibility you may leave tonight with a severed arm."

"I'd still want her even with a severed arm," Jasper screamed from the audience, wearing a devilish grin.

The audience guffawed.

"That's commitment right there," Ian commented. "So, she's already made her mind. Everyone, please give a round of applause for the beautiful Miss. Kiara Reeves."

Claps boomed in the little auditorium as there was another cloud of smoke on the stage. Before the smoke disappeared, Amy whispered under her breath, "When you step into the box, there will be a lever on your right, pull it. You will only have ten seconds. Don't screw this up."

"Miss, would you please be kind enough to step inside the box for us?" Ian asked.

There was a drumroll in the background, I could feel the audience's gaze locked on me.

I stepped inside the coffin-shaped box. Jasper was smiling, and I watched as he waved one last time at me. I smiled and waved back at him.

I stood inside, waiting as Lucas closed the lid shut, leaving me in complete darkness. The sounds from the audience became barely audible, all I could hear were the soft thumps of my rapid heartbeats.

Before I knew what was happening, the box began revolving. As Amy had mentioned earlier, I spotted a small lever that was barely visible.

Only five seconds remaining.

It was now or never. I could take this risk or remain confined in the golden cage with a man who didn't have feelings for me.

I tightened my hold over the lever, and took a deep breath before I finally pulled it.

*　　*　　*

JASPER

I had often wondered what it would be like to be tied down to one woman for the rest of my life, and it sounded rather boring considering the fact that I got bored easily.

At first, Kiara had been someone who was a means to pass time—someone who could provide entertainment into my rather colorless life. A docile woman with a fierce streak, that was what she was and that was what attracted me to her.

When she confessed how much she loved me, a sense of pride swelled in my chest, but it wasn't in my nature to tell her that I loved her back because that was impossible. I could feel obsession, passion, and possessive but never *'love'*. I had been honest when I told her that, although I didn't love her back, I did enjoy having her body under mine.

I thought that had to be enough.

If that woman had been someone else, I would have shown her her place but I couldn't bring myself to tell Kiara off. I was possessed in the music room. I had never intended to go that far, but one thing led to another and before I knew what was going on or what she was saying, I was pounding inside of her. I saw the fear laced with desire in her eyes.

After that day in the music room, I had thought the cravings for her body would stop but that was beside the case. I ended up feeling hard every time she was around to the point where I couldn't keep my hands to myself or concentrate at work.

I was insatiable for this woman, and she was ruining my life.

She wanted more. I could tell by the look on her face that she was sad. If only I could feel the same. I just didn't. It was her fault partly for making me feel fucking horny all the damn time. That delicious body and those luscious breasts were just begging for my attention.

I smiled to myself, remembering Dylan and Tom's envious stares as they appraised the woman on my arm when we walked in. It was beyond them how I could still keep a girlfriend because half of them had run for the hills within a week, and when Kiara admitted that we had known each other for over two months, their eyes resembled tennis balls. She gushed about how much she adored me, and they ate it up with seething jealousy. To add fuel to fire, I kissed her in front of them.

I snapped back to reality as Dylan whispered something to me from the next seat. I smiled politely, having little to no clue what he had been blabbering for a while. I had a certain ability to tune out when a dumpster suddenly started talking. My thoughts went back to the stage where Lucas was performing his trick I had watched over a dozen times, but this time it was interesting because my Kiara was right there.

Kiara waved at me as Lucas shut the door. He revolved the box around a few times while the stage became engulfed with a puff of smoke. I knew what was going to happen next.

When he opened the box, Kiara had disappeared, replaced by a tall blonde assistant. The show ended, and the audience roared into loud cheers and claps. Lucas bowed before the curtains descended. I knew Kiara would be waiting for me in the backstage, so I climbed to my feet and strode out of the auditorium, making my way towards the backstage.

I entered to find Lucas seated in the makeup booth with a topless Amy straddled on his lap. His hand rested on her breast and the other hand held her close to him, their lips locked in a passionate kiss. They either didn't noticed me walk in or were ignoring me on purpose.

I walked across the room and opened the door leading to the props room downstairs where I was positive I would find Kiara. The room resembled a basement, but when I entered, I just saw Lucas's assistant, Jen, packing things back into a chest. When she noticed me, she quickly averted her eyes and concentrated on the task at hand, clearly intimidated.

"Where is Kiara?" I questioned her.

Jen swallowed as she stared at me.

My instinct told me something was not right.

"Kiara, sweetheart, if you're in here, come out now."

The silence in the air thickened.

I scanned the cozy room. "I asked you a question, Jen. Where is Kiara?"

"I don't know, Mr. Lockhart." Her voice was almost inaudible. "I did not see her when Mr. Johnson asked me to pack his things."

I turned on my heels and climbed the stairs leading to the backstage room where it was filled with moans and groans. My anger was going to shoot through the roof.

"Lucas, where the fuck is she?" I was trying to act as calm as possible, but inside, there was a burning volcano ready to explode.

Lucas placed a quick peck on Amy and turned his bored gaze towards me. "Not the first time you've cockblocked me. What's gotten up your ass?" He placed Amy beside himself on the love seat and tossed a t-shirt towards her, buttoning up his own.

"Kiara was supposed to be in the props room downstairs after the illusion. I can't find her there. Where is she?" I asked, digging my hands in my pockets.

Lucas had a knowing smirk on his face, one that I didn't like. "She's gone."

I glared at him. "What do you mean she's gone? Where did she go?"

"Well, my assistant, Ian, did warn you that she'd be transported to an island. I guess that's where you'd find her right now," Lucas made a lame attempt at a joke.

"I'm serious." I glared at him.

"I don't know. After Kiara slid into the props room from the stage, she told me she didn't want to stay for the after-party, so Amy opened the emergency exit downstairs and let her go."

I chuckled. "I don't have time for jokes, Lucas."

Lucas laughed. "Wish I was joking, but I'm not."

I stared at him for a good minute, thinking that he would finally declare this to be a practical joke, but that never happened.

"Kiara's my girlfriend. She's my responsibility and you . . ." I jabbed an accusing finger to his chest. "You let her fucking leave. She doesn't even have a home. Where do you think she's gonna go, huh?"

Lucas had his fingers balled into tight fists. His face had turned red. I thought the vein in his forehead was about to burst.

"She's not some pet that you can play with whenever it pleases you, and then let her fend for herself. She's a woman who has feelings, unlike you, and I think you should save this *"girlfriend"* bullshit for someone else. You and I both know you don't do relationships. It was just plain screwing where you're concerned.

124

The girl didn't want to remain as your slave, so I did her a favor, simple as that."

"Don't you dare psychoanalyze me, you kinky sonofabitch," I spat at him, kicking the chaise off the floor.

"Do you remember Violet, Jasper?"

"Violet?" I tried to rack my brains.

"You don't recall the girl you and Dylan toyed with? The girl you bullied enough in school that she resorted to committing suicide. No? Doesn't ring any bells?"

I snorted. He wanted to dig up old skeletons. "That was ten years ago. What does that have to do with anything now?"

"It has everything to do with it. I loved that girl, Jasper, and if it weren't for your sick games, she would have still been alive." Lucas said, his voice turned menacing.

"The girl died because she was weak. I thought we were friends. You want to ruin our relationship because of some stupid girl you can't get over?"

"Friends?" Lucas snorted. "As far as I know, I tried to become your real friend in the hopes that eventually you'd get the fucking help you need, but it never ends, does it? Playing these childish games, toying with people's emotions, driving recklessly for the thrill of it—it doesn't stop at that, so you convinced a poor girl into becoming a slave. I'm sick with your fuck-ups. If it weren't for me, nobody would want to be anywhere near you, Jasper Lockhart."

My jaw was ticking and my head was pounding which wasn't a good sign. This usually happened when I was mad as a bull, and what Lucas had said hit home, but he was wrong. Kiara wasn't my slave. She was with me because she wanted to be. She loved me. Lucas knew how bad my temper was, and yet he was testing me in the worst way possible.

"I saw how important Kiara was to you. Your shiny new trophy to parade around." He smiled cockily. "I realized it was time you paid your dues."

"So, I take it you won't tell me where she is." I narrowed my eyes at him.

Lucas walked to his mini bar, poured himself a drink, and raised the glass of scotch towards me. "Cheers to Kiara's new freedom."

With Lucas, I never had to maintain a charade. Masks were off because he knew the real me. He stepped on the wrong foot, knowing what I was capable of. It was time he paid his dues as well.

"I warned you," I said, and then everything happened too fast after that. The raging nerves in my head began to burst as I grabbed Amy by the back of her head and bashed her against the wall hard in one swift motion.

I heard a loud thump followed by a bloodcurdling scream, and I pounded her head once more. Her blood was on the wall and her eyes rolled back as her body slipped towards the floor.

"Amy!" Lucas screamed as he launched for her, and she sank to the floor in his arms. "You bastard, how dare you?!"

"Amy, you should watch where the wall is, darling." I couldn't keep myself from laughing.

Her head was matted with a cake of blood. I knew she wasn't dead. Although I wanted to kill her, I thought this was enough to teach Lucas a lesson to not mess with his best friends.

"Jenny! Call the ambulance right now!" Lucas yelled out to his assistant as she rushed into the room, her eyes wide as she noticed the scene that had unfolded.

I fixed my blazer jacket and started leaving the room. "This should teach you not to fuck with me, Lucas."

He fixed his glare at me. "You're going to pay for this, Jasper."

I strode out of the room without so much a glance in his direction, making my way out of the house. A few people were rushing towards the backstage room. I knew Lucas wouldn't press charges against me, because if he did, some of his dirty secrets were going to spill out too. Once it started spilling, my mouth would have a hard time stopping, and that would stir up the media, which would cause good ol' Lucas trouble, not to mention a big blow on his reputation.

I tapped the driver's side of the car and ordered the chauffeur, Morgan, to take the passenger seat. He appeared confused at first, but then decided to obey my orders rather than question me. I slid into the driver's side and pressed the button for the ignition.

I pushed the car into drive and maneuvered it out of the driveway with a loud screech. I felt Morgan stiffen in his seat. My hands were shaking on the wheel as I took a sharp turn.

"Sir, you may want to reduce the speed," Morgan suggested in a meek voice.

"Don't tell me what to do, Morgan, unless of course, you want to be pushed out of a running car."

He remained silent as I drove through the streets like a loose maniac fresh out of prison. I had wasted enough time talking trash with Lucas. I only just realized he had done it on purpose so he could engage me in a frivolous conversation, and Kiara would have the time to get out of there. That one small thing had bitten him in the ass—nothing he didn't deserve.

Now I needed to find Kiara soon. I gritted my teeth hard, and my hand on the wheel tightened until my knuckles were white.

This was going to be a long night.

CHAPTER SEVENTEEN

KIARA

One Hour Ago

I couldn't believe I was going through with this. I had taken a huge risk. I was riding in one of Lucas's cars with his assistant, Dale. He was an angry-looking thug with black hair and black eyes along with a jagged scar running from his cheek down to his neck. He seemed like he could handle fighting a dozen men easily, and that made me feel a little less concerned about Jasper coming after me.

"You need to go faster," I urged him.

"What are you so worried about?" Dale asked.

"If Jasper finds me, he's going to ask me to go back with him. He will grovel and beg, and I don't know how I will refuse him. I'm under his debt, but I'm going to figure out how I can pay him back, but it's definitely not going to be the way he thinks I should." I hugged myself, leaning more into the soft leather seat.

"Is that what your relationship with him was? I don't understand. I mean, it's none of my business anyway," he said.

"It's complicated," I admitted. "I love him, but he also scares me. The things he does and says. He's just too unpredictable. I can't stay with him no matter how hard this is going to be for me to deal with."

"I've known him for the past six years, so I know I'm playing with fire. Once Jasper Lockhart has his eyes on something, he stops at nothing. You need to be strong."

I gave a nod. "I have to first stop at my mom's for a minute. I need to talk to her."

It took about an hour to reach my house in Pine Valley. The time was a little after 11 PM which meant Mom was probably in bed. I hated to wake her up, but this was urgent. I didn't plan to stay here because there was a chance that Jasper would find me and try to take me back to his mansion.

I told Dale to wait in the car while I went inside to have a little chat with my mother.

I rang the doorbell. "Mom, it's me, Kiara."

I waited for a minute, but there was no response.

I knocked this time and called out to her again. When I knocked the third time, I heard the sound of footsteps, and the door swung open.

Standing in the doorway was a middle-aged man with a receding hairline and a protruding belly staring at me in confusion. A frown was plastered on his tired face. He didn't seem to appreciate me standing at the door at this hour.

Who was this man? Had my mom moved on already?

I wondered if I had knocked on the wrong house. *Had a few weeks with Jasper rusted my memory?*

The man leered at me, his eyes scanning me from the bottom until he finally rested his gaze on my face. I could read his thoughts well—he was probably wondering what a well-groomed woman in expensive clothing was doing in this neighborhood.

"May I help you?" he asked, his tone screaming hostility.

"I'm looking for my mother, Julie Reeves. Is she here?"

"Julie Reeves?" The man scratched his head. "Doesn't live here no more."

"Then where is she? Do you know where my mother is?" I was puzzled.

Had things really changed so much while I was away?

The man nodded slowly. "I'm not sure. She used to rent this place before me, but I heard the neighbors say that she moved to Sunny Heights."

That wasn't possible. Sunny Heights was the richest part of this town. How could my mother afford to live in Sunny Heights when she couldn't even afford to pay the rent of this place that I was standing at the moment? I used to work at a restaurant and helped pay the bills.

"Okay. Thank you," I said, and started walking towards the car when I halted and walked back to him. "Can I ask you a favor?"

"Sure."

"If a man shows up, asking you if I was here, just say I did and tell him that I mentioned leaving for Northern Hills."

The man nodded. I thanked him and walked back to the car in a daze. If Jasper showed up here, then he would be misguided to drive two hours into another town to look for me.

I slid into the car waiting for me. "Where to?" Dale asked.

"Sunny Heights."

*   *   *

To look for my mother without a proper address was like looking for a grain in the ocean. I called Casey, the owner of our previous home, and asked her if she knew about the new address that my mom had moved to.

Fortunately, Casey knew about it because apparently, she had helped mom during the move. I was thankful she didn't inquire where I had been for the past few weeks.

"Are you sure you brought me to the right place, Dale?" I asked, looking at the piece of paper and glancing back at the house.

Dale chuckled. "You sure your mom didn't find a genie in the past few weeks while you were gone?"

I started to wonder the same. Maybe Mickey Mouse was a real person too.

My mother's new house was beautiful and nothing like what I had imagined it would be—a brown bricked modern two-story house with a white picket fence. It had trimmed lawns with a private parking area and a cute little patio stood at the center.

This shit was posh. *Had my mother remarried to some rich bastard?*

Dale parked the car in the shadows as I told him to since I didn't want to take any risks.

I rang the doorbell and waited. I rang once again and saw the curtains rustle. The door opened finally and my hands flew to my mouth as I suppressed a loud sob that was about to erupt from within.

My mother stood at the doorway, dressed in a silk maroon robe. Her black hair was dyed blonde, and the tired bags that used to be under her eyes had vanished. She looked so much younger and better, like a posh lady that goes to Sunday brunch with her friends, drove expensive cars, and did charity for fun.

Her eyes swam with tears as I wrapped her in a hug and cried my eyes out on her shoulder. She then closed the door behind me and led me inside. The living area was impressive with furniture that matched with the drapes. A flat-screen was mounted against the wall. It was a home that I had always wished we had.

Mom smiled at me. "Would you like some tea, my dear?"

I shook my head. "I'm good." I had to leave soon. Jasper would probably be here looking for me.

"Mom, I need to talk to you."

We settled on the couch. Mom took my hand in hers. My tears started spilling out. I had questions about her moving to this place. I wanted to ask her where she got the money from, or if she had moved in with a wealthy man, but first, I needed to get everything off my chest and fast. If I had found mom's address so easily, I knew Jasper would too, and I didn't want to think what would happen then.

"I was living with Jasper Lockhart for the past few weeks as his . . . as his mistress."

Mom appeared to be shocked by my revelation.

I shrugged. "You were right, Mom. Someone as wealthy as Jasper wasn't really interested in someone like me." The next few words came out in a strangled sob. "I was in a helpless situation, and he just used me. I mistook it for love. I thought if he realized how much he meant to me, he'd change. I just ended up feeling so disgusted with myself. I was reduced to being his whore. Nothing else."

Mom nodded. Her expression remained impassive. This was all a little too much for her to handle. Maybe she thought I had gone bonkers and was cooking up stories.

"You seem hungry, honey. I made macaroni and cheese. Would you like some?"

"Yes, of course." It had been a while since I had mom's food. I was craving it.

She walked into the kitchen and stuffed a plate full of macaroni and cheese into the microwave oven for heating. A few minutes later, I was devouring it.

"So, how did you move in here?" I finally asked her.

She shrugged. The thin lines on her forehead creased. "Your grandfather left us a small fortune in his will."

"I wouldn't call this small. Did grandpa win some kind of a lottery before he died?"

My grandfather used to live on a farm. To think grandpa would leave tons of money in his will seemed unlikely, considering the fact that he barely made much out of farming and spent most of his time watching television and boozing. Something was not right. My mother was definitely hiding something.

Before I could say another word, the doorbell rang and there was a brief knock at the door. My heartbeat sped up. "It could be Jasper. If it's him, please don't tell him I'm here, okay? I need to hide somewhere."

There was another loud pounding.

Mom instructed me to go into the bedroom and hide in the walk-in closet. I rushed into the master bedroom, slipped into the walk-in closet, and hid behind the hanging clothes.

A moment later, I heard the sound of retreating footsteps. The closet was dark, but there was a small gap in the corner of the door where I could peep out and see what was going on.

I heard the bedroom door creak open and a voice that said, "Where is she?"

My chest tightened with fear. It was undoubtedly Jasper's voice. I could recognize that deep voice even in my sleep.

How did Jasper know my mother's new location?

"She isn't here." I heard Mom answer.

Jasper's eyes darted around the room. His hair was thick and dark. His blue eyes shined like marbles. He kind of reminded me of a raven trying to spot its prey. He dug his hand into his pocket, avoiding direct eye contact with my mother.

At that point, I noticed how young he looked—a gorgeous young man in his late twenties, dressed to impress. The burn mark on his neck did not steal away from his beauty.

"Where is she, Julie?" Jasper asked my mother in a low gravelly voice. I had to press my ear to the door to listen to him carefully.

"I told you. I don't know," Mom lied. "She didn't come here."

"Kiara and I were at a friend's party, and she went missing during that time. Now, if she stopped by here, which I'm one hundred and one percent sure she did, I want you to tell me the truth. If you're lying, you do know what that entails, don't you?" Jasper asked.

Mom nodded. *Why did it seem like they knew each other?*

133

"Here's what I'll tell you, Julie. My team will try their best to track her down, and in the meantime, I want you to do the same. You're her mother, she is going to come looking for you, which is assuming you aren't lying right now and Kiara wasn't already here."

Jasper looked at mom calmly. It was the calm before the storm. "If you can't manage to locate her, I will have to take action which means you are going back to that trashy place that you called home, and you will return me the money. All of it. Is that clear?"

Wait! What?

I froze on the spot; I was practically brain dead.

From this short conversation, I drew the conclusion that Mom had taken some money from Jasper.

But why the hell would she do that?

"Yes, I understand," she said.

"Good," Jasper said as his eyes moved towards the closet, and for a second, I thought he spotted me.

I watched from the small open gap between the doors as he took long strides towards where I was hidden. All he needed to do was open the closet and he'd find me. I was so heartbroken that I covered my mouth with my hands to stifle a sob. I shifted back deeper into the closet, covering myself with the clothes hanging.

He pulled open the closet and moved a few hangers to find nothing. Jasper sighed, finally giving up and backed away. Next, he checked the attached bathroom, only to come up empty.

"I expect you to call me as soon as she contacts you." Those were the final words I heard from Jasper before he strode out of the room. I waited to step out of the closet until I heard the main door shut.

A few minutes later, Mom walked inside the bedroom and declared, "He is gone. You can come out now."

I stepped out of the closet cautiously. I looked to the closet again and searched through the hangers for my old clothes only to find none. The clothes that were hanging were all her new ones.

Every single one of my belongings were gone—the denim, the casual wear, the handbags . . .

"Where are my clothes?" I asked.

"I got rid of it," she said simply.

I nodded. Of course, she would get rid of it, which also meant that she didn't expect me to come home. I tried to appear not hurt by that thought and reached for some of her clothes and dumped it into the bag. She was only a size bigger. I could easily fit into hers.

"Sweetheart, I can explain . . ." she started saying.

I stopped packing midway to turn and glare at my mother.

"Explain?" I folded my arms across my chest because I wanted to see what lame excuses would come out of that lying mouth. "Well, why don't you start with why you took the money from Jasper? I thought you said grandpa left the money in his will. It's all a lie, isn't it? Grandpa never left a dime."

She started rambling on about something, but at some point, I tuned out her voice as the sadness tore at my heart. Jasper's words hadn't hurt me as much as my mother's betrayal. I had known Jasper was different and it wasn't the first time I heard him threaten someone, but I never thought Mom could stoop as low as this.

I heard her whisper, "I did it for us."

I grabbed ahold of her shoulders and looked straight into her eyes. "What did you do?"

I was scared to hear the truth. I was scared of what she might have in store. I realized that I needed to be stronger for this.

Mom swallowed. She was teary-eyed and looked guilty for some reason, and that wasn't a good sign.

"I'm sorry, honey. I didn't have a choice."

"I want to know the truth," I yelled at her, losing my patience.

Mom flinched. "After your father's death, when I told you to leave, I called Frankie, but he refused to help me and that was when I got a call from Jasper."

"What happened?"

She couldn't even meet my eyes as she continued, "He offered to help us."

I gave out a dry laugh. He had taken advantage of our situation. I knew what was going to follow, but I still decided to ask her, "What kind of help?"

"He told me he had connections that would help prove in court that it was an accidental death, and I think he did keep his promise." Her eyes suddenly turned sad. "Jasper provided for everything. He bought this house, Kiara."

"I'm sure he asked you for something in return."

"He helped me cover your tracks. He has good connections, and nothing could ever prove that you did it. He said . . . he said all your father's debts would be paid. I'd get a proper roof over my head, clothes, and everything that we ever wanted. He promised to keep his end of the bargain if I . . . ."

"If you what?"

"If I let him keep you," she finished, and I was stunned beyond words.

How could she do that to me? I was her flesh and blood!

"I didn't see the problem because you seemed to like him, and he promised me to keep you happy. Kiara, we are free of your father's debts. We earned our freedom. Isn't that something?"

I laughed. I laughed so hard that I was back in tears again, hacking loud sobs when the horror of the situation hit me hard.

My mother had sold me for money. All this luxury wasn't because she married Frankie or something we acquired from grandpa's will. It was all because Jasper Lockhart had paid for it, in exchange for helping my mother and keeping me captive.

Yes, that's what it had been.

A kidnapping in disguise.

136

Flashbacks began haunting me from when Jasper came to pick me up at the park.

"Let me help you, Kiara."

Realization struck me like a bolt of lightning. Jasper hadn't come to just help me back then. He had come to collect his dues. It was no wonder he pulled my legs apart with such ease as if he had ownership over me.

Like I was sold to him.

I cried, this time silently wondering if there was a way I could still get out of this mess. I didn't want to go back to Jasper.

I wiped my tears. "Mom, listen. Whatever money you took from Jasper, we will return it, and we don't need this house. We are returning that too."

"We can't." She shook her head vigorously.

"Why not?"

"Because we would go bankrupt!" she snapped in a frustrated tone. I never heard her use that tone with me. "Your father left us in debt of fifty-thousand dollars which Lockhart cleared up for us. If we return everything, we will be homeless. Do you understand what I'm saying?"

"Then what do we do?" I asked.

She took my hands in hers. "You go back to Jasper's."

I pulled my hands away. "Do you understand what you are suggesting?" My hands shook. "He is a possessive man with a controlling streak! Jasper doesn't even love me, Mother. How do you expect me to go back to him?"

"Listen, baby, please," Mom pleaded. She was pleading with me not because she cared for me, but because she didn't want to be robbed off the luxuries. "I did it for *us*, I did it for *you*. We're poor and the poor don't always get what they want if they continue to maintain pride and dignity. If we want that lifestyle, we have to get our hands dirty. Jasper's someone with enough money to buy a country. He made all our money problems vanish. Look at you, honey. You look like those rich women we see in the magazines.

Think what would happen if you decide to stay here with me. This is not your home now. Your home is with Jasper Lockhart. If you don't go to him, he will take everything back."

I shook my head. "You're not ashamed of yourself, are you?" I asked. "You practically sold your daughter to sleep in a king-sized bed, and all this while I thought he'd asked me to live with him because of the goodness of his heart."

I wiped the tears with the back of my hand, stormed into the bathroom, sneaked two bottles of shampoo and some soaps from the cabinet, and dumped them inside the travel bag.

I opened the window of the bedroom, tossed the bag out of the window, and landed on my feet on the soft grass.

"You will go back to Jasper, won't you?" she asked.

"You don't leave me a choice," I said as I climbed out of the window.

CHAPTER EIGHTEEN

"Kiara, if you have some free time from daydreaming, table number four is waiting for you to take their order," the restaurant manager, Colin, whispered to me. I almost jumped out of my skin when I heard his voice.

"Sorry," I mumbled, and walked towards the group waiting to place their order. I walked back to the soda dispenser and filled a tall glass of coke and ice when I noticed Colin's eyes assessing me. He gave me an apprehensive smile and continued with his work.

If anything, I knew I was going to be fired pretty soon.

The clock ticked to 1o PM, and I was almost done with my shift. There wasn't anything else waiting for me at home other than the suffocating silence, so I decided to help Colin with the cleaning duties.

He was cleaning a table that some patrons had just vacated. I offered to help him clean the mess.

"I'll take it from here," I said, taking the rag from him. "You can take care of other things. Chloe already left."

Colin was a nice guy. He was sweet and kind of naïve to believe a sob story I fed him when I applied for the job.

Calling it *applied* would be the understatement of the year, I had literally walked into the diner and begged him to give me a chance, and now that he had, I spent most of my time staring into spaces than working my ass off.

"Are you alright?" He surprised me with that question.

"Yeah." I passed him a smile, one that I knew did not reach my eyes.

He nodded. "You should know, Kiara, that if you need anything, I can help, but I need to know exactly what is going on in your mind."

Okay, maybe he wasn't as naïve as I thought he was.

I wasn't sure he would understand, and I didn't think I even wanted him to understand.

Was I supposed to tell him that my own mother had sold me to a wealthy man for her ticket to a luxurious lifestyle? Or, was I supposed to tell him that I was on the run from the same man for over a month, and that I may have lucked out?

Jasper hadn't found me yet for two weeks. Either he hadn't been able to trace my location, or he had totally given up on me and was out there targeting other women. If that was true, I wondered if Mom was back in the old rundown house, and if he had stripped her of the wealth.

The thought of him with other women repulsed me. These feelings that I had for him wouldn't fade away. You couldn't just turn off all your feelings, and start hating someone all of a sudden.

Yes, Jasper was selfish, and yes, he was unpredictable, overbearing, and self-centered, but there were also so many good sides of him—the part where he fought that man for trying to hurt me in the alley, when he helped me during my most desperate times by stopping me from making a fool out of myself in a strip bar, those moments when he'd looked at me like there was no better woman than me . . .

When I was alone in my room, all these thoughts haunted me and kept me awake in bed.

I often woke up in bed thinking I was still in his house and would be turned on by the thought of him. I imagined his seductive mouth moving against mine and that expert tongue of his suckling against my core. It was just too much, and I missed him more than I wanted to admit to myself. When I finished taking care of myself,

140

I would become utterly ashamed at how my heart was betraying my mind.

It was hard to forget Jasper Lockhart.

I lied to Colin about everything. I told him that my parents were dead, I didn't have anywhere else to go, and I needed a job and a place to live desperately. I felt guilty for lying, but desperate times called for desperate measures.

I was so shaken by the whole thing that I often spaced out. I lived in constant fear that Jasper was going to come after me. The crazy thing was, a part of me wanted him to and another part of me didn't. At one point, my entire world revolved around his axis.

"Colin, I just want to thank you for everything that you have done for me. I really appreciate it," I said sincerely. If Colin hadn't helped me out, I'd probably be homeless.

Colin knew better than to press me further, so he walked back into the kitchen.

I cleaned up the mess, got changed out of my work clothes, and walked out of the restaurant back door into the breezy cool air. I lived in a small studio apartment just above the diner. It was actually Colin's old apartment that had been locked up and collecting dust, so he thought it was a suitable place for me to live in.

I had initially planned on moving to my grandpa's farm and that was where I told Dale to drop me off the night I escaped after the act. The house was small amid a sea of cornfields. It was an old house that looked like it had been featured in one of Hollywood's horror movies—infested with cobwebs and a thick layer of dust. I knew it was still better than staying at Jasper's and feeling like I was his plaything.

The problem was that I didn't have the key, and I was in no position to knock at the neighbor's door for help, so I slept the night in the empty shed by the back of the house and took a bus to nowhere.

I had little money that Amy and Dale both had given me and a pair of earrings which I had acquired from Jasper's that I saved for later. I dropped down on the last station the bus took, and walked into the first restaurant that I laid eyes on.

I quickly changed into my pajamas, fixed myself a glass of milk and settled down on my comfy bed.

I wondered for how long I was going to be able to live like this.

*   *   *

JASPER

I ran my fingers across the keys of the piano and played a piece by *Beethoven*. I won awards for playing this during the various competitions I had taken part in. Never had I been interested in playing the piano, but it was something I did to impress my father to no avail. I eventually enjoyed playing it.

I had always been the son of a mistress—a woman that my father had taken under his wing as a housemaid for the mansion, the same woman who kept him satisfied while his wife was away doing charity functions.

And then one day, the maid told him she was pregnant with his love child. My mother was under the false belief that the man loved her, but she was dismissed into the servant's quarters where I was raised.

My father's sorry excuse for a wife, Faith Lockhart, found out about it, because it was hard not to notice the child's striking similarities to the imposing man. Faith Lockhart used to hit me with a stick as a form of punishment for things I hadn't done, mistakes that I never made. She hit me until my back was tattooed with scars that I carried to this day.

Funny thing was, that bitch would always miscarry her children. I guess that was karma for the things she put me through at the age of four, so my father gave up and made an agreement with my birth mother. She was to never call me as her own, and I was handed over to my stepmom who did continue with the abuse out of jealousy.

I was five when she got pregnant, (a miracle) and a baby boy was born whom I was accustomed to hating.

Vincent thought he was the rightful heir to this property, only I wasn't going to let that happen.

Nobody took what was rightfully mine.

So I did what I had to do. I competed with my younger brother, and finally drove him away. Being the firstborn, I had the right over everything. The Lockhart Enterprise would have been in a shamble if it hadn't been for me bringing it back up from the ruins. I had the right over everything.

After the death of my father and stepmother, it was just me and my mother in the house while Vincent went to medical college to be a neurosurgeon. My mother insisted that things should remain the same, and that it wasn't her place to have any right over the house.

For years, I had tried to cut out all the memories of abuse from the hands of my stepmom by taking in girls that I liked, but they never helped with my pain.

And then there was Kiara—sweet, beautiful, Kiara Reeves—who somehow broke down the walls of my heart. I thought she was here to stay. She said she loved me. I knew she wasn't faking the moans of pleasure as she wiggled under me in bed.

Women always wanted more. Kiara wasn't a gold digger by a long shot, the diamond necklace that I had gifted her was left in her bedroom on the dresser, and that was proof enough. It also meant that she had planned on leaving the same day as Lucas party. The box came with a note in her loopy, cursive handwriting.

Dear Jasper,

You may find this letter when I'm long gone. I feel like a complete idiot writing this letter because this is a little too old-fashioned, isn't it? But, I'm writing you this because I never got a chance to tell you how I really feel.

I love you, and it will never change. I've loved you since the day we first met in the alley, and as we spent time with each other, my feelings for you kept growing until I didn't even recognize myself. This is not me, Jasper. I've never asked for diamonds, or fast cars or expensive things. All I ever wanted was you.

I don't expect you to love me back, but I also can't let you treat me the way you've been lately. I respect you, and in return, I want to be treated with respect. I have these uncontrollable feelings, and the more I live with you, the more my heart breaks, thinking that we could never have a future together. I sound pathetic, and no matter how hard this is going to be, I have to go.

I understand that you're not a normal man, although I don't know what you are exactly. I sympathize with you. I love you for the man that you are.

After much thought, I've taken this decision to leave. Thank you for everything you've done for me from the bottom of my heart.

Yours,
Kiara.

I noticed the little dried blotches on the paper at the end of the letter and realized she had been crying while she wrote it. I read the letter over a dozen times. The mind-blowing sex, the billionaire life . . . it wasn't enough for her, and I knew what she wanted, it was pretty apparent in the letter.

Kiara wanted me to love her.

It was the one thing that I couldn't give to her, not because I didn't want to, but because I couldn't. I knew I was different, my mother kept telling me that. I had consumed a lot of alcohol so my head felt fuzzy, but my fingers continued to assault the piano. Drops of blood trailed down my fingers and stained the white keys.

"Jasper, honey, that's enough!"

I ignored the voice and stopped playing the piano. I smacked myself hard on the right cheek.

That's for trusting Lucas.

I smacked my left cheek.

That's for losing Kiara.

I smacked my right cheek again.

That's for still wanting to be with her.

My mother, Margret, placed her hand on my shoulder. "Stop punishing yourself."

I smacked her hand away but she pulled me close, and I felt her fingers running through my hair. "What's so special about that girl?"

"I don't know, Mom. I just want her," I admitted.

There were a lot of other women I knew who would throw themselves at me. I just needed to throw them a bone. They'd even kill to be my woman, and I had given Kiara that chance, but she ruined everything. I always got what I wanted, and I wasn't going to stop now.

Kiara was mine, and I wasn't going to have it any other way.

I had looked everywhere for her. I even checked her grandfather's farm and every possible place I thought I could find her, but I came up empty. This wasn't a good sign. It only meant she was laying low in some other town.

I would go into the pits of hell to find her if that's what it took.

Kiara, you better be ready because I'm coming for you.

PART TWO

CHAPTER NINETEEN

KIARA

Four Months Later

It has almost been four months since I had last seen or heard from my mother. I hadn't even contacted my old friend, Kathy, because I didn't want to involve her into my problems. It was also four months since I last saw or heard from Jasper.

And I would be kidding if I said I didn't miss him.

Although the man was borderline crazy, I knew there was a part of him that fought to resurface, like the nice guy inside him which I had seen on several occasions. He was a good listener, and I enjoyed our little chats during the evening. It was just that he acted strange sometimes. Indifferent. That was the only part I hated about him, and that drove me away.

The next morning, I spent a disturbing amount of time staring at the diamond-studded platinum earrings that I had been wearing on the night I escaped from Lucas's house. I was in dire need of cash because even after all the savings, I didn't have much left.

Although Colin sometimes gave me an advanced paycheck, it just wasn't enough to cover my other expenses, so I decided to sell the expensive pair of earrings that I knew would get me by, at least for a while.

When I went to the shop to sell them and the sales guy inspected the earrings, I noticed that he assessed me with a wary look. I knew that look. He was probably wondering what a shabby girl like me in a cheap suit was doing with an expensive pair of earrings.

He told me the price he was willing to pay for it. I pushed him some more, but he was adamant on the given price, so I decided to take what I could get. I had to literally put a rock on my heart before I traded the pair for the money because the earrings were gorgeous, and I knew that I would never be able to afford them in future. I felt like I had stolen from Jasper, but I guess if I made enough money, I could pay him back somehow.

By the time I was back at the restaurant, it was already past 6 PM, and hidden under my cushion was an envelope filled with cash that could sustain me for months if I used it wisely.

It was almost closing time when the bell dinged which meant another customer had walked into the diner.

Colin patted my back. "Chloe will take the order."

I had forgotten to turn the *"Open"* sign to *"Closed"*, so now we would have to tend to the customer because Colin didn't like to send away a waiting patron.

Chloe placed the order at the kitchen. It was the weekend special—Fish & Chips with tartar sauce and a side dish of Caesar salad.

"Here. Order for table number three." Colin handed me the tray of food, "This is the last order. Would you please turn the sign on the door for me?"

"Sure."

I walked out of the kitchen, towards the table. "Here you go . . ."

I stopped short when I first noticed the familiar shiny shoes. My eyes then traveled up towards the face of the man seated in the booth. My breath hitched in my throat.

I didn't know how long I was shell-shocked because I think I heard Colin call out my name. My hands shook, and the tray of food crashed and shattered on the floor.

I took a step back, then another, and dashed into the kitchen and collapsed on the floor by the counter.

Those blue eyes curiously assessed me. He seemed shocked to see me the same way I had, and I wondered how that was possible. It's been four months since I last saw him. His once clean-shaven face had a slight stubble and his usual short brown hair had grown longer. He looked different, but I could never forget that face.

I covered my mouth with my hands and cried. At one point, Colin was kneeling down next to me, whispering something, but I couldn't hear him because my mind had wandered to the man in the booth.

There was no mistaking who it was. It was *Jasper Lockhart.*

"I . . . I can't go out there," I told Colin.

Colin looked concerned and didn't seem furious about the wasted food. "Who is he, Kiara?"

"Ex-boyfriend," I said. It wasn't a lie basically because that was what people thought of our relationship.

Colin nodded. "Stay put. I'll handle him."

I caught his hand. "No. Please. Don't say anything to him. He is . . . he is very dangerous."

Colin chuckled. "I may look like this, but I can fight, babe."

I shook my head. If the guy had a gun, which I'm sure he did, Colin's fighting would be useless, and Jasper was a Karate black belt, Colin didn't stand a chance.

"Just keep him busy. I'm going to sneak out of the back door," I whispered.

"Okay," he said.

"Colin."

He stopped in his tracks and turned to face me.

"I will tell you everything tonight, but please be careful."

He nodded, and I watched Colin make his way out of the kitchen. When I was sure he was already out tending to *him,* I picked up my bag and made my way towards the staff back door.

I heard Colin calling out to me which was when I knew I had made the wrong decision.

I walked out of the diner, and that was when a tall dark shadow who was leaning his back against the wall stepped into the street light.

"Kiara," that icy voice called out to me.

I was breathing heavily.

He reached out towards me but I took a step back.

I knew I was trapped. There was no way out now.

A shudder ran down my body as Jasper watched me intently. I folded my arms across my chest as if that was some kind of a shield to protect me against him. I tried to stand tall, act confident, but I felt my resolve slipping away slowly.

His hand rose towards me. I flinched and backed away. Jasper's hand fell to his side, his expression wounded.

"How are you doing, Kiara?"

"I'm fine," I replied. "What do you . . . what do you want?"

"Do you work here?" he pressed.

Was Jasper back because he wanted me to come back to his house and repay our debt in other ways again?

"You didn't answer my question, Jasper. I asked what you want."

I thought I saw his jaw harden, but I couldn't be sure because it was dark. If he decided to drug me and kidnap me, it wouldn't be very hard, but so far, he hadn't made a move. I had the mace spray in my bag just in case.

I noticed Colin watching us from the kitchen window. He wasn't spying on us but checking to make sure we were fine. He was probably chalking this up as another common breakup between couples—ex-boyfriend showing up at girl's work, convincing her to take him back, blah blah blah. I wished it was that simple.

150

I shifted from one foot to another. "Why are you here?"

"It's a coincidence. I didn't know you worked here. I stopped by for a quick meal and saw you." As much as I wanted to think he was lying, his voice spoke levels of sincerity and his expression remained stoic, then again, Jasper had mastered acting.

"I really appreciate what you did for my mother. You paid my father's debt and got me out of trouble from the law, but I think I've already repaid you by living three weeks in your house and . . ." I could feel the heat warming my neck as I said it. "And catering to your needs." I bit my lip. "If you should know, Jasper, I would never stay with you for your money. I thought I could do what you expected from me—be content with just staying as your mistress, but I can't do that. I'm sorry."

"Your hair has grown longer. It looks beautiful," he complimented with a smile.

"Thanks," I said.

"I didn't come here to make you feel bad about yourself. What you did was correct. I just wanted to tell you that I miss you, Kiara." He dug his hands in his pants pockets, seemingly haggard. "You look well, and I'm really happy to see that."

I stared at him in surprise. It was getting pretty chilly outside, I hugged myself, trying not to freeze my butt and thinking what to make of this conversation. I thought he was going to be angry and ask me to go back to him, but he had totally surprised me with his words.

Jasper stripped off his bomber jacket and placed it on my shoulders. I felt nice and warm, and it smelled like him.

A sense of déjà vu hit me.

Why was he acting so nice?

"I should go," I said.

He nodded again. His blue eyes did not betray any emotion, and that was what scared me most of the time. "Take care of yourself, Kiara."

Still feeling a bit shocked, I watched as he walked away from me towards his car. He opened the door and slid into the driver's side. I stood there until the car disappeared from the street.

*　　*　　*

"I don't understand. How did he know you were working here?" Colin asked me the next day while I was helping him in the kitchen.

"He told me it was a coincidence," I admitted.

"That's a fat lie," Colin muttered.

"It didn't seem that way," I said, squeezing ketchup on the burger patty.

Colin placed his hand over mine. "I've said this before, and I'm going to say it again. If you have any problems, talk to me about it. I can help you."

I passed him a smile. "Thanks."

He placed his hand on my shoulder and that was when Colin's girlfriend, Sasha, walked in. "What the hell is going on here?"

Colin pulled his hand away from my shoulder like he just touched a hot iron rod. "Baby, it's nothing like you're thinking."

Sasha turned a deaf ear to him as she walked towards us and stood right in front of me. She was at least a few inches taller than me which gave her the upper hand.

I didn't really like Sasha. She always had the wrong idea that I had a thing for Colin which was far from the truth.

"You can fool Colin with your goody two-shoes act, Kiara, but you can't fool me," she said, fuming. She always had a bit of a problem with me. I wasn't sure why.

"You're misunderstanding me," I tried to reason with her.

"He stays out until late, and he gave you his old apartment to live in for free. So, tell me something, *Miss Reeves*. Are you screwing my boyfriend as payment for his kindness?"

"Sasha! Mind your language!" Colin yelled.

Sasha smacked Colin's face and stomped her way out of the door. Colin didn't bother to follow her like I assumed he would. Instead, he turned to face me and apologized.

"As soon as I find a good place, I'll move out," I promised.

He shrugged but didn't protest which told me I needed to find a place soon.

*　　　*　　　*

I was mostly being careful after that night with Jasper. It had been a few days since he had been at the diner. Honestly, when he said he missed me, I had the same familiar butterflies take flight in my stomach.

It was hard to admit, but I was still in love with him. After the attempted rape in the alley, I was always careful when I had to run an errand to the supermarket.

I climbed the stairs to the studio apartment quietly. The staircase light was left off. I wondered if Colin switched it off by mistake. My fingers found the button as I clicked the lights on, and my heart almost stopped beating when I saw the man standing near my doorway. The shopping bag I was carrying dropped to the floor.

"Oh my God, Jasper!" I bit back a scream, holding my rapidly beating heart.

"I didn't want to surprise you like that."

"Surprise? Jasper, you scared the shit outta me!" I said furiously.

Jasper ran a hand through his hair in frustration. The unruly curls had grown wilder. His other hand was hiding something behind his back. I couldn't see it. He was dressed casually in an Abercrombie t-shirt and blue ripped jeans. The sleeves of his t-shirt hugged his biceps perfectly.

I remembered him shirtless and the feel of his amazing set of six-pack abs right there. The expanse of his broad shoulders was blocking me from entering the apartment, and his imposing height made me feel even shorter.

He was pure sin, dangerous yet tempting and hard to resist. He was born to ruin women with just one glance. My heart did a quick somersault, and I cursed myself inwardly for feeling this way. If this man begged, I wasn't entirely sure if I wouldn't cave in.

"How did you know I lived here?" I asked.

I was starting to feel a little curious and scared about what he was hiding behind his back.

Could it be a knife? Was he going to threaten me?

He shrugged. "Just saw you walking back here yesterday."

"Are you stalking me?"

He didn't answer. "I was wondering if maybe we could, you know, start over."

"Start over?"

"Yeah," he admitted. "Do what normal couples do, date each other."

I was speechless. He had been waiting here outside my apartment for who knows how long to ask me if we could date?

"Why would you want to date me? You don't even like me. You just like fucking me, that's the last thing I remember you said," I threw his words back at him.

He sighed. "I don't deny that. I've always liked being intimate with you and I apologize that you felt insulted, but you already know that I'm always honest with you," he said, and my eyes widened at how he never made an attempt to deny the facts thrown at him. He was brutally honest as always.

"So why are you here? If you're going to ask me to sleep with you, Jasper, please don't bother. The money you lent me, I know it's a lot, but I'm going to try and pay you back even if it means working two jobs. I just need more time."

With that said, I turned towards the door, retrieving the keys from my bag. Suddenly, his hand wound around mine as he pulled me against his chest. His strong arm snaked around my back and the familiar scent of his cologne filled my nostrils. His other hand finally revealed what he was holding.

A bouquet of lovely red roses. The flowers were huge and perfectly bloomed. "These are for you," he whispered, softly.

I took the bouquet from him because I was a sucker for roses and stuff like that. "Thanks."

He was still holding me close to him. "I need one more chance, Kiara, to make it right. I want you back in my life."

I tried to wiggle out of his embrace, but his hold on me tightened.

I said, "I can't give you what you want because we both know we want different things from each other."

His thumb slowly caressed my cheek and lingered near my jaw. "For months I tried to forget you. I tried to tell myself that it's okay to move on, but I couldn't do that," he whispered in that deep husky voice. "You don't have to answer me right away, you can take your time."

He didn't say any more after that and made his way downstairs out of the building.

It was exactly what I had wanted to hear him say, and for months, I replayed it in my head a lot of times, but I had been heartbroken before and I didn't know if I was ready to make another mistake again.

*   *   *

Jasper never took no for an answer, I knew that much, and so he continued to show up at my workplace during the evenings and stayed until closing time, watching and waiting, a half-eaten sandwich on his table. His gaze would dart towards me before he moved his attention back to his laptop screen.

It went on for over a week until one day, Colin approached Jasper's table. I wondered if he had sensed the tension.

I followed him. "Is there a problem?"

Jasper's stare got ice cold, and the softness that I had seen a while ago was getting clouded by menace. "You tell me. I'm just a customer having my coffee."

Colin tried to match Jasper's hard stare but I knew Jasper would win this show of epic stare-down. "I noticed how you've been insistently trying to court Kiara."

Jasper barked out a laugh. "*Court* Kiara? Does anyone even use that word anymore?"

Colin ignored the jibe and continued, "I think she made it clear last time that she didn't want to see you, and I've been noticing you here every single day since then, even when she told you off clearly which tells me that you are causing us trouble. I want to know if I need to involve the police."

Jasper chuckled. If Colin was smart, he would let this go.

I placed my hand on Colin's shoulder to tell him to shut up before it was too late.

"Mr. Davis, I really appreciate you looking out for *my* girl, but that doesn't mean it gives you or anyone the right to insinuate that I'm indulging in criminal activity. I was just merely trying to fix the misunderstandings by persuading her."

"More like stalking rather than persuading. And I do have proof."

"Colin," I warned him.

"Are you sure it's alright, Kiara?"

I nodded. "Yes."

"Whatever it is that you need to talk about, take it outside," Colin said and walked away.

Outside in the parking lot, we stood by his car which was a new shiny red Maserati. I wanted to believe he had brought it to impress me.

"I'm sorry about Colin. He gets a bit defensive sometimes."

"Are you free Saturday night?" he tried to change the subject all of a sudden.

I was free but I didn't want to seem too eager. "Guess I will be."

"Alright. I'll pick you up at eight and we can go out to dinner," he was acting bossy again. "I won't screw it up, I promise."

I nodded and smiled. "I'll look forward to it, Mr. Lockhart."

That night, I received a text from my co-worker, Chloe, asking me to come to a club downtown called *The Vault*. It wasn't the weekend so I knew the club wouldn't be packed.

Twenty minutes later, I was dolled up in a short back dress, and my hair curled up. I had watched some makeup tutorials and managed to do a smokey eye-makeup look. When I reached the club, it was easy to spot Chloe dancing between two men. She usually enjoyed all the male attention, and I wondered how I ended up with the same type of friends. Kathy had been similar.

Chloe tried to get me to dance but I strictly declined her offer, and instead, ordered a margarita and cheesy nachos. It was past midnight, and I was bored out of my mind even with Chloe trying to make conversation with the loud music blaring in my ears.

It was a weeknight so the club wasn't packed. There were more people sitting on the sidelines watching than dancing on the floor.

I was sipping my margarita when I noticed a tall blond guy leaning against the wall and looking straight at me. I thought it was a mere coincidence that we happened to exchange glances at the same time, but a while later, I looked again and I noticed his eyes were still on me, serious and intense.

A shiver ran down my body and I looked away. After the third drink, my head felt woozy, and I instantly regretted having so much to drink.

"I have to use the restroom," I informed Chloe.

"Should I come along?"

"No, it's okay," I said, and made my way towards the restrooms.

The restrooms weren't as bad as I thought if you got past the stink of piss. I walked out of the stall, washed my hands, and applied some lip-gloss.

When I walked out of the passageway, I was caught off guard by a strong hand that covered my mouth.

A man was dragging me somewhere.

Could it be Jasper?

CHAPTER TWENTY

The man loosened his grip on my mouth as he dragged me out of the club through the back door. I tried to scream, but he pressed his hand back again on my mouth. I got a glimpse of his face when the strong strobe lights reflected on him. It was not Jasper or anyone I knew. He was the same blond man who had been staring at me a while ago.

We were in an underground cave. The strong whiff of smoke and alcohol almost made me gag. There was a different crowd of people down here, the type you were supposed to stay away from. I saw a woman passed out on the floor. Her eyes were rolled back, and there was another man smoking at the arm of the couch.

They were doing drugs. *Why had this man brought me here?*

"I'm going to scream," I warned him.

"I need you to trust me, Kiara," he said, and pointed at a door at the far end. "We can go outside to the parking lot where there are fewer people and have more privacy to talk." His eyes darted around the room cautiously.

"I'm not going anywhere unless you tell me who you are," I said, folding my arms across my chest and trying to appear tough even though I was scared from the inside.

"Lucas Johnson sent me here. Does that name ring any bells?"

Of course, it did. How could I forget the man who had helped me with no questions asked?

"What does Lucas have to do with this?" I asked.

"If you follow me, I'll tell you everything," he said, and then added, "You have to trust me, Kiara."

I didn't have a choice so I followed him out towards the door that had a huge *Exit* sign in neon lighting. The curiosity building inside me outweighed the fear I had for this man even though his method of getting my attention was wrong, although I admit I wouldn't have talked to him if he hadn't dragged me downstairs.

As the club doors closed behind us, the chaos got quieter. He grasped my elbow, and pulled me towards the corner near a blue Lexus sedan.

"My name is John, and I work for Lucas. He sent me here to warn you about some things," he got straight to the point.

"He knows where I am?" I asked him, surprised.

John nodded. "And he also knows what Jasper is up to."

"I don't understand."

John glanced around as if to make sure we were actually alone, and whispered, "Is he being unnecessarily sweet? Did he tell you that he has changed? Did Jasper ask you for another chance?"

"He did, but—"

John gave out a hoarse laugh. "That bastard is playing you."

"How can you be so sure?"

"Because that's his plan all along. He wants to trap you in an elaborately sketched plan and drag you back to that hellhole."

"I don't believe you." I shook my head.

It was true that Jasper acted indifferently, but he had apologized for his behavior. He was sweet by giving me roses even though I didn't appreciate how he almost scared the bejesus out of me. I had seen and felt how he really wanted me to accept his apologies. He had been trying for almost two weeks straight now.

160

"He's using you," John said.

It was time for me to laugh. I laughed so hard that tears formed in the corner of my eyes.

"I'm sorry, what was that?" I asked in-between laughs. "Jasper is using me?"

John clearly appeared pissed. "Is there something funny in what I said?"

"Let me get this straight. You're saying Jasper Lockhart, CEO of the Lockhart Enterprise, billionaire and owner of hotel chains and resorts is using Kiara Reeves, a nobody, a waitress who works at a diner. Please forgive me if I find that utterly laughworthy." I couldn't control my laughter. Maybe it was the alcohol working its wonders.

"It's your call. My job was to warn you, and the job is done, but it seems like I may have just wasted my time," he said.

"In all seriousness.. . . ." I continued. ". . .I find it quite hard to believe that Jasper could be planning to use me in any way. I'm sure there are far more influential women lying in wait for him to spare a minute of time of his day."

"It would be in your best interest to move somewhere else. Stay low for a while," John suggested.

"You don't understand." I shook my head. "I have a job here, and a place to live. I can't afford to move anywhere."

John didn't seem convinced.

"Besides, Jasper had apologized to me, and he's trying to fix our differences. He's trying to change himself."

A few seconds passed and then he said, "Lucas told me to warn you, I've done my job. Goodbye."

He turned on his heel, walked towards his car—a sleek black Jaguar, and left me to ponder over our conversation.

It was a little hard to believe that Jasper would go to the extent of apologizing and doing things for me because he thought I was useful to him in any way.

As far as I knew, Jasper had everything and didn't need a woman like me by his side. During the numerous parties that I had posed as his companion, I had seen beautiful women, single or married, openly flirting with him. Those were the women with high statuses and heavy bank accounts—the kind who didn't need a man to provide for them.

He surely didn't need me.

Jasper had paid my father's debts, and I paid my dues in Jasper's bed. There was only one reason why he would go all the way to track me down . . .

We all were humans. We make mistakes, and we learn from them. If Jasper had developed feelings for me, I knew he deserved a chance.

*   *   *

JASPER

Lucas thought he was really smart, sending someone like John to warn Kiara. What he didn't know was that I was always one step ahead of him. If Lucas was desperate to fuck my life, so be it. He was going to get what he asked for.

John was a big imposing man with a face that seemed like he had a permanent case of constipation. He had ash-blond hair and eyes as green as an apple.

John was about to open the driver's side door of the car when I stepped towards him. His gaze met with mine, and recognition registered in his face.

I watched him swallow hard. I could smell a person's fear from a mile away, and this one was beyond terrified.

"What did you tell her?" I asked him.

"I told her the truth about you," John replied.

I wound the cable cord in my hand that was hidden behind my back.

"What truth?" I could feel my jaw harden. I was trying very hard to keep my anger at bay.

"That you're putting up a façade so the girl can fall for your charms."

I chuckled, showing off my impressive set of white teeth. The lines of worry deepened on John's forehead.

"I told Lucas to stay the hell away from my business," I said. "He never learns, does he?"

"If you try to do something to that girl, Jasper, Lucas will inform the police. I hope you are clear on the fact that he isn't your friend anymore," John reminded me.

"Of course," I agreed.

Lucas screwed up our friendship the day he helped Kiara take off from his mansion. I grinned as I was hit by an old memory. John appeared to be more than a little intimidated or knew about me enough to understand how this situation could escalate. If he was smart, he would leave. If he was as blond as the mass of hair on his head, then he would stay and argue.

"Some things never change I guess," I continued, still smiling. "Things like people's ability to poke their noses where it doesn't belong. I like Lucas. Don't get me wrong. He used to be a lot more fun to hang around with until he started to preach about how I'm supposed to live my life, take my decisions, stuff like that. He thinks he's a saint—akin to the Dalai Lama, but we both know he's far from it."

John was confused. He wasn't sure what that meant. "What do you mean?"

"It means that I want him to start remembering about the favors he owes me. Maybe his memory is a bit rustic . . ." I said. "So . . . I'll remind him this once."

As if John had a bit of a premonition, he took a step back and then another, making his way towards his car when I threw a blow at John's face.

Even though John was a strong man with muscles, it was a piece of cake for me to tackle him to the side of the car. The feeling of having my fists join his jaw was ecstatic. Surprise registered on John's face which turned to fury and then terror.

I glanced at the surveillance cameras just to make sure we weren't in the line of sight, pulled on my leather gloves, and wound the cable cord around John's neck, giving it a swift little squeeze. I felt John's body thrash and wiggle under me.

The temptation was wild.

Ecstatic.

A little more hold on the squeeze would dim the light in his green apple eyes. How fun would it be to watch as the flicker of life faded to death?

I loosened the cord around his neck. "I change my mind. I think this is enough for a warning."

John collapsed to the floor, holding and rubbing both of his hands to his neck.

"So here's the story for the police, dear John. Are you with me?"

John coughed and nodded. The parking lot was surprisingly empty. I knew there was a popular local band playing tonight in the club, it was no wonder that no one was around to witness what went down.

"When the police ask you what happened, you are going to tell them that you came to the club and was mugged in the parking lot. The person was wearing a mask so you couldn't see his face." I reached for John's denim pocket and pulled out his wallet. "The thief took your wallet and . . ." I took the keys. " . . . your car keys."

John coughed some more.

"Is that story very clear or do you need me to repeat it for you?"

John shook his head.

"The man was going to kill you, but Mr. Lockhart somehow happened to stumble upon the situation and the thief took off. Repeat it for me, John."

John repeated it. One wrong word and John would have been awarded with another punch.

"Good," I said, quite pleased with myself.

I could smell bullshit from a mile away just as I could sense the clear insincerity in his eyes. I knew that as soon as I was out of sight, John would call the police and tell them everything. The wheels were already turning in his head as he planned how he was going to get out of this situation unscathed. His eyes widened when I reached for his wallet and pulled out a small picture from beneath the debit and credit cards.

I smiled, inspecting the picture. "Daughter? Cute as a button."

"Please," John pleaded.

I chuckled. "I don't hurt children. Did you really think I would stoop so low?" I shuffled through the rest of the wallet contents. "Let's see . . . ah, it is here."

I pulled out another picture. "Thought there had to be a wife tucked away somewhere or is she a girlfriend?"

At that moment John had his hands joined together. "Please, I'll do anything you ask me. Don't hurt them."

"She's pretty. Well, not as pretty as my Kiara, but she's nice." I got ahold of his jaw and forced him to make eye contact.

I continued, "You try to act smart with the police, and I'll make your life a living hell. I don't bluff. I can do whatever the fuck I want when it comes down to maintaining my reputation and protecting what's mine." I squeezed his cheeks with my fingers so his lips were puckered. "You better tuck that little tail between your legs and tell Lucas not to mess with me again."

"I will do as you say. This never happened. I didn't see anything," John repeated like a robot that hit reboot. "Please don't hurt my family."

John was terrified. If I didn't know any better, I'd say he was quaking. People usually had that effect when they saw the real me.

I nodded, satisfied. "You have my word. You do as I say and no one gets hurt."

I slid behind the wheel of John's car, taking his wallet with me. John lay down on the ground, his eyes looking sunken. According to the plan, he'd yell for help from the first person walking out of the club and narrate the story we had decided on.

"Oh, and John,"

He looked at me. I said, "Tell Lucas I said hi."

CHAPTER TWENTY-ONE

I had done this a dozen times before—not stealing a car, but manipulating people into following my rules. And with time, I had gotten better. Whatever I wanted in life, I got it, and if I didn't, I made sure to steal it using any means necessary.

I drove through town, thinking how stupid it was of Lucas to send someone to warn Kiara, and it had to be someone as dumb as that fucktard John, who was probably whining in the parking lot like a pussy, thinking I was going to kill his wife. I would if dear John didn't take my warnings seriously.

I had come so far to convince Kiara, and I wasn't going to let some idiot ruin it. If anything, John was going to make things right, and for that, I needed to hatch a plan.

I ditched John's Jaguar in a secluded area and walked to the nearest train station. During my train ride, I emptied John's wallet which consisted of his debit and credit cards. I threw them in a dumpster on the next station and pocketed the cash. Not because I wanted to steal money, but because if John decided to file a complaint against me, I had to make sure it looked like a case of parking lot nabbing.

If there was an investigation, the police would think the thug robbed John in the parking lot, took the money, and left town. I was walking out of the train station when I saw a homeless guy on the side of the street. He was dressed in old clothes and a beanie hat. A cardboard sign was placed aside that read, *"Struggling. Need help."*

I pulled out the money I had taken from John's wallet which was roughly two-hundred dollars. With a smile on my face, I handed it to the homeless man. "Here you go."

The man took the money, thanked me, and then counted the amount. Relief and suspicion crossed his face as he asked me, "Are ya really sure, sir?"

"Positive. The money is yours," I said.

Suddenly, he took both my hands in his and squeezed. "I can't thank ya enough. God bless ya, kind sir."

I just smiled back at him. Once he was out of sight, I pulled out a hand sanitizer, doused it on my palms, and rubbed them together.

I texted my chauffeur, Morgan, and sent him my location so he could drive here and take me back. Morgan was one of my best employees. He was a trustworthy man and mostly got every job done, no questions asked.

Thirty minutes later, my Aston Martin pulled up at the given location. On my way back home, I decided to order dinner. Normally, I hated junk food, but sometimes I craved for it. so we stopped at *Burger Palace* for a quick bite.

I walked into the restaurant and was welcomed by a girl with *Bugs Bunny* teeth which were in dire need of a set of braces. Her thin dark hair was pulled back in a ponytail, and there was barely any makeup on her face while her eyebrows didn't seem to have known a beautician in its lifetime.

I always thought women needed to properly keep themselves groomed. It's the least they could do. Kiara used to be shabby when I had first met her, but after spending a few weeks at the mansion, she learned how to keep herself presentable.

The girl behind the counter, whoever she was, if she didn't get any work on her face done, her eyebrows were going to ruin her life or any chances of getting laid.

168

"Good evening, sir. What can I get you?"

I plastered my sweetest, most charming smile. "I'd like two cheeseburgers, a large fries, coke, and a double chocolate chip milkshake," I ordered. "Please."

She punched in my order and told me the amount which I paid.

A few minutes later, she delivered the order. "Here you go," she said with a smile. Her teeth needed a dentist too.

I cringed and decided to tip her while politely pushing a business card towards her. The girl appeared confused at first. I saw the name on the tag. "Felicity, sweetness, do you want to die a virgin?"

Felicity flushed; probably embarrassed by the fact that I knew she was a virgin. Well, it didn't take a scientist to figure out that much.

"No," she said.

"Call this number. She will get you in shape, and I'm sure in a month's time, this wouldn't be the case."

I walked out of the restaurant with a very angry Felicity boring smoke holes into my back. I was glad I hadn't given her the card before getting my order ready. I didn't want the girl to spit at it. I liked women who knew how to take care of themselves, and it ticked me off to see women like Felicity who never put an effort, and had the audacity to whine about men not looking their way.

I slid into the car, passed one package of food to Morgan, and took a huge bite of my burger. Sometimes I needed a break from all that healthy gourmet bullshit.

"Take me home, Morgan."

If only every day of my life was as interesting as today.

*   *   *

On Saturday, I invited Kiara over for a dinner date. She had been a bit reluctant at first, but surprisingly, she agreed. It wasn't like she could help what she felt for me. I had seen how her eyes would never hold my gaze, and instead, stray towards my hands and the rest of my body. I could sense when a woman desired me.

I was parked outside Kiara's apartment building. She wore a knee-length, off-shoulder olive-green dress. Her creamy shoulders were exposed, and it infuriated me. I believed that a woman should only expose herself for a man she was supposed to be with, and not attract the attention of a dozen.

However, I needed to stay calm and concentrate on my goal. Lessons could be taught later.

"Good evening, Jasper," Kiara said as she slid into the passenger seat of the car. She quickly straightened out her dress.

Good girl.

I smiled and despite my brewing anger, I kissed her cheek. "Good evening, sweetheart. I'm glad you decided to give me a chance. I swear you won't regret this."

Kiara blushed and gave me the smile that had drawn me towards her. Sometimes, I didn't understand what was so special about her. If I needed a warm body in my bed, I knew that could be acquired easily. It didn't have to be Kiara. Women threw themselves at me all the time, but there was something different about *her.*

It was our history together—the way I had saved her from the bad guys, how I had sheltered her for a couple of weeks. That couldn't be undone with just a few mistakes. Everyone had flaws, and Kiara knew that everyone was flawed one way or the other, and she decided to look away from it. She was willing to give me a chance because she loved me for what I had given her. I had been alongside her when no one else had.

Kiara looked at me like I was God.

And that really satisfied me.

It blazed a passion within me knowing how she felt in my presence. I had the urge to possess her completely.

I drove to a nice quaint restaurant by the lake that was famous for delicious Lebanese food. I was never the type to try local restaurants, although this particular one was recommended by Kiara, and I wanted her to know that I kept track of her likes and dislikes.

The place was packed when we arrived, the faint aroma of Lebanese grilled chicken and Falafel permeated the air. I hated crowded places. It was not easy to read people's expressions, but over the years, I had learned the art of slipping on masks and say what was expected of me.

The waitress argued that it was a *'Reservations'* only, and Kiara appeared to be upset by the fact that we wouldn't have dinner here, so I quickly slipped some cash towards the waitress without having Kiara notice, and that did the trick. The best table was ours, and who said money couldn't buy happiness? Kiara seemed happy.

Kiara would occasionally glance towards me, and look away like she was analyzing me, trying to read my expressions. The food arrived a few minutes later, and true to Kiara's word, it smelled wonderful. The rich flavors of the Arabic *khubz* bread complimented the *hummus,* and it melted in my mouth. I felt like I was walking down the bustling streets of Beirut.

Kiara was less chatty today, and it seemed like she was constantly on alert mode whenever I tried to say something. She was asking me everything, leaving out one particular topic that interested her the most.

The waitress that I had tipped earlier passed me a flirtatious smile—one that said, *'Come fuck me whenever you're ready'.* She bent down on purpose so I could have a full view of her assets. A casual fuck would've been nice, but I was being a total gentleman tonight. No amount of tits, no matter how big the size, were going to distract me from my plan tonight.

This was the problem with being too attractive. Women couldn't keep their eyes off me. Men wanted to be me.

We ordered *Kunafa* for dessert, a pastry soaked in sugar syrup, layered with cheese, and sprinkled with pistachios. It tasted delicious, but it wasn't as good as the one I had when I traveled to the Middle East.

I had eventually gotten tired of Kiara trying to be evasive and decided to take matters into my own hands. It was funny how she jumped from one topic to the other. I laughed and her expression changed.

"What's funny?" she asked.

"I like how you're trying to change the subject every time I mention '*Us*'"

"Well, that's because I know there's not really any point in discussing it."

"Then why are you here with me?" I asked, scrapping the last bit of dessert from my plate.

Kiara threw me a questioning look. "Because you invited me over for dinner?"

"Let's be honest with each other, Kiara. You wouldn't be here on this dinner date with me if you weren't expecting something more."

Her cheeks caught fire. I liked watching her squirm and deny when I was right. "Last time you said that you couldn't give me what I wanted because we wanted different things from each other, correct?"

She nodded.

I took her hand in mine and interlocked our fingers, palm up. "What if I said that I changed my mind?"

She concentrated on our adjoined hands. "What do you mean?"

"It means that I love you," I confessed. "I've loved you ever since the day I met you in that alley. I was lonely Kiara, until you came along and brought so much happiness into my life."

I went on, "I want you to know that when I helped your mother to clear your father's debts, it was because I genuinely

172

wanted to help the situation. I don't know how to say this, precious . . ."

"What is it?"

"Your mother, Julie, she told me that I could keep you with me in the mansion if I paid for her a home and a secure life. She said you wouldn't mind since you liked me anyway."

Kiara closed her eyes and opened them. Her chocolate-brown eyes sparkled with unshed tears. I knew she was brewing with anger towards her mother, but it was for the best.

"I promised Julie that I would take care of you, and it had never been my intention to have anything serious between us until you left me alone, and I realized that I had fallen in love with you. I don't want to feel miserable again. Whatever your decision is going to be, I'll accept it. I just wanted you to know how much you mean to me."

I knew I had said the right words because her eyes were blazing with adoration, and I knew she was hopelessly in love with me. She started to say something when another voice interrupted her . . .

"Mr. Lockhart, it's so good to see you here," John said, forcing a smile. A well-dressed lady stood beside him.

"John, how are you doing now? What a pleasant surprise!" I decided to play along.

John continued to smile. "I'm doing great, and it's all thanks to you."

The acting was something that came to me naturally. "Kiara, let me introduce you to John. He works for Lucas, and John, this is Kiara."

"We've met," Kiara said, keeping a stone face.

"You have?" I decided to play dumb. "What a small world."

The lady accompanying John came forward and took my hand in hers. "Thank you so much for saving my husband that day, Mr. Lockhart." Her eyes were beginning to tear up, "John told me how you stopped the man in the parking lot from assaulting him and chased after him. I can't thank you enough."

I smiled back and waved my hand in dismissal. "It was nothing. When I witnessed what was going on, I thought that was the right thing to do. Anyone in my place would have done the same thing."

Like a true gentleman, I handed the woman my handkerchief. The irony of the situation was amusing. John stood watching from the sidelines, very much aware of the gentleman in disguise, the fake charade. I couldn't help but smirk.

John's wife introduced herself as Ally.

"I have to invite you over for dinner, whenever you're free that is," Ally said.

"Alyssa!" John warned her.

"I insist," Ally pressed.

Jasper nodded. "Of course, Ma'am. It would be a pleasure."

Ally turned to Kiara, and with utter sincerity, she said, "You're very lucky."

Kiara giggled. "Everyone seems to say that."

"You are the cutest couple I know," Ally said. "Have a good night ahead."

They made some more small talk, and I sneaked a glance at my wristwatch. I wanted them to fucking leave as soon as possible. I threw a look at John, and thankfully, he got the signal.

I paid the bill with my Platinum Am Ex card, and we made our way out of the restaurant in silence. I knew Kiara was both appalled and impressed by the encounter. A small smile tugged my lips. I played the cards right.

I tried to act casual through the entire ride back to her apartment. The streets were deserted, people were already in bed, unaware of the monsters that prowled the streets wearing human skins.

When Kiara hadn't uttered a single word through the ride, I wondered if impressing her was going to be tougher.

She looked gorgeous in that green dress and I had noticed how even married folks threw appreciative glances towards her. She was a trophy. There was no denying that. Her body was designed to be worshipped by a deserving man, someone like myself. And I knew I'd kill before I would let anyone have a taste of it.

The silence in the car was becoming unbearable. "A penny for your thoughts?" I asked.

"I'm just thinking about how amazing you are." Kiara's tone was genuine. "Amazing, selfless, and honest. You did it again. You saved someone else's life."

I made an attempt to appear embarrassed by her compliment. The key to not sounding like an asshole was to act modestly even if it killed you.

"No, I'm not. I'm far from amazing, Kiara." That was actually a fact. I wasn't amazing; you might as well replace those three words with narcissist, selfish, or a big fat liar.

I continued, "In fact, I think you're the amazing one."

She laughed. "Me? Amazing? How so?"

I always sensed the right time to make my move. Fortunately, I was already pulling over to the side of her building. I parked the car and cut the engine. The car was filled with silence.

I slid my arm around her waist and dragged her into my lap possessively. Kiara gasped as she straddled me in the car. Her short green dress rode up her creamy thighs.

I cupped her face, brushing the dark locks of hair away from her forehead. In an irresistible voice, I said, "I think you're an amazing and strong woman who has been fighting her own battles for a long time. Life put you through so many harsh situations, and yet you never wavered. I love that quality about you. You're an incredible woman, and I want to be the one to give you everything you deserve."

"Oh God, Jasper . . ." Her eyes were brimming with fresh tears. "No one has ever said something like that to me."

I closed the remaining distance between us and pecked her lips softly, and when I was sure Kiara wouldn't protest, I drew her bottom lip into my mouth, bit gently and suckled. I felt Kiara's arms going around my neck, her fingers moved to caress my hair. She moaned as my tongue worked deep inside her mouth. I wanted to bite hard on her lip, but knew that would catch her off guard or even scare her, so I controlled my urges.

My hand roamed at the hem of her dress. I dipped my fingers inside, and brushed the thin fabric of her panties which were now damp. I was sporting a raging hard on and all I wanted to do was haul her in the back seat, turn her around and plow into her until she screamed, but I was a patient man, and all my wild fantasies would have to wait. If she was getting back with me, it would be on her own terms.

I trailed hot kisses down her collarbone and whispered, '*I love you*' several times. Her seductive mouth came down on mine in a passionate kiss.

She whispered, "I love you, too, Jasper, so much. You have no idea. I have never loved another man as much as I love you."

"You're going to be the death of me, I've never wanted a woman so much," I admitted breathlessly. "You're so fucking sweet. The thought of you with someone else kills me."

My hand lingered near her inner thigh, and I knew she was craving my touch and obviously wanted more. To tease her a little, I drew my hand out of her dress, and I could clearly see the instant loss she felt on her face.

Kiara's eyes were laced with desire when she whispered, "Come upstairs to my apartment."

I grinned, unable to control myself. "Are you sure?"

She bit her lip, and nodded. "Yes. One hundred percent."

*   *   *

176

As soon as the door of the apartment shut behind us, Kiara's mouth was already on mine and moving urgently. Clothes were off within a few seconds, and before I knew it, we were having hot raw makeup sex where neither of us had time to talk to each other. We were a blur of hands, mouth, and teeth.

Back when she lived with me for a few weeks, Kiara hadn't been this responsive. I realized that things had changed because I'd told her that *I loved her.*

Those three simple words were the key. I only said those and her legs were open and eager. Soon, she was in bed, under me, and my thick cock slid inside her wetness. She gasped and moaned, and it was good to know I was having that effect on her. We moved together, matching our rhythm, and reached the peak for a climax soon after. My eyes rolled back as the first orgasm hit, and I came inside her hard and fast. Kiara's soft melodic voice was music to my ears.

Minutes later, we were spent and lying in bed, and she was snuggled in my arms. Two hours later, I woke up with a raging hard on, and I slid inside of her body once again. We took it to the shower in the morning.

I hadn't felt so sated in a long time.

There was one thing that was jarringly obvious after that night.

Kiara was a keeper.

CHAPTER TWENTY-TWO

One Month Later

At the crack of dawn, I felt Jasper kissing his way down my spine, soft adoring kisses that I never thought he was capable of giving.

I turned my back to see him staring at me with his piercing blue eyes. He smiled.

"Good morning, precious," he whispered, pecking my cheek as he slid his hand around my waist and pulled me against him under the covers.

The past two months had been pure bliss with Jasper pampering me with expensive gifts that I didn't need, taking me out for breakfast, lunches, and dinners and finally making love in bed. No matter how many times I told Jasper that I didn't want gifts, I still found diamond necklaces, clothing, and shoes from luxurious brands popping out after each of our dates, and now they were stacked in my sorry excuse for a wardrobe.

I was still living in Colin's apartment, and I knew I had to move out soon. Colin had noticed how Jasper visited me often, and asked me if everything was alright now. I knew he was concerned for me, but I assured him that everything was alright.

I was momentarily distracted from my thoughts when his long, skilled fingers strayed underneath the covers and moved towards my inner thighs.

I laughed and said, "Pervert."

Jasper appeared amused. "You don't want me to?"

I sighed. "Can't say I hate it."

He ran his fingers through my hair. "I love you, Kiara. I don't know why it took me so long to realize that."

I touched his cheek. "I love you, too."

Sometimes it felt like a dream because I never thought that the man I loved would love me back one day. It felt too good to be true, but it was a reality.

"So, do you also forgive me?" he asked, kissing my hand.

"Forgive you for what?"

"For treating you like shit before?"

I laughed. "I find your bluntness very attractive. Yes, Jasper Lockhart, you're forgiven."

"Do you want to hear a story, Kiara?" he asked.

"What story?"

He jumped out of bed, and made his way towards the attached bath. "Let's brush our teeth first and then we'll talk."

It was a good thing I kept a spare brush in my room. This was the first time that Jasper actually stayed until the morning.

We brushed our teeth side by side before we eventually ended up in the shower together and then back in bed. Jasper sat up straight, his back against the headboard. The sunlight streaming through the window made his dark hair seem chocolate brown, and I loved it. I loved every little detail about him—the teasing curve of his mouth, those expert set of hands, the broadness of his shoulders, and don't even get me started on the long fingers and those delicious abs.

Jasper was too handsome for words. When we walked together on the street, people would stop and turn. It was like a magnetic attraction. Even though he wasn't an actor, people still recognized him through social media. If they failed to recognize him, they'd still stop and ask if he worked in some movie, and I basked in proudly at their attention because this man was all mine.

He pulled me into his arms as I sat sideways in his lap, eager to listen to this story he was going to tell me.

"Listen carefully now. There was a housemaid appointed by a very influential man. He was no billionaire, but they were wealthy at that time. The man wasn't happy with his marriage and constantly quarreled with his wife. One evening, when the wife was out, enjoying her parties, the housemaid decided to ask the master what was wrong. The two talked for a long time and they knew that they had an instant connection."

Jasper paused as I drew circles on his chest. "What happened after that?"

"Things escalated between the two, and the man started having an affair with his housemaid. He repeatedly cheated on his wife, and one night, the wife caught them together. She tried to fire the housemaid but it was too late. The maid was pregnant with his son. When the son was born, he was sent to live in the servant quarters together with the other house servants. He started doing small jobs around the house at the age of four, and at times, underwent abuse at the hands of the cruel wife. She was a jealous woman because she couldn't have a child of her own."

I looked into his eyes and tried to see if it was a real story. Jasper caressed my face lovingly.

"The wife of the wealthy man couldn't have children, so the man decided to give his bastard his name while the maid was fired from the job and given a hefty settlement. The couple pretended to adopt the boy from an orphanage and even made fake documents. Life was suddenly better for the boy. He went to a good school, got the best grades, and his stepmother started to treat him a little better until a year later, the wife got miraculously pregnant. A son was born, and the cycle of abuse for the maid's son began. The boy had gashes over his back, bruises on various parts of his body, and a lot of times, he was starved."

Suddenly, Jasper's hands were shaking, and I could see that he wasn't with me. He had drifted off somewhere else, looking everywhere but me. He rubbed his hands together.

"Fractured . . .fractured bones."

I cupped his face in my palms and forced him to make eye contact. "What's wrong?"

"Karma came for them in the end," Jasper said. "And the boy grew up to build an empire. He was a child who never got the love and affection that every boy deserves and then he met this really beautiful girl who was selfless, strong, and didn't care about his money."

My heart began to beat faster. It was like I already knew where he was going with this.

"Are you that son, Jasper?"

181

Jasper's gaze was fixed somewhere far, but he kissed my forehead. "Yes."

My hand flew to my mouth. "I'm so sorry, baby. No child deserves to be treated like that."

"It's in the past," he said in a monotone.

"Your biological mother, where is she?"

He smiled. "You didn't guess?"

"Margret?"

Jasper nodded. "I contacted her again after the reins were passed down to me. She's a stubborn woman and told me she would continue to work as a housekeeper because she thought it wasn't her place to be taking one of the master bedrooms. I just hired her instead, and she's just like any of my other staff except she is my birth mother."

"It must be so hard for you," I said and pulled him in a tight embrace, raining kisses over his forehead, his cheeks, and his mouth.

"It actually is very hard for me to talk about this. I told you about my past because I wanted you to know why I am the way I am. I can be very possessive about things, about you, and I love having sex."

I giggled. "Not complaining about the last part."

Jasper grinned. "I want to be inside of you right now, Kiara, only deeper this time." His lips slammed into mine, and I moaned loudly into his mouth. The need to possess me was very apparent with the way his lips assaulted mine. He was sexy, and his mouth was dirty, not that I had any problem with that.

Jasper always did well on his promises. A while later we were both breathless, covered in perspiration, and our bodies were satisfied. I hadn't felt this happy in my life before.

Reluctantly, I pulled myself out of the bed and began picking up my discarded undergarments.

"Where are you going?" Jasper asked.

"I have to go to work," I said.

"I told you I'd provide for you," he reminded me.

"And I told you I didn't need you to," I said politely, trying my best not to sound rude or hurt his feelings.

"Well, I'll find a way to stop you." Jasper sniggered.

"What are you going to do? Tie me up in your bed?" I stuck my tongue out to him. I was being totally childish, but I liked teasing him.

"You're forgetting something," he called out to me, still grinning like an idiot.

I snapped the bra into place and turned to face him. "What is it?"

"I'll show it to you if you climb in bed for a minute," he said, running his hand through his hair.

I sighed and climbed back in bed, only wearing a bra and panties. "What are you hiding? If it's my phone, you can go through all the chats. You won't find anything."

"Oh, honey. I already did that. Don't you worry," Jasper retorted, and I couldn't be sure if he was joking or being serious.

Suddenly, the jokes and all the other retorts that were bubbling on my tongue disappeared when I saw what he was holding.

A blue velvet box.

I stared at him in surprise. "You can't be serious," I choked.

Still sporting that charming smile, he said. "Open it."

Jasper placed the velvet box into my shaky hands, and I took a few deep breaths. Was this really happening? Or would I wake up tomorrow and find myself rolling on the floor with this beautiful dream?

"Come on, Kiara, open the damn box," Jasper encouraged.

Still shaking, I opened it.

Inside the box . . .

There was nothing.

Jasper doubled over with laughter like a child whose prank had been successful.

I threw a pillow at him. "I hate you."

I started climbing out of the bed when his arm slid around my waist and he pulled me against his chest.

"Were you looking for this?" he whispered, holding up a breathtakingly gorgeous diamond solitaire ring between his fingers.

Completely unable to form speech, I continued to stare at him and the ring in shock.

Reading my expression, he said. "Kiara, I know I'm not the perfect man out there." I watched as he slid down from the bed and lowered himself to one knee. "But I know that if there's anyone who can keep you happy, it's me. I want your smiles, your tears, and your love all to myself. I promise to cherish you and provide you with everything. Most of all, I want to spend the rest of my life with you."

He paused to take a deep breath.

"Kiara Gracie Reeves, will you marry me?"

*   *   *

I never thought that when I get married, it would be so sudden. We never even got time to arrange a proper wedding. Jasper insisted that we have a private ceremony on the family-owned Lockhart Island beach. The altar was decorated with colorful flowers. It was simple yet lovely.

Jasper had done a lot of work in the past week, from wedding planners to getting a custom-made wedding dress from one of the best designers in the country.

Not many people made it to the guest list. All of Jasper's friends with their wives were present excluding Lucas, and that made me a little sad. Lucas was a good man, and he had helped me when I needed it the most. Colin and Chloe were invited too, along with Kathy, my best friend from the previous diner I worked at. She was my maid of honor. When Jasper suggested inviting my mother to the wedding, I had been reluctant but after much thought, I cooled down and decided to toss the weapons aside.

She was my mother after all. She had done what she thought was the best alternative. Mom was seated at the front row of the aisle, teary-eyed while wearing a beautiful peach gown, smiling proudly at me. She looked so much better, younger even. Those bags under her eyes were gone, and I had Jasper to thank for that too. Mom looked happy and healthy. He had done for her more than what I could have been able to.

I couldn't even recognize myself in the white dress; I looked like a completely different person, and the thought that I was finally having happiness in my life brought tears to my eyes. I didn't have a brother, so I asked Colin to walk me down the aisle, and he gladly obliged.

Standing at the end of the aisle was Jasper. He looked everything like I imagined he would. A lot of times, I had fantasized getting married to him, not realizing that it would actually happen in the future. It was so much better in reality. Jasper looked drop-dead gorgeous in his black tux, clean-shaven, and his usual unruly hair was tamed to perfection with a few wispy waves curled over his forehead. He had the familiar teasing glint in his alluring blue eyes.

The vows were taken and rings were exchanged. Jasper kissed me full on the lips, and looked lovingly at me when he pulled back. I wondered how I had gotten so lucky.

The ceremony ended, followed by a short celebration after which Jasper and I slow danced to Elvis Presley's, *"Can't help falling in love"*. Jasper's moves were measured and sensuous, and I wasn't that bad either. It was so romantic how he sang along, keeping his eyes on me. He was my own prince charming.

We didn't stay much longer during the reception as Jasper carried me bridal style to the car. He said he had to get back to work by Monday, and that didn't leave us much time together as a married couple. The car took us directly to the airport where I experienced my first time in a private jet. It was named *'Lockhart'*

By the time the plane landed within an hour, I was completely overwhelmed. During the ride back to the mansion, my husband kissed me on my cheek and whispered, "You look like a gift tonight that's waiting to be unwrapped. I can't wait until we get home."

I laughed. "You're so cheesy."

CHAPTER TWENTY-THREE

"Welcome back home, Mrs. Lockhart," Jasper said as he ushered me inside the mansion. Suddenly, I was hit by a wave of nostalgia.

Who knew I'd be walking inside the house weeks later as Mrs. Jasper Lockhart?

Butlers and maids were all standing by the door to welcome us, but there was no sign of Margret. Why hadn't she attended her own son's wedding? I had a hard time wrapping my mind around it. She was his mother after all.

"Where is Margret?" I questioned as I ascended the stairs.

"She decided to move into our Villa in Santa Clara. I'm sure she would have loved to welcome you darling, but that home needs some renovating, and she's supervising." Jasper said, placing a quick kiss on my lips. In one swift motion, he scooped me up into his arms and continued up the stairs.

Panic and excitement surged through me in equal measures. I had never been in Jasper's room before. For the entire duration of the one month that we had been dating, we had mostly crashed at my studio apartment and sometimes at a hotel. He turned the knob and stepped into the room with me still in his arms.

Once inside the room, Jasper placed me on the bed that was covered in rose petals. A bottle of champagne was beside the nightstand, along with what I assumed was a box of expensive Belgian chocolates.

I scanned the room. It was going to be our bedroom from now onward. The thought made me giddy. This beautiful mansion was my home now.

The room was enormous. Its walls were designed in gray wallpapers. The dark drapes were in contrast with the walls. The large French window overlooked the spectacular view of the woods and the lake at a distance. The bed that I was seated on was massive and matched with the dresser and the wardrobe.

I loved the décor, it was modern and so masculine. It defined Jasper—dark, dominating, and attractive.

Jasper closed the door behind him and turned the lock. My heart began to pump against my chest with anticipation. It wasn't like it was my first time with him, but there was a completely different aura in the room. I watched as he removed his blazer jacket and let it fall on the ground, loosened his tie, settled down on the leather chair opposite the bed, and lowered the light.

Instead of attacking me as usual husbands do on the first night of marriage, he settled down in the chair, crossed his legs and smiled at me. His eyes were still unreadable.

"Strip for me, baby."

"Strip?"

There was something blazing in his eyes; something that resembled the predatory look when we were in the piano room last time.

"Yeah, give me a striptease," he said. "You didn't seem quite reluctant to take off your clothes that day in the strip club in front of all those men. Why the hesitation now? I'm your husband, and isn't it your duty as my wife to give me what I want?"

"I thought you wanted to be the one to undress me."

He shook his head. "I'll watch."

It wasn't the first time that Jasper made a bizarre request. However, I recalled the requests used to be more polite. Now, it was downright commanding.

The dress wasn't too complicated for me to undo which was a good thing. I let it slide to the carpeted floor and proceeded to take off the corset. My shaky hands reached for the clasp of my lacy beige bra which added to the growing pile.

I knew my cheeks closely resembled a tomato. It wasn't like Jasper was seeing me naked for the first time, but it was kind of embarrassing when he was staring at me like I was a very unique painting at an art gallery.

"Jasper . . ."

"Come here," he ordered softly, raising his hand towards me in invitation.

And as soon as I walked to his chair, all my worries dissolved. His lips swallowed me in a long kiss and then they were everywhere.

Maybe he was a little crazier than the average man. Maybe he did make me feel a bit uncomfortable a second ago, but right now, I felt like a man of his caliber knew how to please a woman too well which made me wonder how many of them he had been with before me . . .

The thought of my husband with several other women disturbed me.

*   *   *

JASPER

I had been waiting for this day and it called for a celebration. Throughout the entire wedding, I had been watching Kiara parade around in that sexy white dress, and all I wanted to do was take her back home. I watched how her creamy breasts were spilling out of that lacy bra, the way those frilly panties were holding that little pussy in place.

Not that this was the first time I was seeing her naked, but every time, there was a certain hunger for the next.

I was totally and completely insatiable for her. Without further ado, I unhooked her bra and let it fall to the pile of discarded clothes. I cupped her right breast and squeezed it gently. Maybe it was a little too aggressive because I watched her wince. I took her left breast in my mouth and teased the tip of her nipple gently, making it pebble hard which caused a reaction from her as she moaned and arched her back to give me more access.

At some point, we were on my bed, minus all the clothing. She unbuttoned my shirt hastily, and flung it towards the floor to add to the pile. My body hovered over hers as she ran her hands through my toned abs down to the waistline of my trousers. She unzipped it and her reaction was no surprise. She had a hungry look in her eyes, much like mine. They all

190

lusted over what was packed in my pants. Once they got the taste of it, nothing was better. I had ex-girlfriends begging me to come back just for my impressive cock. It needed a good stroking, much like my ego.

Kiara took me in her hands and my brain exploded.

It felt so fucking good.

She had taken one look at the scars from my childhood and didn't even make a fuss. I peeled off her soaked panties, flung it to the ground, and nudged her creamy legs apart. I touched her core that now glistened with arousal. I rubbed her nub and she came undone within seconds, begging or praying, or both.

"Jasper, please." she whimpered.

I guided my cock to her center, unable to control much longer. I was married to Kiara now which proved she was mine—body, mind, and soul. I'd fuck her whenever the hell I wanted, and she wouldn't be able to complain. That sweet little pussy was mine to devour.

"Hope you're ready for this Kiara because I take no prisoners tonight. I'm going to fuck you really hard tonight, and you're not going to complain."

Her eyes widened, and I didn't give her time to respond as I drove my entire length into her with such power that she was pushed back. The intensity was so strong and the need so primal that I didn't care about anything else. I pulled out and slammed back into her, groaning so loud I hoped the servants weren't going to wake up. I heard her soft whimper, but I didn't know if it was due to pleasure or pain, and frankly, I. Did. Not. Care.

Not enough. I caught her buttocks in my palms, drove into her harder, and continued until I felt my seed seep inside of her. I panted, opened my eyes, and saw her expression was masked between confusion, hurt, and pleasure.

I rolled off from her body. "Good night, precious. I'll wake you up in two hours again. Get your rest."

It was a good thing I was sometimes bad at reading reactions. I needed my animalistic needs met and I got what I wanted. It was as simple as that.

*   *   *

KIARA

I woke up the next morning feeling sore but oddly satisfied. Jasper was nowhere in sight, so I assumed he was getting ready for work. He was a workaholic, and there was nothing anyone could do about it.

Yesterday night had been an orgasm fest, and we had been on it for several hours until we eventually fell asleep. I knew Jasper had an appetite for sex, and yesterday, he hardly let me sleep. He was a little rough, but it wasn't the first time that he wasn't a gentleman in bed. He had always been a bit demanding when it came to satisfying himself.

I stared at the beautifully designed ceiling, thinking how luck was oddly in my favor to land a billionaire husband.

I raised my hand to the sunlight pouring from the window, the solitaire glimmered, and I smiled. I wasn't a gold digger, but after living a difficult life, it was kind of nice to think that things were finally getting better.

Before I could climb out of bed, there was a knock at the door.

I sat upright and covered my front with the bed sheet. "Who is it?"

Jasper poked his head in, "It's me, love. Good morning." He laughed as he walked into the room, holding a tray of food in his hand.

"I brought breakfast in bed for my beautiful wife."

Wife.

The word made my heart flutter.

He settled down on the edge of the bed and placed a silver tray over a pillow. The food looked delectable with fresh toast, sausages, sunny side omelets, and croissants. It was Instagram-worthy. He picked one toast and brought it to my lips. I took a bite.

"I . . . I haven't brushed my teeth yet," I said between small chews.

Jasper smiled. "It's alright."

He looked gorgeous dressed in denim and a simple off-white t-shirt. The ray of sunlight streaming from the window made his olive skin glisten. I touched his cheek, and he kissed my palm in turn. "I have a surprise for you."

I giggled. "I don't like how you spend so much money."

"I can afford it, Kiara. Now, lift the plate up."

I did as I was told, and to my astonishment, there was a pink envelope on the tray.

"Open the envelope" he said calmly, his expression betraying no emotions.

I opened the envelope slowly to find a hotel booking in Cape Town, South Africa.

Relief crossed my features. "Is this . . . ?"

"For our honeymoon," he completed.

I launched into his arms, and once again, I felt the wetness pool in my eyes. "Thank you so much, Jasper. This means a lot to me. Not just the honeymoon trip, but the fact that you are trying to change so much for me."

"Of course. You're my wife now; you deserve all this and so much more." Jasper smiled.

"But what about your work?" I inquired.

"Actually, I have some business in Cape Town, but it would be rude to leave my gorgeous wife in this house all by herself, right? So, I thought, "Why not take you along?". That way I can get my work done and we can spend time together. I'm sure you'll like the place, but if you have some other destination in mind, we could schedule it too."

"You would do that for me?" I asked, wide-eyed.

"Of course, precious, I would."

I closed my eyes and shook my head, "Punch me. Tell me this is not just a beautiful dream."

Jasper chuckled. "If I punch you, we'd have to cancel the trip, and a bride with a purple eye doesn't sound attractive."

I laughed as I elbowed him playfully. He pushed the tray of breakfast towards me. "Come on, eat your breakfast and get ready."

"Where are we going?" I asked.

"It's a lovely day. I thought we could chill at the beach."

"Okay," I said excitedly.

*   *   *

I was still having a hard time getting used to all of it. Maids and butlers were always ready at my beck and call. I didn't have to cook my own food, and didn't have to worry about paying bills. It's been a few days since our marriage, and so far, I was content.

Today, Jasper was taking me out shopping because he thought I needed new clothes for our honeymoon trip. I showered and dressed within twenty minutes and made my way downstairs. Morgan told me that Jasper was waiting for me inside the car.

When I stepped inside, Jasper passed me a hard glare.

"I think I told you to be ready in fifteen minutes." Jasper scowled at me.

There was nothing scary about his tone, but I didn't like the look in his eyes. It was almost like the old Jasper was back, the one who was rude at times and disregarded my emotions.

"I'm sorry. I didn't expect to find a whole closet full of clothes. I was just confused on what to wear," I explained and then further added, "And I really have no idea that you were waiting in the car with a stopwatch."

His expression softened as he pulled me into his lap and ran his hand through my hair. "It's alright. You look stunning by the way."

"Thanks."

Jasper took me to a street filled with shops with only designer clothing. It seemed like the salesperson knew who Jasper was, and would always politely usher me to the displayed clothes to help me choose.

When I checked the price tag, I was shocked. My annual income at the restaurant didn't even come close to the price. Jasper shrugged it off like it was only natural.

We made our way to a café after the shopping. Jasper's fingers interlocked with mine.

"Jasper . . . it's too expensive, and I really don't need so many outfits. My closet is already . . ."

"Kiara," Jasper said in warning. "Your husband is a billionaire. Trust me, I can afford this. Where you shopped before, what you ate, where you lived, it's in the past, and shouldn't concern you now. With me, you're a queen, and queens don't settle with satisfactory but only the best, so get used to this lifestyle," he said it with such authority that it frightened me a little to argue any further.

"I'll order for the coffee," he said, and stormed away towards the barista without even asking me what coffee I preferred.

I settled down in a chair, and pulled a book out of my bag to read. I had just finished reading one chapter when I heard someone say, "Well, if it isn't Kiara Reeves."

I looked up from the book to find myself staring at a familiar face. Mason Wright, my ex-boyfriend. He looked the same as before—tall, copper hair, and grey eyes. He always reminded me of a character from a video game.

Mason grinned, and before I knew it, he wrapped me in a hug. He pulled back, and there was a wide smile on his face as he gave me a brief once-over and whistled.

"You seem to be doing really well."

I laughed in response. "Well, you don't look bad yourself," I replied, poking a finger in his chest.

Mason and I had a bad breakup because I found out that he was secretly getting back together with his ex-girlfriend. Fortunately, we didn't have a shouting match or name-calling battle. It was just like two friends who had grown apart and that was one reason why this reunion was less awkward.

"How's Elaine?" I asked.

His smile was bright, and that was the answer I needed. "We probably would get married next year."

I smiled. "I'm really glad it's working for you, Mason."

There was an awkward pause. "Look, Kiara, I'm really sorry for what I did to you."

I shook my head. "You're happy, and that's all that matters."

He nodded in understanding. "So, what are you doing here?"

"I'm actually here with my husband," I told him.

"You're married!" Mason grinned. "That's great news, so who is this lucky guy?"

Before I could point towards Jasper, he was already by my side, his arm snaked around my waist possessively.

"Who is your friend, Kiara?"

Mason pulled his hand out towards Jasper for a handshake. "Mason Wright. An old friend of Kiara's."

That lopsided grin suggested otherwise, and it was a dead giveaway for what he wanted to imply.

Jasper would have to be stupid not to notice, but that was the problem. My husband wasn't stupid. In fact, he was smarter than the average man, and Mason liked being sarcastic. I used to love that about him but looking at Jasper's changing expressions, I was starting to hate it.

Jasper shook hands with Mason. "Jasper Lockhart."

Mason was studying Jasper now, and this whole situation was making me uncomfortable. "Why don't you join us for coffee, Mason?"

"Oh no, I have an errand to run. Gonna be late, but maybe some other time. Appreciate the offer, though."

"It was nice to see you again, Kiara," he said, and his gaze locked on my diamond ring. I knew what he was thinking, that I was a gold digger—a woman who married a rich man so that she could mooch off him and finally live a better life without working for it, but that was far from the truth, and I didn't think Mason deserved an explanation.

"You too," I said politely.

As soon as Mason was gone, Jasper thrust the cup of coffee in my hand. "Let's go home, baby."

Jasper didn't seem like he was in a bad mood, but I was still getting some strange vibes.

When we reached home, I was headed for the kitchen to see what they were planning to make for dinner, but Jasper called out to me.

"I want to see you in our room. Right now," he said and stormed upstairs.

I knew from personal experience that if Jasper needed to summon me, it had to be an important matter. I climbed up the stairs, and made a beeline for our bedroom.

As I opened the door, I noticed Jasper was making himself a drink.

When the door closed behind me, I was fired with a question. "Who was that man?" Jasper asked, taking a swig of his drink.

I didn't think lying was a good start if I wanted a good married life. "Mason was my ex-boyfriend."

Jasper turned his icy-blue eyes at me and stared. "So, what was it like?"

I blinked. "What was what like?"

Jasper had an expression that I didn't recognize. "Sex with Mason. Was it better than what you have with me?"

My face caught fire. "You've got to be kidding me!"

"Answer me, Kiara." His voice was deadpan. "I want to listen to what you have to say." He leaned against the island bar, regarding me over the rim of a glass of scotch.

I clenched my fists in anger. "You're being very disrespectful."

Jasper snorted. "It would be disrespectful, honey, if I asked you if his cock was bigger, and if you enjoyed taking him as much as you do me, but I didn't ask you that. I just want to know how the sex was."

"Go to hell!" I snarled.

In one quick stride, he was hovering above me, his fingers digging into my jaw. Hard. "When I ask a question, you give me an answer."

With my cheeks still in a death grip, I whimpered. Tears trickled down my face. "It wasn't great. It was average."

"And how is it with me compared to that?"

"Lovely," I said. "I can't get enough of it."

Which wasn't a lie.

Jasper grinned with that response. "Good, and baby, please don't talk back to me again. I really don't like to be angry at you. Okay?"

"Yeah," I said.

"You're supposed to say *"okay"*, when I say *"okay"*, okay? You know, like *Fault in our Stars* and all," he joked.

"Okay."

"I have some work pending in the office, but when I get back, I want to see you in our bed wearing the sexiest fucking lingerie that you can find and your sweet little cunt wet and ready for me because I'm not gonna waste my time in foreplay. Got it?"

And then Jasper stormed out of the room, shutting the door behind him. I heard the lock turn, so he was making sure I wasn't leaving the room.

I slid down onto the carpeted floor, the feeling of shame washing over me.

For the first time in a week, I wondered if I had married the same person.

CHAPTER TWENTY-FOUR

The next morning Jasper acted like the previous night never happened, like he hadn't embarrassed me with questions about my past relationships. He was acting like he hadn't walked in drunk as a sailor way past midnight, woken me up from my sleep, and thrust inside of me until he was satisfied—making me feel utterly hopeless and used.

I thought marriages were more than that. I thought marriages were about sharing and caring for the other, but the definition of marriage for Jasper seemed completely different. It was like he owned me.

Body, soul, and it was legally on paper.

"Kathy had called this morning," I informed Jasper when we were having breakfast at the kitchen table.

He glanced up from his iPad. "Yes?"

I thought I was going to lose my appetite if he refused.

I casually took a bite of my eggs and avocado toast with blueberries, and continued, "She wanted to know if I could catch up with her today. For lunch and some shopping. So, I was wondering if I can . . ."

Jasper stared at me for a minute, his blue eyes glinting in the sunlight. "It's going to be just you and Kathy?"

"Yes."

Jasper smiled sweetly. "Of course, precious, you can. She is your friend."

"Thank you, Jasper."

Funny, how he calls me *precious* all the time and then calls me a *dirty little whore* in the bedroom.

Jasper handed me the keys to a *Porsche* convertible and his debit card and then kissed my forehead.

"Have fun, Kiara. After yesterday, I guess it's the least I could do."

At 12 PM, I picked up Kathy from her apartment which took me about thirty minutes to reach. She whistled when she settled into the passenger seat of the car.

"Perks of marrying a rich man." She laughed, and I laughed with her.

We decided to go to a movie, a romantic comedy. We were laughing throughout the movie, and Kathy ate most of my popcorn, but I didn't protest. I enjoyed the girl time, and I really wanted to forget about what happened yesterday. I also hoped to never get on Jasper's bad side. If I managed to keep him happy, there weren't going to be any problems. He even let me take one of his cars and allowed me to take his debit card which was proof that I meant a great deal to him.

Kathy and I were doing some window shopping for clothing when she pointed at my jawline. "Kiara, what's this mark?"

Crap! I forgot to hide the red fingerprint mark that he had given me when he pressed too hard. "Um, it's some kind of allergy I guess," I lied.

Kathy passed me her *'I-don't-believe-you'* look. "Are you sure?"

"Yes." I gave her a tight smile.

Quickly, I managed to steer the conversation into a safer territory. I asked her about her life and her new job, and that did the trick. Kathy liked talking about herself, although she was a great friend, I wasn't comfortable talking to her about my marital issues. She suggested a restaurant nearby that served great seafood. I wasn't a huge seafood fan, but Kathy seemed really excited about it, so I thought why the hell not give it a try.

The restaurant had a nice ambiance with some chic décor and cute lights suspended from the ceiling. Kathy was a sneaky woman and had already made a reservation, so the waitress led us to a secluded table in the corner.

When we approached the booth, I was surprised to find two more men already waiting for us in the booth. One was a lean blond man with long shoulder length hair and serious eyes, while the other one was chubby with dark hair and striking topaz eyes.

I threw a look at Kathy, but she seemed oblivious to my gesture. Lunch with strangers was not on my to-do list.

"Kiara, I want you to meet my friend, Ethan." She pointed at the lean blond guy. The way she was smiling told me he was more than just a "friend". She was eccentric and bizarre. I wouldn't be surprised if she was doing some friends-with-benefits kind of thing.

She continued further with the introduction, "And this is Ethan's friend, Michael. They are going to join us today for lunch. It was a last-minute kind of plan. I hope you don't mind."

I shrugged. "I guess I don't."

It wouldn't hurt, plus, it was just lunch. I wasn't doing anything wrong.

This seemed more like a double date than a girl's lunch. I was so mad at Kathy for dragging me into this. If she had planned on bringing other men, she should have at least informed me first. I didn't think Jasper would like this.

Michael was pushed right beside me, so far, we were making small talk. I tried to avoid talking about myself and gathered more information about him. Michael was almost the same age as me, and he worked at a nearby store as a manager. He went as far as to tell me how Ethan and he were such good friends and blabbered about their stories from high school.

The waitress approached our table and took our orders. We decided on mixed seafood pizza, mozzarella sticks, and salad. She served our drinks while we waited for the food.

"So, what do you do for a living, Kiara?" Michael inquired. He had slipped right beside me in the booth, while Ethan kept Kathy busy. She was on a giggling spree, and that proved that the two definitely had something going on.

Before I could answer his question, Kathy chimed in, "Michael, a woman doesn't need to make a living if her husband is the owner of supermarket and hotel chains. Unless, of course, she thinks going back to the waitressing job is better." She laughed at her own joke.

Michael's brows arched up as he took a sip from his drink. "Really? Your husband is a wealthy man?"

"I don't like to brag."

"What's your name again?"

"Kiara Lockhart," I replied.

"Your husband is Jasper Lockhart?"

His name sent a bolt of fear through my body. "Yes."

Michael appeared surprised. He chuckled. "Well, at first glance, I did think you were wealthy, but to think that you're the owner of Lockhart Legacy Hotel, Lockhart Resort & Spa and Crystal Plaza malls . . . wow."

"He owns everything. I'm just his wife."

He laughed. "You seem down to earth than most rich wives."

"Thanks," I said awkwardly, circling the ring on my left hand.

Michael smiled. "I must say you're an interesting person, and I'm not saying that just to flatter you."

I thought my face was reddening, not because I was attracted to him, but because I was not used to anyone flirting with me so openly.

All of a sudden, he grazed my cheek with his finger and leaned in. "I hear rich husbands like to take short work tours, and they are mostly unable to give much time to their wives. Does that happen with you too?"

I inspected his face to see if I could depict some kind of hidden invitation to his question but came up empty. I was saved from answering that question when the waitress arrived with our food. True to Kathy's word, the food was delicious. I made a mental note to bring Jasper here next time.

Before the pizza slices could disappear, I reached for another slice and took a bite. From the corner of my eye, I noticed Michael's gaze fixed on me, and it made me feel uncomfortable.

Michael's gaze then shifted towards my ring finger. "So, how did you guys meet?"

This was my cue to stare blankly at him. I tried to come up with an excuse to avoid explaining to him. What was I supposed to say to him anyway? That I was almost raped in an alley when Jasper saved me? Or should I mention that my mother insisted on getting our debts cleared in exchange for a luxurious life?

"It was . . . it was love at first sight. I used to be a waitress before. Jasper met me at the restaurant, and we fell in love," I said as if I had rehearsed those lines before.

I climbed to my feet before he could think of any more questions. "Excuse me. I'll be back in a minute."

I made a beeline for the ladies's restroom. When I walked out of the cubicle, I stared at myself in the mirror and barely recognized myself. Below all those layers of designer clothing and expensive jewelry was a suppressed woman. I was still the same old Kiara Reeves, only restructured and molded into a different lifestyle.

When I was about to exit the restroom, my phone buzzed in my handbag. The iPhone was a gift from Jasper. I wasn't really surprised to see his name flash on the screen.

I answered the phone.

"Hey precious, miss me already?" Jasper spoke from the other end.

I laughed. "Always."

He seemed pleased to hear that. "How's your lunch going with Kathy?"

"It's going fine," I said, trying very hard to appear calm.

A pause later he asked, "Is it just you and Kathy?"

"Yeah," I lied.

"Enjoy your time. Tell Kathy I said hi," he said, "I'll see you in a few hours. I love you."

"Love you too."

As soon as I hung up, I huffed a breath of relief. It seemed like a normal phone call, but for all I knew, Jasper could be checking up on me, and I believed that I hadn't given him any reason to think that I was doing anything suspicious.

And I really wasn't. I could have told him the truth and said that Kathy had already invited two other men, but that would have caused some unnecessary questions and more drama.

I splashed some water over my face, reapplied some makeup, and walked out of the restroom to find Michael at the bar.

He smiled when he saw me approach. "Can I order you a drink?"

I sneaked a glance at Kathy, and it seemed like it was getting steamier in that booth. No wonder Michael was out here hanging out alone, all by himself. He openly tried to flirt with me with his corny one-liners even though he knew I was married. Before I could protest further, he ordered a *Bloody Mary*.

Then, I thought, *what the hell*. It's been a while since I last visited a bar. One drink wouldn't kill me.

Michael inched closer, and I felt a little uncomfortable. "So, you didn't tell me."

"Tell you what?"

He passed me the kind of cocky smile I didn't like. "Let me be very straightforward. A lot of times, wives of wealthy business tycoons get lonely and tired of the same shit.

You know, charity functions, social gatherings, looking after the children, etc., and then they start looking for entertainment outside of their marriage. They need someone who can hold them in bed at night, cuddle with them, and show them a good time. I can be that someone. Nobody would know."

I frowned. Was he being serious?

For emphasis, he placed his hand on mine. I pulled it back abruptly.

"I'm not that kind of a woman," I said.

"You're not really happy with your marriage, are you?"

His question caught me off guard, and I glared at him. "Why wouldn't I be happy? I love my husband, and he provides me with everything that I want. You seem to misunderstand. Now, if you'll excuse me."

I didn't even take a sip of the drink that he had ordered and made my way out of the bar. I would text Kathy later that I was never going to hang out with her again if she was going to bring men that I didn't know, and she could take a ride home with one of those idiots for all I cared.

I rummaged my *Louis Vuitton* handbag for the car keys while walking and bumped into someone. "Ohhh . . . I'm so sorry . . . I didn't . . ."

My ability of speech was lost when I saw who was standing before me. He was all dressed up in a navy suit, and not a hair out of place. It looked like he walked right out of a set in Hollywood. Although his body seemed poised, his stare gave me the chills. I was scared, and by the looks of it, I knew this could go to shit right this moment.

"Jasper . . . I . . ."

"Who was that man?"

"Kathy's friend."

He ran a hand through his hair. Morgan summoned himself out of nowhere. Jasper and he exchanged some signal, and Morgan nodded.

Before he could say anything, I said. "I'm sorry, Jasper."

"Sorry about what, Kiara?"

"About lying to you," I said. "I just thought it wasn't a big deal."

He raised his hand towards me, and I flinched, expecting a blow this time, but he pulled me close and placed a quick kiss on my lips. "It's alright, sweetheart. I know you were scared."

I stared at him incredulously. What just happened?

Jasper outstretched his palm towards me and asked me for the car keys which I handed him. He drove the Porsche home while I was seated in the passenger seat. The clouds were turning gray, indicating a downpour. The wipers slashed at the windshield, wiping off the water droplets.

I turned on the radio only to hear a weather forecast and something about a truck skidding off the road. Jasper was silent most of the way and that made me anxious.

When we reached home, he made a beeline for his office, leaving me confused. That evening, I didn't see Jasper at all. In fact, I was seated alone at the dining table downstairs, eating creamy burrito casserole and Greek salad. I knew he was upset, but he was acting like it didn't affect him.

I prepared a plate with food, and decided to visit him upstairs. I knocked on the door, and Jasper asked me to come inside. I placed the tray of food on the coffee table. He was seated behind the mahogany desk, looking out towards the dark woods.

"You didn't come downstairs for dinner, so I brought you food here."

"You're a good wife, Kiara."

Out of all of the things, that was something I least expected to hear. "Uh . . . thanks."

He smiled. "It's nice to know that your wife would never cheat on you even if you're traveling or can't give her much time. I'm really pleased about your loyalty towards me, but I hate liars as much as I hate politicians."

My blood turned to ice. As if to answer my unvoiced question, he picked up the Porsche keys, and pressed a button on the keychain. The room filled with the familiar conversation.

"You're not really happy with your marriage, are you?"

"Why wouldn't I be happy? I love my husband, and he provides me with everything that I want. You seem to misunderstand. Now, if you'll excuse me."

Jasper pressed rewind and played some of our previous conversations. I was boiling with rage.

"You were spying on me. Why did you bug the car keys with an audio surveillance?"

Jasper chuckled. "Actually, I didn't. The key was bugged way before you took it. I had installed the audio surveillance when I lent the car to a friend whom I assumed was getting into illegal activities. I wanted to make sure I wouldn't get into trouble for it. I told Morgan to get rid of the audio surveillance, but I guess he forgot all about it."

"Oh," I said. "I see."

Jasper walked slowly towards me and placed his hands over my shoulders. "I love you so much, baby. You're my precious little cupcake. Why would you think I would even consider getting your car keys bugged?"

I sighed with relief. "I'm sorry I said you were spying on me."

Jasper pressed his warm lips against mine. "It's okay. We're good. Although, I really don't appreciate how you lied to me on the phone, and said it was just you and Kathy. I'm really disappointed you did that, Kiara."

"Let me explain," I pleaded.

"You don't need to explain anything. I said we're good."

Once the conversation was over for Jasper, it was absolutely done. That subject wasn't open for discussion, and I knew whatever I wanted to say would just be a waste of breath.

Jasper took off his jacket, and let it fall on the bed. He then he straightened his shirt, and ran his hand through his hair. "I will stay here in the office to work for a while. If you need anything, call me on my cell phone."

"We should talk about this, Jasper. Work can wait," I insisted.

He kissed my forehead. "I won't be gone for long."

Without another word, he stormed out of the room, and closed the door behind him.

Jasper usually worked until the late hours, mostly in the home office. Sometimes when I woke up to drink water past midnight, I'd see him lying beside me in bed, but tonight, when I woke up at around 3 AM, Jasper still wasn't in bed.

Strange.

Maybe he had a lot of pending work that needed to be taken care of. I pushed the comforter away, slid my feet inside the cushiony slippers, and pulled on a night robe as I walked out of the room to find the pitch-black darkness leading down towards his office.

I switched on the passage light and walked to his office.

Softly, I knocked on the door. "Jasper, are you still busy?"

There was no answer.

"Look, I said I was sorry. I shouldn't have lied to you."

I opened the door and peered inside to find him nowhere in sight. The Gramophone sang a soft opera song. I walked into the room and stopped the song from playing. The room basked in an eerie silence. Feeling like a little adventurous, I closed the door behind me and tiptoed towards the imposing wooden mahogany desk.

The drawers wouldn't budge. If the drawers were filled with office work, why would he have to keep it locked?

"Do you need something?"

Jasper stood at the doorframe, his eyes darting from the drawer to my face.

"Just . . . just looking around. I was just going to ask you to come back to bed and then I saw you weren't here and the gramophone was still on."

My heart was racing in excessive overdrive.

He regarded me suspiciously. "Come, sweetheart, let's go to bed."

When we lied down in bed, Jasper whispered. "Next time, Kiara, let the gramophone continue to play even if I'm not present in the room, and in case you were looking for the keys to the desk drawers, I keep them with myself."

He had been watching me. I remembered the surveillance cameras in the office . . .

How could I have been so stupid?

CHAPTER TWENTY-FIVE

The honeymoon seemed less like a romantic getaway and more like Jasper's business trip. We were staying at a resort in Cape Town, South Africa, and so far, I hadn't done any sightseeing.

All I did was sunbathe by the pool, dine in the hotel bar, and sometimes go for a swim. I was bored out of my mind. I always thought that turning into a billionaire's wife was going to change my life completely, but in fact, it had gotten a lot worse.

Working as a waitress, at least I had goals to achieve in life. I could go out freely and do whatever I wanted, but after getting married, I realized I had lost sense of my freedom. Jasper controlled the reins.

Sometimes he was charming and loving, while other times, he was brooding over minor things. I had tried to drown my loneliness by doing shopping and other things rich wives did.

Sometimes, I went out for lunch with Penny and Cecilia, whose marital lives weren't bright either—not when Cecelia had fresh marks over her arms and neck every time we met, but she liked to pretend she was fine.

Days began passing at a snail's pace, and during the two months I had been married to Jasper, I noticed how he would sleep at irregular hours, and when I inquired about it, he would shrug it off as being due to his pending work. He arrived home late usually and always failed to come up with a good excuse. When his mood was off, he went out for long walks after dinner and came back seemingly cheerful.

The most suspicious was his sweet behavior. Jasper had a way of talking and making the argument seem like it was my fault. He also said some really hurtful things, coated with extra whipped cream and sugar.

It was too confusing and exhausting to witness the mood swings and be at the receiving end of it. Jasper liked the control. If I moved his things a bit, he would go into a fit of rage and put it right back to where it used to be. I had to take permission to go anywhere outside. If I had to make phone calls to my friends, Jasper needed to know. He also checked my phone from time to time, and yet he never let me check his. If that wasn't suspicious behavior, I don't know what is.

My house was like a golden prison, and I was a prisoner with a fancy title called *Wife* to go with it.

Was Jasper having an affair? The thought of him having a lover tucked away somewhere made me ill. It wasn't like he wasn't capable of having one. Most rich men had a family wife, kids, and yet still feel the need to screw around with other women.

On Monday evening, Jasper came home after work and stepped into the shower. I quickly checked to make sure the water was still running and picked up his phone from the dresser.

I punched in the passcode that I had usually seen him put in, but it didn't work out. I tried putting in his birthdate and then reversed it, I even tried my luck with the numbers on the number plate of his favorite Lambo but nothing was working.

I needed to transfer the data into the computer, and check if it worked that way.

"Type in zero, three, ten, ninety-six."

I spun around to see Jasper standing in the doorway of the bathroom, a towel wrapped around his waist and his hair soaked. I had a chill run down my body as his azure eyes stared at me.

"I was . . . I was just . . ." I stammered.

"It's okay, baby. I understand you'd want to check my phone too. Type the code. It's your birthdate," he said, grinning.

I punched in the code, and the phone unlocked. He laughed. "Please browse through to your heart's content," he added in a mocking tone, "Oh, and don't forget Facebook Messenger. That's where I get a lot of messages from ladies asking me out on dates, one-night stands, and they sometimes send me their nudes." He chuckled.

I wasn't shocked to see that Jasper wasn't lying. He did have women messaging him all the time, and most of those conversations weren't even viewed. After checking everything that I wanted, I handed him back his phone.

"Are you sure you got everything covered?" Jasper asked.

I nodded. "Yes. It was really stupid of me to think—"

"That I was having an affair?" he completed the question for me.

216

"Sorry. I just got a little carried away," I admitted.

"It's not your fault, precious. I'm too damn gorgeous. Any plain wife would have second thoughts."

I laughed and hit him with a pillow. "I'm plain, huh?"

Jasper pulled me close, and drew my lower lip into his mouth. He whispered, "Oh, did I say plain? I think you heard me wrong. I said the most beautiful wife on this planet."

I giggled. "You're so corny."

"You mean charming, don't you?"

It was moments like these that made up for all the shit he put me through. Jasper had some control issues, and he told me before that he was different than most men. I didn't know what he meant, but I knew it wasn't anything I couldn't handle. Marriages included compromise and sacrifices for your loved one. I wasn't perfect and neither could I expect him to be.

"Jasper, I want to tell you something. I know we hadn't discussed it before but it's something that just happened." I said.

I had been holding it in for the entire evening, and tonight he was in a good mood, so this was a perfect time.

"What is it?"

I wet my lips first. I felt like my throat was getting dry. What if he didn't take the news nicely?

"I'm pregnant," I broke the ice and tried to gauge his reaction.

He appeared so dumbfounded that I rambled on, "I missed my period this month and I asked Rita, one of the housekeeping staff for a pregnancy kit. It turned out positive. I know we hadn't discussed children before, and I was on the

217

pill, but I think I forgot to take it regularly, and yesterday morning, I got a little sick and . . ."

Jasper placed his hand over mine. "Kiara, that's the best news anyone has ever given me."

"Really?"

He pulled my mouth to his and kissed me long and hard. His palm slid towards my belly. "My precious little baby. Sweetheart, it's the best gift and you have no fucking idea how happy you've made me."

"Shh . . . the baby shouldn't learn your profanity. I think it's high time you cut it down a little when you're talking to me."

He hugged my stomach and laid his head on my lap. "I love you so much, Kiara. I swear I will give you and our baby everything you both deserve."

"I know you will, and I love you, too."

I had never seen Jasper this delighted before. "Tell me what you're craving, and I'll bring that for you."

"Double chocolate ice-cream," I said.

Jasper was on his toes, his hand raised towards me. "Come on, we'll go on a long drive and have ice-cream together."

"Jasper, I can't go on a drive when I'm . . ."

He had an amused expression on his face. In a baby tone, he asked, "Do you think I would let Mommy into my Lambo and drive one-eighty per hour? I wouldn't do that because I want Mommy to be safe."

I laughed about how he always found out what I was thinking. It was funny that Jasper did mind reading sometimes.

"Come on, Mommy. Daddy's gonna keep you safe."

"Then let's go on that drive, Daddy."

*   *   *

Nine Months Later

After that day, Jasper took good care of me. I was on a strict diet, and the Cook only prepared meals that were nutritious and healthy for me and the baby. Jasper was so happy, he would take me out for drives, dinner dates, and even showered me with gifts.

He had also decorated the room beside ours with a cute little white crib, toys, and children's books. He had some of the best interior designers redecorate the entire room.

I was content. I couldn't have been happier about my life at this point.

"I think the baby just kicked." Jasper's ear was stuck to my protruding belly.

I laughed. "How long are you going to sit like that?"

Jasper kissed my stomach, staring at it in awe. "I'm so excited to see my baby. When are you due?"

"In two weeks."

"I wish it was today." He placed his head on my lap, still hugging me, and I played with his hair.

It's been nine months since I first announced my pregnancy, and nine months since I've been anywhere outside the property. During the first month, when Jasper realized I was pregnant, he was really sweet and even took me out for dinners and did everything I asked on a whim, but after that, his possessiveness towards the baby and me heightened where even the most minor things upset him.

I was getting bored eventually of just watching TV, reading books, and having nothing interesting to do. That evening, I was organizing our bedroom, putting things back into place when I noticed a pair of keys left on the dresser. Jasper had forgotten to put them back. I grabbed the keys and inspected it. They were keys to the third floor which I had never explored in the year that I have been married to him.

I was curious to the point where I decided to take the elevator to the third floor. The last time I had asked Jasper about the space, he said it wasn't anything important, and mostly consisted some of the old furniture.

Since I was bored out of my mind, I thought a little house exploration wouldn't hurt, plus the doctors told me sleeping all day wasn't such a good idea. My body needed some activity.

The mansion was enormous and I had yet to explore some of the other rooms as well. I stood in front of one closed room, but when I turned the knob, it wouldn't budge. I tried the next and it was locked too, and the keys wouldn't work for them. Now there was only one last room remaining. I approached the door slowly and turned the knob.

Surprisingly, it gave away easily.

I stepped inside and looked around, staring at it in awe. It was a lovely bedroom—a four-poster bed dominated the center with a matching dresser at the side and a lovely oval mirror. I reached towards the wardrobe and pulled it open. The wardrobe had beautiful dresses lined up.

I grabbed one lacey violet-colored gown that had studs embroidered all over the bodice. It was so pretty. There was also red, navy blue, pink, and various gowns of other different colors.

I wondered if I had spoilt one of Jasper's surprises for me.

I opened one of the drawers from the dresser and found some jewelry sets, and decided to sneak some into my room. I was just browsing through all the contents when a few photos slipped out and landed on the floor.

I gathered the pictures which lay face down on the floor and casually turned them over. A young woman was staring back at me, her glossy straight blonde hair grazing her shoulders, and a radiant smile touching her beautiful green eyes. The next picture was of the same woman in a white bridal gown, a veil over her face.

The picture after that made my blood turn to ice. My hands started to shake as I stared in horror at the groom standing beside her.

*   *   *

It was past dinner time, and I was tired of waiting for Jasper. I had been sitting for over an hour which felt like an eternity. I watched from the bay window as he got out of his BMW and made his way towards the mansion.

I climbed to my feet and walked towards the railings, looking down as he made his way upstairs. My patience had already run out, and I knew he would make a beeline for his study and spend hours on end behind closed doors.

I decided to confront him before he does that.

"Hey, sweetheart," Jasper greeted me as usual. He was smiling even though he seemed tired. "Why aren't you asleep yet?"

I pulled out the picture I was hiding and showed it to him. "Who is she?"

I wasn't going to beat around the bush.

The spark in his eyes went off in a second and turned into a hard stare. "Where the hell did you get that?" he asked in a mellow monotone.

Now I was the one who boiled with rage. I showed him the other picture I had found in which he was the groom for the same blonde girl that was dressed in a white wedding gown.

"How about this? I'm sure you've got another solid reason for this one."

"Did you go to the third floor?" I hated how menacing his voice sounded.

"I asked you a question first, Jasper! Who is that woman?"

"How dare you?" Jasper's jaw tightened. "How dare you go to the third floor without my permission?"

Tears began to spill from my eyes. "You are a liar and a cheat. She is the same as me, isn't she? She's also your wife! Where is she now? Tucked away in another one of your mansions?"

He didn't utter a word, and that was even scarier.

"Am I a home-wrecker?" I shouted, tears spilling uncontrollably. "Answer me!"

Jasper just continued to stare like I wasn't even crying or demanding answers. "Ava's dead, alright? She committed suicide."

Blood rushed to my ears, and I didn't listen to a damn thing he said after that because I was making my way towards our room. I threw open the wardrobe and started pulling out

222

all my clothes. I unzipped a suitcase and stacked it with my belongings.

I've had enough.

"Where are you going?" Jasper asked.

"Anywhere that I want, just as long as I'm away from you. I'm not living in this house for another fucking minute."

"You don't have a house, precious. Look, it was a long time ago, and the marriage didn't even work." I felt Jasper's hands on my shoulders as he rubbed them, trying to soothe my anger.

"Baby, I didn't love Ava. She was quite power-driven, using my debit cards for careless shopping spree, and she was exceeding the limits. When I told her to cut it down, she refused and became depressed. She was so far into her depression that she committed suicide," he continued, "I didn't tell you this because I didn't want to upset you."

"Well, you've already upset me. I don't care about your excuses. I just don't want to stay here anymore," I said firmly as I picked up the suitcase and made my way towards the stairs. If I didn't have a protruding belly, it would have made my flight downstairs a lot easier.

Suddenly, I felt a jerk from the back. Jasper had grasped the suitcase and was pulling at it. "Let the bag go, Kiara. You're not going anywhere."

"Leave me alone!" I said with tears streaming down my face.

I didn't remember how it happened later, but all I could recall was my body rolling down the staircase with a shriek from a housemaid, followed by Jasper's footsteps and his voice booming in the mansion.

I felt the blood rush to my ears, my eyes registering Jasper as he ran towards me. All I could think of was my baby. I hoped my baby was safe.

"Oh God, Kiara . . . No!"

I was dazed, but I could see him chanting something to himself.

"Call an Ambulance!" Jasper yelled. I felt him pat on my cheek. "Kiara, wake up. Kiara . . ."

His voice began to seem distant, and then there was total blackout.

PART THREE

CHAPTER TWENTY-SIX

KIARA

Four Years Later

"Mommy, can we stay here longer?" Tyler pleaded with me.

I kissed his little hand. "It's getting late, Ty. Daddy will be home in some time."

"Please, Mommy. Please." Tyler scrunched up his mouth. He was clearly annoyed. He hugged his favorite teddy bear closer. "I don't wanna leave."

"Sweetie, we can come again next week. I promise."

Tyler climbed to his feet, almost destroying the sand mountain that he had made. He liked to call it a sandcastle, and I didn't correct him.

He got hold of my hand and waved his friend George goodbye. George was a sweet boy living just down the street. He and Tyler had become really good friends in a short while, and I enjoyed the company of George's mother from time to time.

I brushed the mud off Tyler's pants. He liked coming to the park often, and I sometimes took him to kid's amusement parks and aquariums. Jasper never had time for us, so I had it taken upon myself to enjoy watching Tyler grow up.

I helped Tyler into the car while I took over the steering wheel and turned on the music. Tyler was looking out the window, and I realized he was sad to go home. He always hated going back home.

"What's the matter, honey?" I asked him.

"I don't like to go home," he complained.

I kissed his cheek. "How about we take a detour to your favorite ice-cream place?"

His face lit up at once. "I want strawberry."

I drove towards Tyler's favorite ice-cream place where we had our own mother and son conversations. He mostly liked talking about his school friends and some imaginary friends as well. I listened to him with interest and sheer adoration.

"Hmm, and then what happened?" I wiped the ice-cream dripping from his chin.

Tyler laughed. "And then I told him he was being silly."

Tyler's blue eyes twinkled, the same large expressive blue eyes that he had gotten from his father. His curly hair was a shade of dark brown. Tyler was a miniature version of Jasper.

A few years back, when I had fallen down the stairs during my ninth month, I had suddenly blacked out, and after a while, I woke up in a hospital bed, having gone into early labor. Tyler was a premature baby at the time, but I literally cried my eyes out when I saw how beautiful and precious he was.

Tyler had been strong enough to survive that fall. He walked into my lonely life like a lamp in the darkness, and I cherished every moment with him. Everyone in the mansion loved Tyler, from the cook to the maids, and even Morgan was quite charmed by the little boy.

Tyler already had nuggets and fries for dinner which was a change from his usual meals at home. When we reached the mansion, he was heading straight to his bedroom when he bumped into Jasper. The smile that Tyler had on his face quickly disappeared like switching off a light bulb.

Jasper, at thirty-one, was still breathtakingly gorgeous and appeared more rugged than how he used to be. He passed his son a heartwarming smile.

"How's my buddy, today?"

"I'm fine, Daddy," Tyler responded.

"Where did you and Mommy come from, Tyler?" Jasper asked.

It was a trick question.

Tyler's little body shook. He glanced at me then back at his father. "We went to the mall."

Jasper nodded. I was glad Tyler hadn't said anything else. Parks were completely off the list. Jasper didn't like Tyler getting along with the town children. Being just a kid, he liked playing with the kids his age. I felt bad on how lonely he usually was, so I promised the boy we would sneak out to our secret hangouts.

Tyler was a vibrant child. He liked going out often, playing in the sun, getting dirt on his face, and doing other activities boys his age did but because of Jasper's strict rules, Tyler was often sad and acted detached from his own father.

The love that Jasper and I had for each other was almost nonexistent after Tyler's birth.

I was more of a convenient tool—a wife kept for the purpose of showing off at parties or charity functions, and warming a bed, not to mention, *breeding*.

Jasper had packed and left for a business trip the next day, informing me that he'd return in a few days. Knowing Jasper, I knew he could return an hour or two later, saying that he forgot to take important files, but that was hardly the case. Jasper came back to see if I sneaked in a lover or if I was up to something that I wasn't supposed to. He thought I was oblivious to such things.

Tyler had an odd ability to sneak into Jasper's study where he usually pulled out all his papers and scribbled all over them with crayons. Jasper didn't mind as long as he could duplicate them but there was one time when Tyler tore these pages, and I was blamed for it. When I had seen the look in Jasper's eyes, all I wanted to do was run away. I wanted to pack my bags and leave the house with my son.

I knew that wasn't possible. I couldn't stand up to a man with so much power. He could ruin me. Even if Jasper hadn't voiced the threat, it was clear as day in his alluring blue eyes.

When I didn't find Tyler in his bedroom or the mansion garden, I realized he was back in Jasper's study, creating another mischief.

I made my way to the study and wasn't surprised to find the adorable boy sprawled on the floor, drawing on a heap of papers with colorful crayons. When he heard me walk in, his gem-like eyes found mine.

"Mommy, look. I drew a kitty!"

"Honey, how many times have I told you not to come inside Daddy's room? This is where he works. You can't come here."

My eager little boy ignored my pleas and rushed forward to show me the art with his little hands. "See."

I took the paper from his hand and inspected it like it was a work of Picasso. "It is so amazing. You're so talented, Ty."

Tyler appeared pleased by my shower of appraisal and passed me a two-toothed smile, one with dimples.

"Thanks." He picked up another blank paper. "Let's draw a doggie now."

After we finished doing our drawings together, I put Tyler to bed and decided to clean up the mess in Jasper's office. I picked up all the papers and put them back in order which took me over an hour. A small bottle of colored pills caught my eye.

Jasper never took any medication. That was odd.

I picked up the bottle and examined it. I pulled out my phone and typed the name of the medication on the search bar. I needed to know what kind of pills these were.

When I saw the results of the search, I was appalled. It couldn't be possible . . .

Jasper couldn't be . . .

I pocketed the bottle and hurried out of the office. I needed to find out the truth. Luckily, I found Morgan loitering around the passage area.

"Morgan," I called out to him.

The butler halted midway. "Yes, Mrs. Lockhart?"

"You've been with the Lockharts for ages." I knew my hands were shaking. "I need to know something." My pulse had quickened, without wasting any time, I showed him the bottle of pills.

He looked at the bottle and then at me. His expression was stoic, one couldn't guess what was actually going on in his head, either that or Morgan knew everything and was pretty good at feigning innocence.

"What of the pills, Miss?"

I stopped before saying anything as a maid bowed at me and passed us.

When I was sure there was no one else within earshot, I continued, "I found these pills in Jasper's desk drawer, and when I searched about it on the internet . . ." I choked, looking heavenward to keep the tears at bay.

This wasn't happening to me!

"Please tell me it's a misunderstanding," I managed to say.

"Miss, I'm not sure what conclusion you've drawn, but Mr. Lockhart is a very kind man. He is not—"

"Morgan, I understand your loyalty towards him. I really do." I cut him off midsentence. "I've lived for four years in the dark, confused about my husband. If there's anything I need to know . . . please. At least for Tyler's sake, I have to know the truth."

He seemed like he was torn between wanting to speak his mind and not betraying his employer.

"It's not my place to say this, but you're quite aware of how eccentric Mr. Lockhart can be. Forgive me, but I'm afraid I wouldn't be able to comment regarding his personal affairs or his mental health."

"Very well, then. I will find out on my own, one way or the other," I said, turning on my heel.

"Mrs. Lockhart . . ." I heard Morgan call out to me.

I stopped in my tracks and looked back at him. Morgan stared at me as if having a dilemma.

"*His* grandmother . . ." I didn't need specification as to who he was referring to as '*His*'. "She was diagnosed with antisocial personality disorder and spent the better half of her life in an asylum. When she was finally free, she was found hanging in the barn, but since she was highly manipulative, it was unlikely she would take her life. It was rumored that Grady Lockhart, her husband, had her killed by a servant and then hung her body to make it look like a suicide. Since the Lockharts have been an influential family with a considerable amount of wealth and power, no one in town questioned it."

This was new. Apparently, the family had a history of deaths and violence. I knew Jasper's father was a cunning man, but I had no idea his grandfather was same too.

"What does this have anything to do with Jasper?"

Morgan continued in the same monotonous tone, "Like I've said before, Miss, I'm not one to comment on Mr. Lockhart's mental health, but I can tell you as much. His grandmother was charming, witty, manipulative, and ruthless, much similar to Mr. Lockhart. As far as what I know, the disorder is generally passed down from a family member. It could be that Mr. Lockhart is a—"

"Thank you, Morgan," I said.

Morgan didn't need to spell it out for me. He hadn't spoken in clear words what exactly Jasper was but had hinted on it which was more than enough for me.

CHAPTER TWENTY-SEVEN

It was past midnight, and I just sipped my third cup of coffee. There was still no sign of my husband returning from his business trip. I was seated in his study desk, waiting anxiously. I needed answers, and fast.

Sometimes, it made me wonder. Did Jasper really go on business trips for weeks, or was he attending to some other personal trip? Perhaps he had a lover tucked away somewhere with an illegitimate child. What if he confessed to having another family?

For a man like Jasper's caliber who was ridiculously wealthy, handsome as the devil himself, and charming like no one you've met, it wasn't hard for him to get whoever he wanted. If Jasper could wish, he could have two or three or even a dozen women scattered across countries, living lavishly and have absolutely no financial issues by a long shot. If not a dozen, I suspected at least one.

I stared at the empty cup of coffee and wished I could ring for a maid to make me another cup, but it was already too late, and I didn't want to disturb the staff at this hour, neither did I have the patience to walk downstairs to make myself one.

Just when I decided to go back to my room, I heard the knob turning. The hair on my back stood up.

The lights switched on as his imposing form walked inside the room. Jasper's alluring blue eyes rested on me.

"Oh, hey precious. Didn't expect you here so late, thought I'd see you in the morning."

He approached me. His fingers slowly wrapped around the nape of my neck as he began to lower his face towards me for a kiss, but I pushed him away.

"I want to talk to you about something."

"The talking can wait, don't you think?" He grinned. "We could utilize the time for some other activities which includes a bed and absolutely no clothes."

Without further delay, or before he could manipulate me to comply with his wishes, I showed him the bottle of pills. There was just a hint of regret in his features—regret of being caught, I believed—and it was gone in a flash. He smiled, almost relieved to have finally lifted off the mask.

"You lied to me," I finally said. "These pills are for antisocial personality disorder."

He chuckled. "A polite name for antipsychotics."

I was seething, feeling like a total idiot. "Why did you hide it from me?"

Jasper still appeared to be indifferent to my inner turmoil. Either he was choosing to ignore my distress, or he just didn't care. "If I told you about the disorder I was suffering from, would you have stayed with me?"

He knew the answer to that question, so he smiled knowingly and leaned against the desk. "I thought so. It took Ava one year to find out, and she threatened to expose me.

Poor girl. A few days later, she was lying on the cold ground in a puddle of her own blood."

Jasper said it with such a straight face and a tone of indifference that one would think he was merely discussing tomorrow's lunch menu. I felt like my ears were bleeding. A deep emotion clogged my throat, raw and real. The tears streamed down my face. The world might as well be upside down.

All wasn't lost. There was still hope. It wasn't entirely his fault he was born this way. I could help him.

"We can go to the best psychiatrists in the country and get you into psychotherapy. We can get the help you need, Jasper."

Jasper looked straight to my eyes. "There's no treatment or a cure for it, Kiara." He twirled the heavy paperweight on the desk. "Besides, cure is for people who want to be treated. I certainly do not need or intend to get help. In fact, I'm quite content with my situation at present. You should be too. Nothing should change from merely you finding out my true nature. I'm still the same loving husband and you my obedient, loyal wife. It's all the same."

"So, you don't want to be treated?" I asked.

"I'm perfectly well," he said proudly. "Don't look at me as if I'm sick with some life-threatening disease."

"If you wouldn't get yourself treated, I will . . ."

"You will what?" His expression turned hard. "If word got out, my reputation will be in ruins, and the company will suffer. The last thing I need is getting attention from the tabloids. I can't allow that to happen. Do you understand what I'm saying, Kiara?"

I couldn't control the outburst of fury waiting to resurface. My hands were balled into tight fists. "You've been lying throughout this marriage. First your ex-wife, and now the fact that you're a psychopath." I gave out a little laugh. I finally said the word. "This entire relationship was built on your lies. The way you offered to help me, used me for your personal needs and then confessed your undying love. You're a good actor, Jasper. You should win an *Oscar*."

"Oh, come on, Kiara, you know better than to display theatrics. I did everything in my power to keep you away from the truth. Can you blame me? I pretended to be someone I wasn't. I tried to blend into the community like every other ordinary man, and I know I'm pretty good at it."

"Good at deceiving people," I muttered. "Do you even have any feelings for me?"

The corners of his mouth twitched upward as if he had expected this question sooner or later.

"I'd like to confess that I lack empathy, guilt, or remorse. I don't even feel love. That's the way I function, but with time, I've learned to control my emotions and do what's needed. I show people what they want to see. I do love you, Kiara, just not in the conventional way. I like to be in control. Now that you know me, I hope we understand each other better."

"Fuck you!" I snapped, climbing to my feet. "I'm leaving, and Tyler comes with me, and I don't care where we're going as long as I'm away from you. I'm not staying in this house with someone like you!"

Before I could get up, Jasper pushed me down onto the seat with one harsh shove and blocked my way.

"What are you doing?" I asked him, my heart thudding against my chest.

"Something that I should have done years before when you disobeyed and broke my rules. I explained it to you nicely, but you want to test the devil in me, so be it."

His palm cracked against my right cheek. It was like waking up from a beautiful dream, only to realize you've been living in a nightmare. Surprise registered only for a second, followed by betrayal, and finally, the horror of the situation.

I dared a glance at his face, and his eyes were nothing like I had seen them before. His fathomless blue eyes were replaced by an unspeakable darkness, his expression vicious.

I touched my cheek. "Why would you hit me?!"

"I make the goddamn rules in this house!" he said with icy calmness, digging his fingers into my cheek until I yelped. "Listen to this, Kiara. I possess you—mind, body, soul. And if you try to get away from me, I promise you, I will hunt you down even from the pits and bring you back here. The punishments you will receive after that will be a bonus."

"You killed *her*, didn't you?" Realization dawned on me. I didn't need to say her name. He knew I was talking about Ava.

"I'll leave that to your imagination. You do know what I'm capable of. You've seen me tear and devour even the strongest of people," he whispered. "It's not going to be difficult for me to do the same to you. Think about it."

My breathing intensified, and I began slapping and scratching him in a desperate attempt to free myself from him. My long fingernail dragged down his right cheek, and when he touched it, there was a trail of blood on his fingers.

That's when all hell broke loose.

I had unleashed the beast living inside him.

*   *   *

All those years that Jasper had humiliated me, put me in uncomfortable situations, and even displayed the lack of interest for certain things were clear signs of being a psychopath. He had been a master of manipulation, making me believe that his feelings for me were real when it had all been just for blending in with the society. In reality, Jasper was a handsome man with horns, and I couldn't believe that I had fallen in love with such an ugly person.

In the heat of the moment, I slapped him and scratched his face. Jasper stared at the blood on his fingers.

"You little bitch!" he bellowed as he reached for my chemise and jerked the fabric so hard, it broke free.

"Jasper! Stop it!" I yelled at him.

He tore it all the way down, almost revealing my right breast. "Stop . . ." I pleaded.

But Jasper wasn't listening. He was possessed by a demon I didn't even know existed. There was a hunger shining in his eyes, a monster unleashed that had been waiting for the right time to showcase its true colors. His eyes, devoid of pity or any emotion, were vacant. The blue eyes that I had always thought to have been beautiful now terrified me to the core.

"You can't ever leave me!" he whispered. "If you do, I'll ruin your life! You're mine."

I was begging him to stop, but before he could violate me any further, the office door creaked open, and I quickly covered my front with what was left of my ruined nightie when I saw who was standing there.

Tyler stood there, holding a teddy bear to his chin, his eyes moving from me to Jasper and back. His face was white as a sheet as if he had seen a ghost. Tyler was too young to realize what was going on, but he noticed my crying face and Jasper pinning me down on the chair.

"Tyler . . ." I whispered, wiping the tears with the back of my hand. "Go to your room, honey."

He hiccupped and then started crying, pointing at Jasper. "Bad Daddy!"

"Tyler! Go to your room! Now!" I yelled at him.

But the boy was glued to the spot. "Daddy . . ." he sobbed. "Please don't hit Mommy."

How had he realized that I had been hit?

I turned my face towards the transparent glass panels of the mini bar where I could see my reflection clearly.

I saw a woman who had been abused at the hands of her husband. My right cheek was a glaring red color.

Jasper let go of me at once and his expression changed. He was putting his civil mask again.

"Ty, buddy, who said I was doing anything to your mom? We were just playing a game, weren't we, Kiara?" He dared me to say otherwise.

I nodded. "Yes, just a game. No one's hurting me."

After Tyler had left the room, Jasper fixed his shirt, ran a hand through his hair, and began inspecting the damage I had done to his lip. He didn't even pay me attention, like I wasn't even his wife; as if I was just another piece of furniture in his office.

"Fix yourself," he told me. "And don't even think about leaving me. Be a nice wife, and go to sleep. I'll be back in an hour."

Despite myself, I asked him. "Where are you going now?"

"I have some work," he said in a tone that told me I wasn't supposed to ask any more questions.

He was already back from a business trip so what work could he have past midnight? I was actually tired of Jasper making excuses at night to get out of the house. Was he going to another woman? At this point, he could have a mistress, another wife, or more of them for all I cared. If I was going to stay in this marriage, it was only for Tyler because I couldn't risk crossing someone as influential and dangerous as Jasper.

I had married the devil, and I was paying the price.

*　　*　　*

That night, I couldn't get much sleep. I was lying down, thinking about how my life had turned out this way. I wasn't going to sleep in our bedroom tonight, so I had taken the guest room on the same floor. I didn't want to breathe the same air as him.

For years, I had wanted to free myself from the reins of my father's abuse until I met this man who was no one like I had ever met. He was charming, handsome, kind, caring, and most of all, he was honest, and he spoke his mind . . .

And that's what drew me towards Jasper. He saved me that night. I loved him with all my heart, and to have him say he felt the same, I felt like the luckiest woman in the world. I couldn't believe that person could be a psychopath. Someone who wasn't capable of having any emotions towards anyone. Did that mean he didn't love our son too?

I contemplated packing and leaving with Tyler, but then remembered Jasper's threat. He would hunt me down and maybe something worse could happen.

Maybe Jasper would keep me apart from my baby.

Maybe he would hurt me again.

I knew the outcomes would be bad, and I wanted to avoid it at any cost. The thought of suicide crossed my mind, but when I looked at Tyler, I wondered how he would survive alone in this world. I was just about to doze off when I heard a knock on the bedroom door.

I looked up to find Tyler at the door, hugging a stuffed bunny to his chest as usual. Some of the maids had mentioned about Tyler talking to his toys, and that made me realize how lonely Tyler must be feeling.

"Can I sleep with you, Mommy?"

"Of course, honey. Come here," I said.

Tyler hopped onto the bed and slid inside the covers, pulling it to his chin. His round blue eyes stared at me. I had seen Jasper's picture album of when he was little, and I couldn't help but notice how similar Tyler was to his father, but I hoped that's where the similarities ended.

"Mommy?" Tyler started saying.

I snapped out of my thoughts. "Yes, honey?

"Can I ask you something?"

"Go ahead."

"Is Daddy a bad man?" he asked.

I was taken aback by this question. No matter how badly he was going to treat me, I would never turn his son against him.

"No, Tyler. Your father is a good man."

"Then why are you crying?" His eyes searched mine for the honesty. His little hand stroked my cheek where it was turning red. "Daddy hit you."

I froze. Of all the things, I hadn't thought Tyler would say this. I pulled him close as the tears began to spill. God, I was so pathetic. "I'm so sorry, Tyler."

I was sorry because I was falling out of love with his father.

"It's alright. I don't love Daddy, either." Tyler said as if he read my mind.

"Why would you say that, sweetie?"

"Because he made you cry."

I didn't say anything, then, he continued. "That day after school when I went to George's house, I saw George's mommy and daddy smiling. George's daddy didn't hit his mommy. I don't see you and Daddy smiling like that."

I shook my head. "We do. Sometimes."

Tyler stared at me like the kid was calling it bullshit. I couldn't believe I was having this conversation with my almost four-year-old son. His birthday was in two days.

To change the topic, I asked him, "What do you want for your birthday?"

Tyler inched closer. He smelled of baby soap. I had come to love that scent. "Chocolate cake."

"Well, you're going to have one of the best cakes for your birthday, you know. Daddy made sure of it."

"No, I want the one that you make. George's mommy makes for him too."

I kissed the top of his head, smiling. "Alright. I'll bake you one."

"I love you, Mommy."

My heart soared with happiness. Tyler was the only one in this world who truly loved me.

"I love you more, honey."

CHAPTER TWENTY-EIGHT

"That's a lovely necklace, Kiara," Mary complimented me, her were on my neck piece.

Mary Whitman was the wife of one of Jasper's business associates and usually accompanied her husband, Mark, in all the elite parties.

I touched my necklace. "Thank you. It's was an anniversary gift from Jasper." I forced my best fake smile, not that she noticed.

Mary nodded, her eyes glinting with sheer envy, even though she spent a hell of a lot more on clothing and jewelry than I did. I was also under the impression that she had a crush on Jasper. I wish I cared.

"How lucky. My husband barely has any time for buying me gifts. It's just me shopping for stuff alone, which reminds me, what are your plans for Thursday?" she asked me.

I was free on Thursday, in fact, I was free most days. You didn't have much work to do around the house if there was staff to do the tiniest of house chores, plus the only job I had right now was to look after Tyler, and I took great pleasure in it.

Mary had a very bad habit of dragging me along to her little escapades where the cocktail parties mostly ended up with male hookers trying so hard to make Mary feel loved. I had been smarter since and avoided that at all costs, knowing the such events would be infested with Jasper's men who reported to him my every move, either that or one of the things in my handbags would be bugged.

"Actually, Tyler's got a school thing going on, so . . ." I lied.

"Aw, honey. You could always ask Morgan or someone else to do that job," she said, as if attending a son's school event was the last thing a socialite woman should be doing.

"I prefer doing it myself, Mary."

"You're no fun." She giggled. I noticed she was waving her hand in my face for the past hour, so I decided to give her what she wanted.

"Love that new ring. Where is it from?" I asked her, faking enthusiasm.

Mary giggled. "Tiffany & Co. Mark told me to choose the best."

Mary blabbered on and on about a new mansion they were planning to buy this year. I was trying to think of a good excuse to ditch this conversation. My cheeks were hurting from all the fake smiling, and my feet were killing me because of the high heels. I needed a break.

I excused myself and started making my way out of the house, away from the crowd and the chaos. I was in a hurry to get out of these stilettos. I didn't understand why Jasper thought it was fine to parade me around in these. It wasn't like I was having a freakin' runway show.

My mind was preoccupied with a lot of things, and maybe that's why I didn't see the waiter with a tray of drinks. I bumped into him which sent the flutes flying. They crashed on the floor, and a bolt of excruciating pain shot through my ankle. It twisted as I stumbled and plummeted towards the floor.

I closed my eyes and willed the pain to subside. I wondered what punishment Jasper would give me for being so clumsy in public. Some ladies scrambled to help me up to my feet, but I just couldn't stand up. It hurt too damn much.

"Try to move your ankle, Kiara," Mary suggested as she touched my leg.

"I can't," I yelped.

"May I have a look?"

That voice. I had heard it somewhere.

All heads turned towards the owner of the voice. Clad in a royal-blue suit, he stood before me. His dark wavy hair matched his familiar brown eyes and concrete jaw that had once been babyish and smooth. He was a boy who had followed his brother's instructions; who used to be weak and powerless. Now, his demeanor screamed power, and if that wasn't enough, he looked even better now. He was breathtakingly gorgeous.

"Vincent?" I whispered. I couldn't believe my eyes.

Was I dreaming? Or was he really back after so many years?

He passed me his familiar friendly smile, but the worry was clear in his eyes. "Let me see."

I felt a bit intimidated by him, so I glanced back down.

Vincent knelt down to where I was sprawled on the floor and inspected my ankle. I whimpered at his touch, but he was being gentle as he pressed the spot.

His eyes met mine and he caught me staring. "It's a sprained ankle. You need to ice your foot twice a day for once a week. Don't exert pressure on it. I'll write you some pain meds which will help to reduce the pain."

"Thank you, doctor," I teased my brother-in-law.

"You're welcome, Kiara." He smiled again, but it felt guarded. "You need to take some rest now, and also, avoid high heels."

I laughed. "I can surely do that."

"Come on, I'll help you up," he offered.

"No, it's fine. I just . . ."

I didn't have time to protest as Vincent scooped me up in his arms, bridal style. I couldn't even stand with the sprained ankle. He carried me upstairs, and threw open the doors of the guest room before he placed me on the mattress. I noticed he had closed the door of the room behind him.

There was silence in the room; the only sound I could hear was my own breathing. Vince's once boyish features were now masculine and sharp. The air between us was different. I remembered it used to be friendly and easygoing. So many things had changed. Now, I couldn't even look in his eyes without feeling like I was being analyzed, as if I were a rare species in a science laboratory.

"Didn't think I'd still see you here. Can't say that I'm pleased," Vincent commented.

I gave out a mocking laugh. "Funny that's coming from someone who never attended our wedding even after the invitation had been sent out."

I thought there'd be a hint of guilt or even shame, but he seemed appalled by my little revelation. "I'm sorry. Did you say wedding?"

Confused, I asked him. "I thought Jasper persuaded you to come to our wedding. He said he'd tried his best but you wouldn't listen."

All the remaining color drained from his face, "You're saying you married Jasper and I didn't make it to the wedding because he couldn't get in touch with me?" Vincent chuckled. "I call that bullshit, and you're naïve if you believed him."

"I had no choice but to trust his word. I lost your contact number, and you never stayed in touch," I exploded. "You said you would come back, but you never did."

"If I had come back for you, Kiara, would you have chosen me over *him?*"

I couldn't even meet his eyes because the unspoken truth was right there. I had been smitten and in love with Jasper. I hadn't seen Vincent as anyone other than a good friend and Jasper's younger brother.

"My brother is a lucky bastard," Vincent murmured. "I'll get you an ice pack for your leg, but we're still not finished with our conversation."

Just when Vince was making his way out of the room, Jasper walked in. Jasper's hard stare was glued to me, and that forced me to look away. He was about to create another scene. I sure could use one of Lucas's disappearing acts right now.

"When did you come back?" I heard Jasper ask.

Vince laughed that masculine boy-next-door laugh that any woman would fall in love with.

"Well, I'm doing great, Jasper. Thanks for asking," Vince said, sarcasm dripping in his tone. "I don't even get a bro hug?"

"I don't have time for this childish conversation. Until when are you planning to stay here?" Jasper asked him, eyes fixed at Vince with what seemed like murderous intent.

"As long as I want," Vince answered.

"You can't!" Jasper said.

"I'll have to remind you, as much as this house is yours, it's mine too," Vince continued. "In paper. If you want me to drag my attorney into this, that's fine with me too, but I will stay here."

"Stop overreacting. You weren't here all these years. Why now?"

"There were things that needed to be taken care of. Since I'm here now, we can look after the company together just like old times. Don't you think it's a fabulous idea, Jasper?"

Jasper was fuming, but he hadn't lashed out on his brother.

Not yet.

I remembered the young man who didn't make a lot of eye contact with his brother, who was easily intimidated and bullied. The Vincent that was standing before me now appeared confident and in control, not at all fazed by Jasper's dominating hard stare.

When Jasper didn't answer, Vince turned to look at me. He was only a few inches taller than Jasper, the difference in their height was hardly noticeable.

"I'm sorry, my lady, I just got carried away when I met my dear brother after a long damn time. I'll get what you need."

"It's alright, Vince," I insisted.

Vince had already left the room, leaving me alone with Jasper who shut the door behind him.

"Are you not going to throw some confetti now that your best friend is here?" Jasper mocked.

"You said you invited him for our wedding! You lied!" I hissed. I was more disappointed in myself for being a gullible little idiot than I was with my husband.

"Yes, I lied," Jasper admitted. "I realized he didn't need to be part of the ceremony. I couldn't risk him screwing up my plans."

"What plans?" I asked.

"Plans of marrying you, of course," he stated.

I could no longer keep the questions to myself.

"Why me?" I asked. "You could have had anyone you wanted."

"Those women you see during the parties, they are wealthy and independent, and I despise them all. I like someone who is docile and would depend on me which is exactly what you were. No offense, Kiara, but when I saw you in the restaurant the first time, I knew it had to be you."

"You never really loved me, did you?"

"I do love you, in my own way. I have an attachment towards you. It's just not the same as everyone else. I wanted to survive in this community as a normal person, and you seemed like a good decoy."

An attachment like one would have with their pets.

I had accepted my twisted fate that night when I found out that he was a psychopath, so hearing him admit that he loved me in an unconventional way didn't surprise me much.

"And stay the fuck away from Vincent. He's no better. The company is what he is after."

Before he could continue further, Tyler threw open the door followed by Vincent who was holding a pack of ice and some medicines.

"Mommy, what's wrong?" Tyler walked towards the bed. His eyes were sad, and it darted up towards Jasper. I knew what he was thinking. He thought Jasper hurt me.

"It's my shoes, honey. I just slipped and fell."

"Mom?" Vince glanced from Tyler to me and back. "You're Tyler's mother?"

"Yes," I said.

The sleeve of my dress slipped off my shoulder, and just as I tried to cover the marks, Vincent's eyes narrowed into menacing slits when he looked at Jasper, and I knew right then what he had seen and assumed.

Vincent turned to Tyler. "Hey buddy, tell you what, Mommy's not feeling well at the moment. How about you go down to the party, and enjoy with your friends, then we all open your gifts together."

"Okay," Tyler said excitedly and exited the room.

After Tyler was gone, Vincent shut the door and took a swing at Jasper. A trail of blood trickled down his mouth and there were spots of crimson on Vincent's fist.

This was the second time he had been punched in a week. First by me, and now by his brother. We were setting up a new record.

251

"Next time, Jasper, I won't stop at a punch. You hurt a single hair on Kiara's head, and I'll make sure everyone finds out your true face. We both know how good Lockharts are at keeping their word."

Jasper pulled out a white handkerchief from his jacket breast pocket and wiped his mouth with it. I felt a sense of triumph at seeing him get hurt. I should have felt bad but I didn't.

Jasper's hands were balled into fists, he was wearing the same deadly expression from when he had hit me in his office the other night.

It was a clear indication that a storm was coming soon.

CHAPTER TWENTY-NINE

I hardly saw Vince since the birthday party. The only times I met him was when he visited to check up on me for my sprained leg. Whenever he visited, he spoke professionally like a doctor and left at once.

When the leg got better, I started to move around the house and we bumped into each other now and then, but all we exchanged was a smile or just a simple hello over our regular meals. I was disappointed and glad at the same time. Disappointed because I wished to see him more often, and glad due to the fact that I didn't want to involve Vincent in my marital issues.

One night, Jasper and I had a fight, and like normal couples, our fights didn't end in silence. It just got worse, and it ended up becoming a screaming match with Tyler brawling at the top of his lungs.

Before Jasper could backhand me like he had done before in the past, I slipped on my silky robe and made my way downstairs. Breathing in the same room as Jasper had gotten hard.

All the shouting had made me thirsty so I made my way into the kitchen to get myself a drink. I didn't bother to switch on the lights as I pulled out a chilled bottle of water from the refrigerator and took a sip. I coughed up some water, but I was able to keep it from spilling.

My heart almost stopped beating when I heard a sound in the room. I turned around to find Vince pulling out things from the refrigerator—a bottle of mayonnaise, tomatoes, and cheese. He noticed me on the bar stool. His eyes crinkled as his lips formed into a smile.

"My lady, how nice of you to have graced me tonight with your presence in the kitchen."

I couldn't help but laugh. "My lord, it's late. What are you doing here?"

"Making myself a snack," he said as he struggled with cutting the long French loaf. "I have midnight cravings when I'm studying in my room."

"We're similar. I get midnight snack cravings too."

"And yet you decided to marry the older brother rather than wait for me."

I knew Vince was joking, but it still sounded like a quick jibe.

I smiled, unable to come up with a response, and climbed down from the stool. "You suck at this. Let me help you."

Vince stood back and watched as I sliced the bread and decided to prepare the sandwich for him. I began slicing the tomatoes and lettuce, all the while watching from the corner of my eye how he observed me doing it.

After I was done, he said, "Thank you" and I knew he meant it.

Those words hardly came from Jasper's mouth. He placed the plate of food on the island counter, his back towards me. "Jasper's still awake?"

I shook my head. "He is asleep."

Vince patted the stool beside him. "Would you mind joining me for a little chat?"

"Sure," I said.

I sat down beside him and watched him eat. In a soft voice, Vince asked, "How is your leg now?"

"Better," I said. "All thanks to you."

Vince waved his hand like it wasn't a big deal. "I like helping people."

I let those words sink in. *Vince liked helping people.* That was so unlike Jasper who took pleasure in hurting people close to him. Then again, Jasper had offered a helping hand during my difficult times, hadn't he? But it had all come with a price. Vince didn't seem like the kind of person who'd keep someone close for a hidden agenda.

A few minutes passed in silence, but it wasn't awkward or forced. I felt oddly comfortable in his presence. Vince was the first to break it, "I didn't mean to eavesdrop but I heard you and Jasper argue tonight."

I failed to come up with a suitable answer. Yes, we were fighting, and yes, we were having issues.

"Tyler tells me how scared he feels around Jasper," Vincent said as he placed his hand on mine. "I understand if you don't want to talk about it, Kiara, but I've seen the fear in the little boy's eyes, and he reminds me of myself when I was his age. I know I made a mistake by not getting in touch with you sooner, but I want to help you now."

"Did you know Jasper has antisocial personality disorder?" I asked, keeping my voice low in case any servants were still awake and loitering around.

I knew his answer would either destroy me or relieve me from my doubts.

"I suspected it. There's no man who could say the most outrageous things in public and have people think it's charming. He used to do that since we were kids, and I looked up to him like he was God. Whatever Jasper did or said, it was always the right thing. When we grew older, he continued to manipulate people into liking him, and it worked."

"Can you tell me more?" I asked curiously.

"As you're aware, Jasper was our father's illegitimate son, born out of an affair with a housekeeper. Father wasn't really fond of him, but he was fair. Jasper convinced our father to let him help in the company, and before we knew it, he used some magic wand. Everyone was under his spell. The company was doing far better after Jasper was part of the board."

"And how did he meet his ex-wife?"

"Ava and Jasper went to college together. She was from a good family as well. Her father owned several car dealerships. They were happy together, and then she committed suicide. Jasper wasn't himself for a long time. I noticed he became more detached, but I realized it was just a phase. He used to be far worse before he met Ava, and then when he met you, I told him he shouldn't play with your feelings, but he assured me he had developed real feelings for you. I believed him, Kiara, just like old times." A pause later, he said, "He's still my brother after all, and we had only each other after our parents died. I realized I was so stupid. He used me just like he had used everyone else around him."

Vincent looked away as if he couldn't fathom to look into my eyes.

"I'm glad you're here now," I said, pressing his hand.

"Morgan," he murmured.

"Morgan?"

"Morgan called me one night and told me that you needed help."

I was shocked. Why would the housekeeper even care for me? Morgan, the man who'd never defied Jasper's word; the man who would listen to us argue in our car endlessly and pretend he hadn't heard a word.

"I had been busy trying to set up my hospital, but I wanted to come home as soon as I could," he continued. "You can't stay with Jasper. He's toxic."

"He would never divorce me. If I even speak of that, he would keep me away from my child. Jasper knows a lot of things from my past, and he will use them against me. I can't take that risk."

"I will help you."

"I'm so scared," I confessed. "He doesn't even love me."

"I may not be too experienced where love is concerned, but I know that if he loved you . . ." He wiped a tear off my stained cheek. ". . . he couldn't bear to see you cry like this. If I was in his place, Kiara, if I had the chance to love you, I'd want to see you smiling all the time. I would sit with you and talk to you for hours about nothing in particular and then if I made you cry, I'd lick your tears dry, and if that still didn't work, I'd set you free."

*   *   *

The pattern of my life had changed in just a few days. Whenever Jasper would lash at me and disappear to do some work, I found myself in the kitchen where Vince waited for me during the wee hours of the night, when the kitchen staff were already back to their quarters. It was the only time I could converse with Vince without any barriers. During the exact time Jasper returned to the bedroom, I'd sneak back in and pretend to be asleep.

It had been years since I had spoken so openly to anyone, and it felt better to talk to a person who really understood me.

Vince told me some of the things he knew about Ava. He told me how Jasper had driven her nuts by watching her every step, mentally torturing her, doubting her with the gardener which finally led to Ava taking the final leap off the third floor.

One night, when I woke up to meet Vince, I found Jasper missing from our bed as usual. In place of him were the wrinkled sheets, so I walked into his study and found it empty. I noticed a shadow outside, so I approached the window and saw Jasper walking through the courtyard.

Something was fishy. I climbed down the stairs and walked into the kitchen. Vince was seated at the island bar as usual. As if he had sensed something, he stilled.

"I saw Jasper walk through the courtyard," I whispered to him.

"At this hour?"

I nodded. "I've been noticing this for a long time. He says he's going into his study, but the last time I checked, he wasn't there. Even now, I couldn't find him there so I looked outside the window and saw him."

Vince climbed to his feet. "I'll check what he is up to."

"I'll come with you," I insisted.

He shook his head. "It's really late, Kiara. Go to bed, I'll follow him and see where he is going."

"But—"

He placed a hand on my shoulder. "I'll tell you all about it. Don't worry."

I was tired and didn't feel like arguing with Vince. It was nice to finally rely on someone and not have to burden all the problems. I had already mentioned my concerns about Jasper being unfaithful in the marriage, and Vince assumed the role of a private investigator, one who did all the work free of charge, merely out of family obligations.

That night, Jasper returned about two hours later and I pretended that I wasn't aware of his disappearance, but I remained vigilant, and sometime around dawn, I heard the door creak open.

Jasper walked inside, and then I heard the sound of the shower in the bathroom. I remained silent all the while. In the afternoon of the next day, I asked Vince what he found out and was disappointed to learn that Jasper was seen in the stables, tending to his favorite mare, Bonnie. Vince added that Jasper was brushing the mare with precision and care.

I knew at once that it wasn't a mistress but Bonnie who he had been visiting during midnight, and I couldn't help but wonder if all this time I had been competing against a horse for my husband's affections.

"Do you really think he just goes there to tend to the horses?" Vince asked me in a whisper.

"I don't know what to think," I said. "It is pretty clear he doesn't leave the property."

"I'll find out. If he is associating with a drug lord and hiding drugs in the forest to smuggle them out, I'll know. I'm going to get to the bottom of it."

"Just be careful, Vince."

CHAPTER THIRTY

It was decided that we were having dinner tonight in Lockhart's Legacy Hotel which was one of the many hotels owned by the family.

I threw on a simple off-white dress, the bodice decorated in beads while the skirt had pleats. It made my waist look trim and gave my look an elegant touch. I picked a matching *Dior* handbag to go with it, and since Vince had told me to avoid wearing high heels, I picked a pair of *Jimmy Choo* flat sandals.

The hotel was grand and opulent like a palace. We had a lot of dinners here, but each time was a different experience. Jasper sat beside me, Vince in the seat opposite ours, and Tyler wedged between Jasper and me.

Since the hotel was owned by the family, the services we received were obviously extraordinary. Jasper was digging into the chef's special steak. Vince glanced at me and back at Jasper, it was a clear indication that he wasn't comfortable with this family dinner.

I took a bite of the salad and pushed it down with a glass of white wine.

"Doesn't seem like either of you are enjoying my company," Jasper said, his expression unreadable.

"What would you like for dessert, Kiara?" Vince ignored Jasper like he was the air.

"What were you doing yesterday in the kitchen after midnight?" Jasper asked, analyzing me, waiting for me to speak.

My stomach lurched with that question. The fork in my hand dropped to the table with a clank. I didn't dare look at Jasper.

"You think I don't know what's been going around since last week?" Jasper asked in his icy voice. I looked up to see the brothers's gazes locked in a stare down.

"Excuse me?" Vince asked.

Jasper gritted his teeth and lifted an accusing finger towards Vince. "You have been fucking my wife behind my back."

"Jasper!" I covered Tyler's ears with my hands but it was too late.

Vince passed him the same angry look. "Trust me on this, brother. If I was having an affair with Kiara, you'd know about it, and you need to watch the way you talk to her."

Jasper forcefully pushed a plate aside which shattered to pieces. Vincent closed his eyes. People around us had stopped having their meals, their confused eyes fixed on us. I recognized their judgmental looks. I only hoped there weren't any reporters or the paparazzi sitting around here.

Jasper's jaw was working, his blue eyes blazing inferno. Vince began in a low voice, "People are looking at us, and you're creating a fucking scene. You wanna continue this conversation, let's take it home, because unlike you, I give a damn about my reputation, and I don't think I can allow a scandalous dinner night to be featured in a magazine and ruin it."

Jasper threw his napkin on the table and stormed out of the hotel without sparing us a glance. His stride was so angry that people automatically cleared out of his way.

The waiter approached us cautiously. He seemed worried. "Is everything alright, sir?"

"Yes, everything's fine." Vince sighed. "Please tell Joy that it was a lovely dinner."

*   *   *

262

The ride home in the car was silent. Jasper was in the passenger seat while Vince was driving the car. I was in the backseat with Tyler sleeping on my lap. He had been too tired, and I didn't want him awake for the drama waiting to unfold once we were back at the mansion.

When we reached home, neither of the men said a word, and Vince picked up Tyler in his arms and assured that he would put him to bed. I didn't miss the look of worry that crossed his eyes when we parted ways. I didn't pass him a pleading look because I didn't want Vince to worry about me and feel helpless about the situation.

I entered our bedroom to find Jasper looking out the balcony. I didn't know how to react, so I decided to avoid conversation at any cost. I opened a dresser drawer and began taking off my diamond earrings when I felt Jasper's presence behind me. I stiffened.

"You didn't answer my question." He shifted his gaze toward me from the mirror. "I asked you, what are you doing every night with Vincent in the kitchen?"

"We didn't do anything," I said.

"I have my sources, Kiara. I know what you're exactly doing. Sleeping with my brother. Have you no shame? How could you live with yourself knowing you're cheating on your husband?" Jasper asked in the calmest, most manipulative tone he had.

"You're being outrageous!"

He punched the oval mirror. The mirror cracked and his fist began to bleed.

"Your hand . . ."

"What did Vince tell you about Ava?" he asked.

I didn't understand how this was even connected to her.

Before I could answer, he said, "I'm sure he told you that it was me who compelled her to kill herself which is a goddamn lie!"

"What are you talking about?"

263

"He stole Ava from me!" Jasper shrieked. "He did every fucking thing with her that he is doing with you right now, and when it didn't work out, he pushed her from the balcony."

Suddenly, Jasper's eyes softened. He closed the distance and pulled me towards him. "Listen to me, precious. Vince is not a good man. He is not interested in you. All he wants to do is ruin my life, he wants this company, this house, the inheritance. He is just using you like a little pawn in his game. He is breaking *our* family."

"This family is already broken," I admitted and saw the clear confusion in his eyes. "I wanted to help you get better, but one can't force a person to mend their ways if he doesn't wish to. I lost all hope in keeping this family together the day you raised your hand on me."

"What do you want from me, Kiara?"

Was he genuinely asking what I wanted, or was this a trick question? Regardless, I decided to be honest.

"If you refuse to go for treatment then I want to separate."

That was the last straw. His stare became hard. "You will go against me?"

"If that means protecting my son from you."

In two easy strides he closed the distance between us and caught my jaw in a death grip. "Listen to me very carefully, Kiara, because I won't repeat myself. You can beg from me, run from me, hide in any corner of this planet, but I will move heaven and earth to bring you back. That's how much I want you."

"You can't stop me from leaving," I said, trying to wiggle out of his grip on my jaw.

"Why don't you try?" Jasper said in a challenging tone. "You killed your father. I knew it was by accident, but I have the resources to make it look like you did it on purpose, and then there will be a trial."

"No one will believe what happened four years ago. I don't think you even have proof," I pointed out.

"You think I'm bluffing?" he asked and picked up his iPhone. "I'll make just one call, and we'll see how much of that really is just a bluff. You see sweetheart, when you have a lot of money, everything in this world ceases to be impossible. Money can buy silence, and may as well start a storm."

I was utterly speechless. He was threatening me. "I'll also tell them how unfaithful my wife is. Everyone suspects you were a 'nobody' before you married me. I'll just prove their suspicions correct and then it wouldn't be hard for people to believe that you are a gold digger who jumped from one rich brother to another for personal gains, and if let's say, you managed to file a divorce, I will see to it that my son remains with me."

I had lost the battle. If I thought I had any fighting spirit remaining inside me, it died the minute he mentioned Tyler. My chest tightened with dread. Jasper knew how much I doted on our son. He knew I couldn't live without him, and he was using my weakness against me.

I slumped back on the bed knowing he was right and had me where he wanted me to be. I was helpless and under his reigns. I didn't say a word, neither did I scream nor beg like I wanted to because it was obvious that once Jasper made his mind, there was no turning back.

He would ruin me with a bat of an eye.

I felt his fingers linger on my neck. In a swift move, he unclipped my hair and his warm lips touched my shoulder blade. He pulled my hair, and I heard the sound of the zipper as he peeled the dress off my body with ease.

I knew what was going to follow. Jasper locked his mouth over mine in a hard kiss, one that wasn't slow but displayed possession. This was undoubtedly his way of showing me that he owned me. His gaze was burning with desire as he wasted no time getting undressed and climbing on the bed.

I lay exposed on the bed. In a different circumstance, I would have walked out of the room even before he had time to get

265

me out of my clothes, but the dangerous expression he sported told me I was better off letting him have his way. I didn't want to think what he would do to me if I denied him. He told me I had already seen the real him but not the worst side of his behavior yet, and it scared me to think how worse he could be when he completely let the mask slip off.

I stared into the dilated icy blue eyes watching me intently. His chest was rising and falling. It was unfair for a man like him to have such a perfect body. He hooked his finger into my panties and I heard the sound of it tearing. He was acting really primitive, and I realized it was because he suspected something was going on between me and Vincent.

My ability to think was momentarily paused when his tongue did delicious things to my nipple. I whimpered until I felt a sharp pain and realized he bit a little too aggressively.

"Jasper, you're hurting me," I complained.

"I just got started," he whispered.

"Stop it."

Jasper caught a fistful of my hair and brought his mouth crashing down to mine, kissing me so hard that I could hardly breathe. I tried to push him back but his body pressed against mine. When he pulled away, my lips felt swollen.

"Turn and lie on your stomach," he commanded. He didn't wait for me to move, and he flipped me over himself. "Bend your knees and spread your legs wide."

I did as I was told, keeping my hands on the side. "Wider," he said in a hoarse voice.

His fingers traced my folds and I cried in a mixture of frustration and ecstasy. I heard him chuckle. "You demand a divorce from me and yet you're dripping wet. Why, Kiara, you're just a glutton for punishment."

I tried to sit up but he pushed me down. His fingers grasped my skull and pushed it on the mattress. He wasn't slow, and neither did he care about my needs. He was rough as he thrusted inside me and withdrew, and continued to plunge in and out until I heard him say my name amidst heavy breathing, "Kiara . . ."

When he pulled out, I instantly felt the loss. Shame washed over me because I was glutton for punishment. One look from Jasper with his silky voice whispering dirty things into my ear, and I was a puddle on the floor. I deserved this treatment because I had let him walk over me time and time again.

He climbed out of bed and walked into the bathroom, leaving me feeling used, and that was exactly what he wanted to do. He wanted to break me if I denied him, and he had been waiting for one word of denial to tumble out of my mouth, but I wasn't giving him that.

Minutes later, he walked out, pulled a casual t-shirt over his head, and slipped into a pair of jeans. He raked his hand through his messy hair, looking like a runway model.

"Are you going somewhere?" I asked, half expecting him to ignore me.

"Need to reply to some emails," he answered.

Yeah. Right.

I clenched my hands into fists in the comforter. "Are you having an affair, Jasper?"

He paused at the doorway and turned to me. His expression did not change; it was still blank and unreadable as always.

"Where do you run off to in the middle of the night?" I pressed.

"Duty calls. I have a billion-dollar corporation to take care of, and I shoulder the responsibility of keeping thousands of employees and their families fed. In case you're still not aware, I'm a company CEO, Kiara, and in order for me to give you the life that you're living right now, I have to make sacrifices even if it means leaving my naked wife in bed at . . ."—a quick glance at his wrist watch—". . . 1:30 AM I don't expect you to understand, but

267

accept it. This is my life, and that's how it had always been and will continue to be."

"I never asked for a lavish lifestyle, for these expensive cars or gifts. I would never complain if we had to move into a smaller house and live a normal life like other people."

"You fancy a house with a leak on the roof? How about an unkempt lawn and the almost falling-down-from-its-hinges house gates? Not to mention, the curtains made of old blankets. Do you like that better?"

My face was blazing hot. He was taking a jibe at my previous living conditions, specifically the house I used to live in before I became Kiara Lockhart.

"You don't have to be so vulgar. All I'm saying is that I wouldn't care if we weren't so wealthy."

"But I do," Jasper said. "And that should be enough to close this topic for any further discussions. As for your allegations over my character, I can assure you that I'm not having any affair. If I did, I wouldn't have been tearing your clothes a while ago. You have what I need, and that closes doors for allegations about me cheating. Although, just a little warning, if I found you going behind my back and fucking other men in my absence, I won't be happy at the slightest."

With that, he slammed the door shut behind him.

CHAPTER THIRTY-ONE

After that day, Vince and I maintained some distance and stopped meeting at night for chats because he had gotten busy with his work at the hospital, plus he also wanted to prove to Jasper that we didn't have anything between us.

We occasionally took lunch and dinners at the table as a family, but that was about it. Jasper's distaste for his brother was pretty apparent.

One night, I woke up to the sound of soft shuffles. When I opened my eyes, I saw the housekeepers packing a suitcase. Confused, I looked at the wall clock. The time was 4 AM. My hand traveled to Jasper's side of the bed and came up empty. I watched as the maids began pulling my clothes from the closet without my permission and packed it neatly into the suitcase.

"What are you doing?" I asked her. "And don't you know how to knock? How can you just barge into my bedroom like that?"

The other girl zipped up another suitcase which consisted of Jasper's clothes and began handing it over to Morgan who took the suitcase and disappeared out of the room.

"I asked you a question. Why are you packing my things without my permission?"

"I'm sorry Ma'am, but those are Mr. Lockhart's orders," Lola said softly before she bowed and resumed her packing.

None of them were even interested to find out if I wanted to have my things packed. It was like they were programmed by Jasper to only follow his instructions.

I climbed out of bed, fixed my hair, and whipped up a silk robe over my body before making my way out of the room and down the dark stairs, only to find Jasper talking to Morgan. It was actually more of Jasper dissing out instructions and Morgan nodding his head to Jasper's every word. Tyler was asleep in Jasper's arms.

I rushed towards them. I needed to know what was going on in the middle of the night. What was so important that he was having the maids pack my clothes? When Morgan noticed me approaching them, he whispered something to Jasper, bowed, and excused himself.

"What's going on? Why are they packing my stuff?"

Jasper turned to face me. "Because we are leaving."

I thought I hadn't heard him properly. "What do you mean? Where are we going?"

"We are moving to our old mansion in Lockhart's Island."

"Why?"

For some reason, Jasper seemed like he didn't want to explain to me in detail, and I hated that. "If Vince wants this house, he can have it, but I don't want us to live under the same roof as him."

"I'm not going anywhere," I said softly.

Jasper stared at me in his usual cold, challenging way. "What did you just say?"

"I said I won't go anywhere," I repeated, pulling Tyler into my arms. "And Tyler isn't going anywhere either."

I started walking away from him, towards the stairs, but Jasper grabbed my arm forcefully and that woke Tyler up. The child began wailing. I pulled away from his tight grasp, placed Tyler down on his feet, and instructed him to run back to his bedroom upstairs. He didn't need to be a part of our daily fights.

270

"Tyler go to your room," I instructed him.

But Tyler remained glued on the spot, hugging his stuffed teddy to his chest. His thumb was in his mouth, sucking the life out of it.

"Tyler!"

I could see Jasper's jaw working, and his gaze turning darker by the second. Calmly, he asked, "Why can't you go with me?"

"Because I've had enough of your lies. This is my home, and I will stay here." I threw his words back in his face.

Jasper chuckled, his tone sardonic. "Is that Vincent talking? What are you? His newest puppet? Do you think I don't notice how you communicate with your eyes at the table, or make subtle conversations while my back is turned?"

I thought I was going to melt under his stare. I folded my arms over my chest, feeling the fire blaze in his eyes, the anger fuming inside him. Tyler had crawled his way beneath a table in the corner and watched us silently.

My poor little boy.

"You know what?" Jasper said. "I don't care anymore. You wanna live here with Vince? That's fine."

Soon after, Jasper powerwalked towards where Tyler was hiding under the table and picked him up in his arms almost too aggressively, forcefully. "But my boy comes with me."

Tyler screamed loudly, his shriek pierced through the silence. His tiny hands reaching out towards me. "Mommy . . . I wanna go to Mommy."

Jasper was walking out of the door. He was going to put Tyler in the backseat of the car. He was going to take Tyler away, maybe even send me the divorce papers and take sole custody of my child. Jasper had enough power to put me in a position where I wouldn't ever see Tyler's face my entire life.

The thoughts that clouded my mind made me hysterical, and I grabbed for a knife from the dining area and stalked after

271

him, pointing my knife at Jasper's back. One jab and it would slice through the fabric and into his skin.

"Hand over Tyler to me Jasper or something really bad is going to happen." My hands were trembling. I tried to hold the knife steadily. "Do not test me!"

"So now you're gonna kill me?" Jasper asked, sneering. Calmly, he continued, "Think about it Kiara. Killing me will get you nothing. You'll only help Vincent with his plan, and once he has what he always wanted, he'll toss you away faster than you can imagine. And when they start investigating, the truth about your father's murder is going to spill out, and you know what happens after that."

My grip on the knife loosened as I realized he was right.

"Let Tyler go."

"What's going on?" Vince strode into the room through the main entrance. He was dressed in scrubs looking tired from his shift. His eyes rested on the knife in my hand. "Kiara, what are you doing?"

"He can't take Tyler away from me," I said.

Vince's gaze shifted towards the luggage being loaded in the car trunk. He looked at me and then at Jasper. "Where are you going?"

"Moving," Jasper corrected him. "We are moving into our old mansion in Lockhart's Island. You can have this house." He rummaged a pair of keys and handed it to Vince.

Vince stared at the keys and laughed. "Oh, I get it. So now you're going to take your family and leave in the middle of the night so that you can make a statement for the tabloids that I fucking threw you out. That's smart."

"You've got a sick twisted mind," Jasper said.

"You're one to talk," Vince retorted. "I wish I had the patience or the energy to stand here and talk until morning, but I don't, so I have another solution."

"You're more likely to create problems, Vincent. It's unusual for you to come up with solutions."

"I hope you had your fill of sardonic comments for the day. I was going to say that Kiara doesn't have to go anywhere, and neither will Tyler or you," Vince said and then turned to Morgan. "Morgan, pull the bags out of the trunk."

"Morgan, don't," Jasper ordered.

Morgan looked at Jasper and then at Vince, probably having an inner battle about which master to listen to. I didn't blame him for feeling intimidated. "Sir, I . . ."

"Morgan, do as I say. Bring their luggage back into the house."

When Morgan stood there staring like a mannequin, Vince took my hand and placed the keys of the mansion in my palm as he disappeared up the stairs. Ten minutes later, Vince was making his way downstairs, holding a suitcase.

He placed it down on the floor and commanded Morgan to load it in his Jaguar.

I was confused. *What was going on?*

Vince was dressed in casual denim over a clean shirt. "I'll move into the old mansion."

Jasper smirked.

What? Vince couldn't do that to us.

I stepped towards him. "Vince, you don't need to go anywhere. This is your home as much as it's Jasper's."

"Kiara," Jasper warned me.

I pleaded him with my eyes and whispered, "Please don't leave us. Tyler and I need you." I sounded so weak.

He brought his lips close to my ear. "I'm sorry, Kiara, but this is the only way."

Tyler made a dash towards Vince and hugged his legs. "Please don't go, Uncle Vince."

Vince kneeled down to Tyler's level. "I'll come see you soon, Ty."

Tyler was already in tears when he looked at his father. "Daddy, please don't let Uncle Vince go."

Jasper sighed and walked away like he didn't want to argue further. Vince looked at the knife that I was still holding in my hand. "Don't do anything stupid."

"I won't," I assured him. "It's late. You can leave tomorrow morning."

Vince pulled me in a hug. I wrapped my arms around him and managed to soak the front of his shirt with my tears. He took my face in his hands and said, "I'm not abandoning you guys. You just have to wait for my signal. Until then, I want you to be strong. Can you do that for me?"

I nodded. "I don't have any other choice."

"I will keep you and Tyler safe, I promise," Vince said, and the way he held us both close, the warmth of his hug, made me trust his words.

He slipped a crumbled piece of paper into my fingers. "This is another one of my numbers that Jasper isn't aware of. Do not hesitate to call me at any hour and try not to make him angry."

I watched as Vince slid into the driver's side of his Jaguar and turned on the engine. Tyler and I waited until we saw the car disappear through the gates.

This was the second time I had watched Vince leave. This time, it was even worse because I realized how alone I was.

All alone with a psychotic husband.

CHAPTER THIRTY-TWO

It was already a week since I last saw or heard from Vincent, and I was starting to wonder if I was going to lose that one friend.

With time, I had completely lost touch with my old girlfriends, mostly Kathy. The last time I remembered talking to her was a few months back and then she stopped replying to my texts. I wondered if it was because she really thought I was a pompous rich bitch. The only occasional friends I hung out with were Cecilia and Penny who pretended to be happy with their abusive and cheating partners. Then again, I didn't have a right to judge their lives when mine wasn't perfect either.

"Mrs. Lockhart."

Ms. Jones called out to me. For a minute, I had totally forgotten that I was here for a Parent-Teacher meeting. Morgan had gotten a call from the teacher, and had been kind enough to pass on the message. The teacher had something to tell me about Tyler.

Her well-manicured nails pulled out a paper and placed it on top of the desk. Ms. Jones's eyes inspected me. "Mrs. Lockhart, I don't mean to pry into your personal life but when it concerns one of my students, I have to step in."

"I understand." I nodded, my fingers knotting and unknotting in my lap. "Did Tyler do something?"

I was feeling nervous about what the teacher might tell me about Tyler. What if she said that Tyler was violent around other children? What if he was becoming like Jasper? I couldn't fathom the thought of Tyler doing something like that.

"Tyler isn't sociable in class, doesn't answer questions, and mostly likes to keep to himself. It's a little disturbing to see him behave like that, Mrs. Lockhart, and I have a reason to believe that it's due to some issues at home."

I hated how Ms. Jones was analyzing me, like she could uncover all the stories in our family by looking into my eyes. "I will talk to Tyler about this."

"I was expecting Mr. Lockhart to be here too so we could discuss this together."

She wasn't going to let this slide so easily.

"My husband has been caught up with some important work so it's just going to be me."

"Oh, that's alright. I can wait." She smiled in understanding.

I tried to come up with a better excuse, deciding to pretend a fake call to Jasper, asking him where he is and then lying to Ms. Jones that Jasper wasn't going to make it. Before I could do that, a tall figure walked inside the room.

It was Vincent. I was shocked to see him here. He was dressed to impress, as usual. The Lockharts seemed to have a gift where style and looks were concerned. He wore a gray suit and a white shirt underneath. His hair was neatly combed.

"Sorry I'm late. There was an important meeting," Vince told me and then turned to the gaping teacher and offered her a handshake which she accepted.

The teacher had apparently lost her ability of speech. I couldn't blame her. Vince could have that effect on people, especially women.

"It's good to have you, Mr. Lockhart. I'm Patricia Jones, Tyler's teacher." Ms. Jones said. "It's about your son."

"Oh, I'm not his father. I'm Tyler's uncle."

Ms. Jones shrugged. "I see."

"Well, I'm afraid Jasper can't make it and he sent me here in place of him," Vince clarified, and his expression suddenly turned sad. "You know, sometimes his illness doesn't allow him."

Ms. Jones appeared confused, and I knew my expression matched hers. What was Vince talking about?

"I'm sorry. I wasn't aware he had an illness."

Vince sighed and glanced at me. "You never told the teacher, Kiara?"

"No," I said. Vince would be crazy to tell the teacher that Jasper was diagnosed with psychopathy.

"Jasper goes through certain mood swings and his depression is getting worse. I would really appreciate if this remained between us Ms. Jones."

"Of course, Mr. Lockhart. Maybe that would explain why the child is usually very quiet and unsocial," Ms. Jones said who seemed to be throwing me looks of sympathy. She placed her hand on mine. "I'm so sorry, Mrs. Lockhart. I wasn't aware of your husband's condition."

I remained silent, wondering why Vince had told the teacher lies.

*   *   *

Vince and I silently walked out of the school hallway. I was struggling to keep up with his long strides. It had started raining heavily outside. We made a dash towards my car and without speaking a word, I slipped behind the wheel while he took the passenger side seat. It was pouring hard by now, and the rain pelted against the windshield with a vengeance, making it difficult to see outside. The wipers swiped violently.

"Believe it or not, I actually got a call from Tyler. He wanted me to see his teacher with you."

"Thanks for the save. It was very nice of you to come to the meeting, Vince," I said. "Tyler really likes you a lot."

Vince smiled. "And what about you?"

I knew he was only teasing me, but I couldn't miss the undertone to the question.

I felt his long elegant fingers coil around mine, I looked up at him and he smiled like he knew how I felt. His arm reached out towards me and tucked the loose hair behind my ear, his fingers caressing my cheek and then he began frantically searching through the car and found something attached beneath his seat. It was hidden away from sight.

Vince placed a finger to his lips, retrieved his phone and typed something. Seconds later, he showed me a message he had typed in his Notes.

Your car is bugged with audio surveillance.

I stared at the message, shocked. He typed more.

There's a car parked at a distance. A black Cadillac. It has been following me since I was back in town.

I looked through the rearview mirror and spotted a black car at a distance parked idly by a tree.

He typed.

I think Jasper is keeping tabs on you while keeping an eye on me, too. He suspects us.

Vince passed me a devilish grin and typed.

He thinks he's really smart. Guess he forgot we share the same blood.

I couldn't help but smile.

"You didn't answer my question," Vince said, louder than necessary. "Did you miss me while I was away?"

"I did," I admitted softly.

He stared at me for what felt like forever. "Can I make a confession?"

I nodded.

"When I was away at medical school, I often wondered where you were, what you were doing, and I wished I was the one who first met you that day in the alley instead of Jasper. I wish I was the one who saved you from the bad guys, Kiara. You have no idea how painful it was to watch you with him." He clenched his hands into tight fists. "I just began to accept that it's life. After everything that you've been through, I'm glad I can be here for you now."

"Oh, Vincent. That's the sweetest thing anyone has ever said to me," I said, almost feeling the tears form in my eyes. "If you had met me on that day in the alley, wouldn't our story be different?"

His brown eyes twinkled. "It's not too late for that. I want you to know something else. Something that I had kept buried deep inside me because I was afraid to say it."

"What is it?"

"I love you, Kiara," Vincent said, and I knew then that the acting had been a disguise. He was conveying his true feelings.

I covered my face with my hands in ~~mock~~ shame, shaking my head. "I'm sorry, Vincent. I can't . . . I can't return your feelings. I'm a married woman, and I have a son. No matter how bad Jasper is, he is still my husband. No matter how badly he treats me, I cannot cheat on him."

He shook his head. "I didn't tell you I love you because I expected you to love me back. Some relationships are complicated, and I've come to accept the fact that you will always love Jasper, and I can't ever force you to fall in love with his brother."

"Vincent . . ."

He sneaked a glance at the car. I followed his gaze and saw as it rolled forward. They were trying to get a better view of us and then the car zoomed past us. Vince and I both saw it turn the corner. It was the same black *Cadillac*. Whoever had been watching us was going to report to Jasper what just transpired.

With Jasper, I knew I had to expect the unexpected. I could never figure out what was going on in his head, but with Vincent, I felt safe. He was someone I could trust. Vincent was my friend.

They were brothers, and yet they had so many differences. While Jasper was stern, charming in ways; Vince was warm, kind and giving. The new information about Vincent having feelings for me didn't change how I saw him.

He looked around, leaned in, and pecked my lips which actually took me by surprise. There was a mischievous glint in his eyes. "Let's keep that our little secret."

He caught my wrist and traced circles over it, "There is something else."

"What is it?"

"You're pregnant."

I was stunned to hear him say that. I was quite happy to hear that at first until I had a reality check. "Another baby. This is not a good life for a child Vince." I looked at my open palm. My hands were trembling.

"If it comes down to the worst, I'll provide for you, Kiara. I'll protect both your children and you."

CHAPTER THIRTY-THREE

"Eight . . . nine . . . and ten. Here I come," I declared as I pulled off the blindfold.

I could hear Tyler's giggle as I tiptoed in the general direction of his voice. Tyler and I played these little games in the evening when Jasper was busy in his study or traveling out of the country.

I walked into the paddock where Tyler normally hid. The property was so large that there was a possibility for anyone to lose track of time and forget their way back to the mansion. Tyler had been lost once or twice when he wandered out of the mansion unsupervised. I hadn't been worried for approximately two hours, thinking he was just looking at the horses or playing with his imaginary friends. After eight hours, I panicked and the house staff was frantically searching every corner of the property, looking for the child. Finally, ten hours later, a maid found Tyler in the attic, matted in dirt and asleep.

After that incident and a few others following that, Jasper had been firm in telling Tyler that he was not to wander around the property unsupervised. Jasper had an authoritative impact over Tyler. He was a loving father, yet he knew when Tyler needed some grilling to keep the boy in order.

I walked towards the stables, all the horses stood tall and handsome, freshly groomed. Next, I checked the shed.

"Tyler," I called out.

I had warned him to stay out of the woods, but I suspected he still wandered there, being the rule breaker that he was. I decided to first check the old barn which remained abandoned. It was a good walk away from the mansion and the courtyard. The lock of the barn was open, so there was a possibility that Tyler was being a smartass and hid inside.

I touched the wooden door and pushed it ajar.

"Kiara." I stopped and spun around on my heel to see Jasper standing a few feet away from me, Tyler in his arms.

"You're back from your trip," I said.

"I wanted to spend more time with my family, and I got Tyler and you some gifts from India," he announced.

"Gifts!" Tyler exclaimed. I was one hundred and one percent sure he had forgotten we were playing a game of hide and seek.

"I went inside the house and the maid told me that you and Tyler were playing in the courtyard. I found this little troublemaker hiding in the old garage." Jasper passed me an accusing look as if Tyler hiding in the garage was my fault.

"Well, then we need a smaller house, one that doesn't include a huge courtyard, stables, a barn and a forest. Tyler is a child, and he likes exploring. How can I confine—"

"You know that family, the Wilson's. Their son used to do the exact same thing—running away from the mansion, hiding in places people can't find him, and do you remember what became of him?" Jasper whispered to me. "His body was found later, floating in the lake waters, purple and bloated, completely unrecognizable."

"Stop it, Jasper!" I said. "I knew the direction he had walked in, and there was a maid here keeping an eye on us. Besides, I'm not stupid."

"Tyler, go inside the house and open your gifts while Mommy and Daddy talk here for a while," I suggested.

"Okay," he said and started walking towards the maid standing at a distance.

Before he could walk away, I pulled out a small device stuck in Tyler's shirt pocket. I showed Jasper my phone. "I had a GPS device attached to him. No matter where Tyler hides, I'd know where to find him. I had to pretend to waste some time before I went into the garage."

Jasper appeared bored, because I nailed it. He didn't have a reason to display his ideals and lecture me about parenting when he wasn't doing a good job himself.

*   *   *

That night, surprisingly, Jasper went to bed on time after dinner. I had watched the clock, and it was at eleven-thirty sharp. I had pretended to fall asleep, but I was awake. I needed to find out what Jasper was up to and why he woke up during the wee hours.

What if the barn was the place where he kept his meth? Maybe it was a secret meth lab like the one *Walter White* had in *Breaking Bad?*

Knowing Jasper, I wouldn't be surprised if he was associated with something dangerous like a mafia syndicate or a drug lord. I was hoping he wasn't. He had connections worldwide, from Royal families to politicians and celebrities, down to the most ruthless people in the underworld.

Sometime in the middle of the night, I felt a weight lifted off from the bed. I didn't budge, didn't even move, and just laid there pretending to be asleep. I waited a few minutes after I heard the door close and the footsteps retreat. I sat up and didn't bother to switch on the lights as I looked out of the window.

I watched as Jasper walked through the courtyard and disappeared.

If that wasn't fishy, I didn't know what was. I quickly pulled on my robe and slipped on a pair of outside shoes. I slipped out of the room, closing it slowly behind me.

I made my way out of the house using the back door of the kitchen. The one good thing about the mansion was the amount of doors leading to the outside. I was still pretty sure I hadn't explored some of the rooms yet. I wasn't really one to feel scared easily, but I had always avoided walking out alone in the mansion grounds in the middle of the night. I could hear the distant howls of the night creatures, but I willed myself to walk forward, heart in my throat. The mansion was a huge intimidating property, and looked almost gothic at night, surrounded by mountains and a forest.

Suddenly, someone grasped my arm, and before I could make a sound, the hand was clamped over my mouth. The person pulled me into a corner. I turned to see who it was, expecting to see Jasper catching me red-handed following him.

It was Vincent.

"Vince, what are you doing here?" I asked in a hushed whisper.

"Same thing you are. I saw my brother walk towards the woods, and I was waiting here for two hours now to see if he would come out tonight and then I saw you," he explained. "If he realizes someone is on his tail, its game over. We need to be careful. I'm going to find out what illegal business he has been keeping from us. You head back to the mansion."

I caught the end of his shirt. "I'm coming with you. I'm his wife and I deserve to know."

A moment of hesitation crossed him. "Fine." Vince sighed. "But only on one condition: If I tell you to duck, run or hide, you will do it, no questions asked."

"Agreed"

Vince nodded. He knew he couldn't protest with me when I was hell-bent on finding out what was going on.

We stayed hidden behind some bushes and waited. A few minutes later, we saw Jasper walk into the car garage, open the trunk of his SUV, and dump something inside. He was at a distance, so we couldn't see. Next, he walked to the driver's side and stopped. He literally turned to face in the direction we were hiding in. I clammed my mouth shut to stop from making any sound. He was looking straight at me, and I thought I was caught, but then he climbed into his car and drove away.

A few minutes later, Vince signaled me that it was safe to come out of hiding. Vince and I walked side by side, making sure we weren't in anyone's line of vision. If Jasper was being smart and recording surveillance footage, he wouldn't see us because Vince and I both knew where all the cameras were installed and were good at dodging them.

Muddy footsteps led towards the huge red barn. My heartbeat was accelerating as I walked further.

Would I find women kept there to satisfy Jasper's sick desires or something more sinister? I had always stayed away from the barn because it was a little far from the mansion, and there were stories the maids weaved that it was the place where Jasper's aunt had been murdered and his grandmother had committed suicide. Upon a closer look, the barn itself was old, unused, and locked.

"Don't make a sound," Vince whispered. "And watch your step. We're going inside."

Slowly, Vince walked towards the barn and opened the wooden door which made a loud creaking sound. I grasped his hand, our fingers interlocked as we walked inside. The barn was large and it was pitch black inside. We could hear our own breathing and the soft crunches of our shoes on the ground. As we walked further, Vincent pulled out his phone and switched on the torchlight.

He moved the light in all four directions, finding the area empty. I scanned around, partly expecting to see a ghost attacking us from the high ceiling above.

Vincent tapped his foot on the barn door, and he threw me a suspicious look. "There's a basement downstairs." He found a tiny hook that he slid his finger into and pulled it open. "You stay here, and I will go down."

I hugged myself. This place was giving me the chills. "I can't stay here alone. I'm coming down with you."

Vincent closed his eyes and sighed. "Alright, but make no sound and stay close beside me."

I gave him a nod. Vince tested a step and slowly descended. The stairs were dusty and rickety, the creaking noise of old wood was eerie. I was debating telling Vince that this was a bad idea and that we should head back into the mansion but it was like we couldn't stop ourselves until we had investigated the depths of this situation. This was maybe our only chance, considering that Jasper had already drove out of the property.

As we stepped on the ground, a stench permeated the air, a very strong odor that I knew I wouldn't forget for a long time even if I wanted to.

"What's that smell?" I whispered to Vince.

"I think it's a dead animal."

Vince brought the phone torch higher, and I screamed when I witnessed the horror that neither of us knew we would see down here. No sound came because my ear-piercing scream was muffled by Vince's hand covering my mouth.

Vince stood frozen beside me, probably too shocked for words.

"What have you done, brother?" he whispered to himself in an anguished voice.

There were countless bodies neatly piled, wrapped in plastic that was stained in blood. Some bodies were hanging against the basement ceiling. The disturbing sound of a swarm of flies buzzed around the area, some feasting over the rotting meat.

Vince took a step forward, then another. I stopped him with a shaky hand on his shoulder.

"Don't, Vincent!" I choked.

"Shhh . . ." He politely shrugged off my hold over him and walked further, throwing the light over each body. I could see the

286

perspiration forming on his forehead, his eyes darting around in horror.

In the midst of the hanging and the piled bodies, Vincent stood there, staring blankly at them. He spun around to face me. In a low voice he said, "Kiara, I need you to come here and identify the bodies."

I tried to say something, but fear had seeped so deep in my bones that my voice felt clogged.

"I . . . I can't," I faltered.

In few easy strides, he was right beside me, his hands holding me steady before I crumpled down on the ground. "You have to be stronger! For yourself and for Tyler! There are probably a dozen of innocent people that Jasper has killed. You've been with him for four years. You could recognize some faces."

I slowly walked into the mess. It looked like a meat farm. Some of the bodies were intact, while others were chopped in half with innards hanging out in the open. I swallowed the bile rising up in my throat.

How could my husband be so despicable?

He killed people so brutally, and for what purpose?

The smell of the decomposing bodies grew stronger as I stood there to look. Vincent pointed at a body in plastic. The woman had an oval-shaped face, similar to my own. Her hair was black, but could be mistaken for dark coffee. What could've been her eyes were now hollows of darkness. The similarities between her and me were jarringly obvious, and I wondered if Vince had noticed too. The woman's arms bore gashes that could've been carved with a sharp blade. Vince quickly took pictures in his phone.

I shook my head. "I don't know her."

He picked a note from the body that read.

Kiara needs punishing for her disobedience.

Vince and I exchanged looks. Both of us had the same thought in our minds.

Did he punish and kill an innocent woman because he couldn't hurt me?

There were black trash bags at the far corner of the room. Vince walked towards it and opened the bags with a pocket knife. There were more decomposed bodies, some with faces so disfigured that it was beyond recognition like Jasper had stabbed their faces multiple times in what appeared to be pure hatred.

I passed other bodies, two women and a man. At the end of the line, I thought I saw a shadow of someone I knew. The figure was so familiar, I rushed forward to have a look, and my hand flew to my mouth. The curly red hair was framing a heart-shaped face. Her green eyes that were so radiant and full of life stared forward lifelessly, her mouth partly open.

Kathy.

I didn't miss how her lips were smeared in an ugly shade of lipstick as if it hadn't been applied by her, but by *someone else*. A small parchment of paper was taped on her head. I pulled it out to read.

'A very bad influence on my wife.'

Kathy's body wasn't old and rotting like the few others, so that meant Jasper had killed her recently. She hadn't responded to my texts, not because she didn't want to, but because she had been dead all along.

A male body was right beside Kathy, but unlike Kathy's, this body was decaying. Maggots crawled out from his open mouth and traveled to the empty eye socket. There was another note stuck on his head in Jasper's beautiful cursive handwriting that I had once envied.

Womanizer and rapist. Swindles wealth from married, rich women. Scumbag.

"Nasty son of a bitch," Vince said.

CHAPTER THIRTY-FOUR

Vince pulled me away from the sight. Even though he was strong and hadn't been repulsed so far, his hand on my arm was slightly shaking. It had to be a shock for him as much as it was for me. Jasper was a pure psychopath.

"Notice how Jasper takes good care of his punctuation," I pointed out to Vince before an erupting sob gave way to a giggle until I was laughing in the dead silence. Vince threw me a quick look filled with concern and maybe some pity for the wife of a *serial killer.*

Yes, I was losing my goddamn mind.

Vince cupped my face and forced me to make eye contact as I laughed hysterically. "Kiara, snap out of it!"

And then the laughter stopped, beginning to give way to fresh tears, and I sobbed.

"It's funny, isn't it? Jasper's been killing people all these years, and I hadn't a clue. If I had just walked into the barn and checked . . ." I rubbed my temples. "So many people wouldn't have died."

Vince's eyes darted towards the staircase and back to me. "Kiara, you have to tell me who these bodies belong to, alright?"

"Okay," I agreed.

When we walked out of the barn, I threw up my dinner. I was silent on our way back inside the mansion. Vince broke the silence when he asked me to identify some of the bodies.

"Kathy and Michael. Kathy was my friend, and Michael was the man who accompanied her boyfriend during lunch one weekend. He was a pushy man, and tried to offer his services . . ." I trailed off, but Vince encouraged me to go on. "He offered his services if I was lonely and needed someone when Jasper wasn't in town. When I came home, it appeared that the car keys were bugged by audio surveillance and all our conversations during that lunch were recorded." I closed my eyes as I remembered how calm Jasper had been through everything and then how he had disappeared that night, saying he had pending work.

They were all lies. His pending work involved capturing people he had grudges against and then killing them. We made endless love on nights and then instead of lying with me in bed, he'd scramble off into his office, making excuses. Each and every time, Jasper had looked me in the eye and lied to my face.

"I'm so scared for Tyler. Dear God, what am I going to do?!"

"Listen to me very carefully. I will not let him hurt you or Tyler. It's my promise, and I'm going to take down Jasper even if it costs my life," Vincent said with such conviction that I believed him. "He will not walk out of this. He's my brother, but he's also a monster." I saw Vince opened and closed his palm, and for the first time, I saw his eyes become moist.

"I will report this to the police," Vince assured me. "Jasper's not back yet, but he may soon. We can't wait much longer and risk him getting rid of the bodies. I captured enough evidence in my phone, so I'm going to report this to the police. Until then, I want you to run upstairs, pack your stuff, and wake Tyler up. We are leaving."

Vince's expression had turned hard. He was a man determined to take care of the situation, even if his own brother had committed a grave sin. He produced a pistol from his waistband and handed it over to me. "Do you know how to use guns?"

I shook my head. Vince gave me a short demonstration of the 9mm pistol. "It's loaded. Use it if you have to, Kiara."

I took the pistol from him. "What if Jasper uses his influence to get away? He will ruin us."

"He won't, because if everything fails, I will not hesitate to put a bullet in his head myself."

*   *   *

We had to move quickly before Jasper came back home. I quickly changed into a pair of jeans and threw on a basic t-shirt and then I opened a duffle bag to stuff whatever clothes I could find along with some cash.

I then went into Tyler's room and woke him up. He whined like any other kid who was disturbed into waking up at the odd hours of predawn.

"Mommy, where are we going?" he asked me while he rubbed his eyes.

"Honey . . ."

And then I heard the sound of shuffling and footsteps. My heart began beating faster. "Tyler, sweetheart, go and hide under the bed. Do not come out until I tell you to. If I don't come back in ten minutes, call nine-one-one."

I saw Tyler's expressions turn wary, his sleep seemingly lost, "What's happening, Mommy?"

I kissed the top of his head. "You know how to do this, Tyler. You're a strong boy, and I love you."

Understanding dawned on him. It was like Tyler knew it was going to come down to this. He was stronger than most four-year-olds. He picked up the phone and crawled beneath the bed. I closed the bedroom door, gun raised in my hand. I walked into the passage. The lights went out all of a sudden. I raised the gun and kept walking.

I used my phone torch to see where I was going, and started descending the stairs. It happened too fast. Before I could feel the presence behind me, I felt something knock against my head.

I vaguely realized that my body was carried in a pair of strong arms, and I couldn't find my voice to scream or ask for help.

I mumbled, "Tyler . . ."

"Hush, my love. You're going to be fine."

The voice was sweet like a melody.

It was Jasper.

CHAPTER THIRTY-FIVE

My throat felt dry like I had been living in a desert without a drop of water in my system. My head seemed like it weighed tons. My arms hurt, and I realized I could no longer move them.

What was happening to me?

My eyelids felt heavy but I managed to open them slowly to find myself in a dark room. Then it all came back to me—flashes of me telling Tyler to hide under the bed, and then walking out into the darkened hallways of the mansion only to be struck on the head into an unconscious state.

How long had I been out?

I looked around myself. I had no doubt about where I was. I was tied to a wooden chair in the basement of the barn. The stench of the rotting bodies was proof enough. The sound of the low moaning opera could be heard in the background, which was one of Jasper's favorite opera tracks.

My breathing intensified. I tried to free my arms but the rope was cutting into my skin. I sobbed. "Why are you doing this?"

Jasper appeared in the room wearing a crisp white shirt, the top buttons undone and the sleeves rolled up to reveal his strong arms. His blue eyes that I had once thought were intoxicating now seemed dangerous and predatory as they were dead on the target.

Me.

His dark hair had been set perfectly. He smiled at me. "You've seen a lot of things that I would have otherwise liked to keep as a secret all my life, but you had to go ahead and become a fucking Nancy Drew, and look where it got you."

"Let me and Tyler go. We won't go to the police. I promise."

"Of course, you won't, because I won't let you. I hope you enjoy the finale, precious, because I have a lot of things planned out for you."

"Tyler needs me. I won't tell a soul about this! You have my word."

Jasper was smiling, the same smile that I had once thought was sexy. Now I knew it was downright evil. "How many times had I warned you about not meddling into my business?"

He walked around a wide wooden table and picked up a long knife. "You were supposed to be a docile wife who obeyed every order of her husband—cook for him, look after him, and warm his bed. You did that for four years, and I'm grateful for that, Kiara. I liked you. I really fucking did. Out of all these skanks . . ." He indicated with his blade towards the lying bodies. "I loved you the most. I never felt even an ounce of affection when I cut them open, but you, precious, you're going to be the hardest one yet."

I knew then that I was going to die. I wouldn't see Tyler, his graduation or what he would grow up to be. What if he learned from Jasper and became a killer?

"I tried to tell myself you were like any other woman, but you continued to surprise me and convinced me otherwise. I've not met a raving beauty like you, Kiara." His predatory gaze moved from bottom to top. His honesty would have made me blush in other situations, but right now, all I was thinking was how to keep the conversation going, so I wouldn't be another body in a trash bag.

I needed to thread carefully. He continued, "You're so fucking gorgeous, and the first time I saw you, I knew I had to have you. You ruined me for everyone else, and once I had a taste of you, you became my addiction, far greater than any drug had ever been."

Vincent could be here at any time. I had to buy myself sometime. Keep Jasper engaged in a conversation.

"Well, if you admired me so much, why did you hit me that one time?"

"I lost control," he admitted. "I want to tell you something since we are at it. This is as honest as I can get in the four years of our marriage. Some nights, I wanted to worship your body, but some nights I had this very strong urge to kill you, and not just kill, I felt like preserving your beautiful body, but I didn't, instead I killed other women."

My eyes were stinging with tears that wanted to bubble up. "How . . . how many people have you killed after we married?"

"Around two dozen, give or take. But don't you worry, I never fucked these women. You needn't worry about me cheating. I just killed them. I was always a faithful husband," he said as if that made up for the fact that he was a serial killer.

He continued, "Do you remember that piece of shit who tried to rape you in the alley behind the restaurant you worked at? I took care of him too, made him suffer a slow excruciating death. A perfect revenge for putting his filthy hands on you. I cut his body parts while he was still alive, and it was fun listening to him beg and apologize, knowing nothing would save him. Although I admit, he was reduced down to a fucking mess that took me ages to clean up."

I closed my eyes for a moment, trying to process that information and the horrors of what he was capable of. Bile rose in my throat.

"Margret? What did you do to her?"

"For fuck's sake, she's my mother. Before we started dating, Margret found out what I was doing and asked me to stop. I refused and I said that if she told anyone at all, she'd end up becoming one of those bodies. I gave her a choice, and she chose to pack and leave."

"I eradicate the people who fail me, but sometimes it's just a hobby I like to purge from time to time. Other people enjoy painting or swimming and such, but I love to see how the light flickers out from one's body when I cut them open. Sometimes I just sit there for hours, read a book or something and watch as they die a slow excruciating death. It's real fun, Kiara. I wish at times that you were like me, so we'd enjoy the same things in life."

I had known Jasper was crazy to an extent—those psychotic tendencies limited to manipulation and getting what he wanted from anyone in any given circumstances—but I never thought he was a lunatic, a mad man who killed for the pleasure of it. It was much like his favorite sport, polo.

Now he was showing his true face. The mask had finally slipped off for good.

He picked up a cleaver. "However, I do have a plan to rectify that particular predicament."

"What do you mean?"

"As I said, Kiara, you're family. My wife. I vowed to support you in sickness and in health. We promised till death do us part, and I won't break those vows because you decided to show a little disobedience. I figured that some things could be taught."

With that said, Jasper cut the rope that tied my wrists together, followed with the ones on my ankles. I stood up from the chair with shaky legs.

"What do you want me to do?" I trembled, frightened of what he was going to ask me.

He pulled the string of a light bulb to reveal a man seated at the corner of the room. His arms and legs were bound the same way mine had been. A black cloth covered his face, like a prisoner ready for his execution.

"Are you ready for the big reveal?" Jasper asked.

I waited as Jasper's hand reached for the black cloth and yanked it off.

I froze when I realized who it was.

The man was Sean Reeves.

My father.

CHAPTER THIRTY-SIX

"Daddy?"

Dad opened his eyes and stared at me in horror. "Kiara? Sweetheart, my baby. Please help me!"

Even now, I could clearly see how he didn't care for me. He just wanted to be out of the ropes. I was appalled that he was even alive. I remembered how I thought I had accidentally killed him.

I turned to Jasper. "All these years, you knew he was alive, and yet you let me live with the guilt from killing him."

"Darling, I'm really sorry I kept that from you," Jasper said. "You see, soon after you hit him, he collapsed on the floor, and your mother called me when you were on the run. She was quite hysterical. I told her to calm down and took this sorry excuse of a father to the hospital because she begged me to."

Jasper grinned. "It's a shame she adores her husband more than her own daughter. I promised your mother I'd take good care of you, and I think you're quite aware of how the story goes from there."

"This is all a game for you, isn't it? Toying with everyone's lives, killing innocent people?!" I shrieked.

"I beg your pardon? Did you say 'innocent people'?" Jasper laughed. "My dear, Kiara, the people I killed were less than innocent. If anything, they were vermin meant to be nonexistent on this planet, and since I'm a good man, I'm doing society a favor by eradicating the waste."

I felt so sick. I wanted this to end, but how? What was Vincent still doing?"

"Now . . ." Jasper clapped his hands together. ". . . we can't waste any more time. I'm going to explain to you the rules of this new game."

"What game?"

"We're family. We stick together. I want you to do something for me."

"And then you would let me and my father go?" I asked.

Jasper gave a nod.

"Name it," I said in desperation. I didn't want to be one of the dead bodies in this barn with a memo stuck on my head. "You just have to ask."

Jasper appeared pleased. "That's my girl."

He walked to the table and brought a cleaver to me. I took it from him. "What . . . what do you want me to do with this?"

"Kill Sean Reeves," he commanded. "For real this time."

My hands shook as I held the cleaver tightly in my hands. "I can't do that. He's my father!"

"Baby, I'm your family now. You're married, and your first obligation goes to your husband. This man's merely a sperm donor. Remember how your mother and you worked your asses to give this pimp some money? Remember how he hit your mother when he was drunk? And you want to tell me you still have fatherly affections for him?"

"Ask me anything. Anything at all. I'll do anything you want, but please don't ask me to kill him."

"That's the only way, Kiara. You and I are very similar. My parents never gave a damn, so I made sure their brakes failed when they went on a business trip. You kill Sean Reeves right now, Kiara and I'll accept that you'd do anything for me. Think of this as an initiation. You and I together, husband and wife. We will make a

300

fantastic team, and eventually, Tyler will learn. One nice happy family."

"I can't kill him!"

"Kiara, honey, I love you. Please don't!" Dad begged.

"Do it now," Jasper ordered.

"Please . . ."

"I said kill him!" Jasper bellowed.

I walked to where Dad was seated, raised the cleaver over my head and swung it towards Jasper. It sliced his cheek and a drop of blood smudged the wooden floor. He touched his cheek and saw the blood on it.

"I knew this was going to be difficult since you were never the obeying type. It's a good thing I have a lot of fucking patience."

I made a run for the stairs leading towards the upper level of the barn and began climbing fast, skipping steps. The door was open and I almost reached the top when a pair of strong arms caught me tightly and dragged me down.

I screamed and tried to kick Jasper, but he was so much stronger. He was all muscle, and I was nothing compared to his strength. He could break my neck in one swift motion of his hand.

"My precious little fighter. I can't bring myself to kill you no matter how disobedient you are," he whispered, dragging me through the floor. My nails had come off and were bleeding. I tried to kick him but he dodged the blow.

Far away, I heard the faint sounds of the sirens. The police.

His eyes widened at the sound, and before I knew what was happening, he picked me up like a rag doll and slumped me over his shoulder. I punched his back, "Let me go!"

But Jasper continued to walk, and he kicked a door which rattled open. It was a little supply room filled with brooms and other equipment. He placed me there and I screamed for help.

He took a ball of cloth and stuffed it inside my mouth. I shook my head furiously as he found a duct tape and wound it over my mouth and around my wrists.

"I'm sorry, but you have to stay here," he said, kissing my forehead and closing the door behind him.

I tried to scream and kick the door until I heard two loud gunshots echo in the air. My breath hitched in my throat, and blood rushed to my ears.

What happened? Had Jasper decided to end his life rather than be caught?

I sobbed in the dark. The cloth in my mouth was suffocating me. I pounded my fists on the door, but I knew no one could hear me. I could feel a piece of fabric brush against my body so I turned, and a rotting body slumped forward in the dark and onto my back.

I tried to scramble away, my screams were muffled by the cloth in my mouth. I had no choice but to stay with a rotting dead body until someone found me. I heard a man's voice from the outside but had no strength left inside me to call him for help. I waited as someone tried to break the door of the supply room.

It was a police officer with a gun pointed at me, followed by Vincent whose eyes were wide with terror.

"Oh God, Kiara!"

A few minutes later, I was sitting inside the paramedic's van. The entire barn was barricaded by a yellow crime scene tape, and bodies covered with white sheets were strapped into gurneys. They were wheeled and loaded inside the vans. The entire property was swarmed by officers, FBI agents, and a team of forensic experts.

A grizzly tale of epic horror had come to an end. A tale about my life being married to a serial killer.

I was the only surviving victim.

It was safe to assume that Jasper was dead, and just to prove my notion wrong, my eyes registered two police officers walking a man to the police car with his hands secured in a pair of handcuffs.

Jasper wasn't dead, so that meant . . .

"My dad . . ." I choked.

"Your father is dead," Vincent declared in a soft voice. "I'm sorry."

That meant the gunshot sounds that I heard were of Jasper shooting my father.

"Where's Tyler?" I asked Vince. "Please tell me he's okay."

"I made sure he was safe. An officer is with him."

I felt better knowing Tyler was safe. A nurse had approached me, and said something about my wounds, but I tuned out her voice.

My eyes followed Jasper as he stood by the police car. As if he had sensed my gaze on him, he looked directly at me. His lips pressed together, the corners of his mouth quirked up in a coy smile.

"You have a right to remain silent. Anything you say can and will be . . ."

I could hear the Miranda rights recited to him as he was lowered inside the car. He hadn't stopped looking at me, the same longing stare.

He mouthed, "I love you." And his next words were also clear.

"You will remain mine. Always."

Goose bumps rose up on my arms as I watched the car leave. Vince stared at me in eerie silence. He rubbed my shoulders.

"It's over, Kiara. Jasper won't come back."

*   *   *

Vince picked up his coffee mug and took a sip, staring out towards the open courtyard—one that held numerous parties when the members of the house were all well and alive. The sky turned a shade of crimson as the sun began going down, hiding behind the lush trees from the woods. The scenery was like a beautiful painting by someone who had spent hours getting the details right. The gush of the wind ruffled my dress as I settled down in the vacant chair opposite Vince.

"It's beautiful, isn't it?" I asked him.

Vince smiled. "It is. How are you feeling now?"

"I'm okay, I guess." I shrugged.

It had been a week since the incident, and I couldn't lie and tell Vince that I was alright because I wasn't. If I was alright, I wouldn't have woken up screaming in the middle of the night, dreaming of Jasper covered in blood.

Vince placed his hand over mine. "I know it's going to be hard, but we will get through his. You and I."

"I hope so. I remembered Jasper told me he's got some of the best attorneys in the country. What if he spins some kind of a story and the court believes him?" I knew I was being paranoid, but I had every right to think that Jasper would be a free man.

Jasper was the definition of dangerous, and when there's a concoction of danger, money, and power, it's usually a very bad combination. He had a reputation of walking out of every situation, and from what had happened last week, it was a given that Jasper would be capable of finding a way out.

Vince sighed. "Kiara, he has murdered people. He played mind games with you for years. We have a lot of proof. Even if Jasper manages to find the best fucking attorney in the world, I don't think there's much he can do."

He scrolled through an iPad. "Oh, look, your husband's still making the headlines. *Billionaire and CEO, Jasper Lockhart of the Lockhart Enterprises, a Victim of Conspiracies.*"

I gaped at him. "Victim of conspiracies? Are you kidding me? The victims here are Tyler and I. Not Jasper!"

"Relax. He's in prison. As soon as the postmortem reports of the bodies are out, it's going to be clear who did it," Vince said like everything was a piece of cake.

I was sure Vince was a little too overconfident and was underestimating his brother even after everything that happened.

Vince continued, "People talk, Kiara, and they make stories. Jasper has done some insane amount of charity in the past. He has always maintained a good reputation in front of the media, and so it's really hard for them to think that he killed so many people. As a psychopath, he is calculating and has manipulated people easily with his charm. He was very careful in public and never had anything controversial pop up in the media. To think someone like him could kill over two dozen people. People believe what they see, and what they see right now is an innocent rich man framed in a crime by his wife and half-brother because they were having an affair behind his back."

"But that's not true!"

"He's nominated you as the owner of the company in case of his death, and I will take over as the CEO of the company from here onward."

My mind was still reeling from that information. "The owner? Jasper would never do that."

"He actually did. If he dies, billions of dollars will be under your name."

"I don't believe this," I whispered.

Vince smiled. "He is making himself look like a victim, and also, if he made you the nominee for the company ownership, I'm sure it's for a cause which we don't know of."

Vince noticed how stressed I was and placed his hand over mine. The brown shade in his eyes were diluting, his look was unwavering.

"Jasper will pay for his crimes, Kiara. I promise you."

I nodded, "Thank you, Vince. If you hadn't called the police, I could have died that day."

Vince stared at me as if I had spoken in Swahili. "It surely wasn't me. I thought you called the police."

I shook my head, even more confused than ever. "If you and I didn't do it, then who did?"

305

Vince thought for a moment then concluded, "Maybe Tyler did."

"He did not. If Tyler had called the dispatchers, I'm sure he would have said something to us."

"Dear God!" Vince exclaimed, jumping to his feet.

I followed suit. "What happened?"

"It's a game, Kiara. Jasper is playing us." Vince stated as he frantically began punching the numbers in his iPhone. "Hello. Connect me to Mr. Davis . . . Yes, Davis. This is Dr. Vincent Lockhart. I want you to keep a close eye on Blackford Correctional Center and report to me if—I'm sorry, what?"

Vince's expression grew dark until his face was the color of a white sheet. He was growing anxious every second of the call.

"Tell the police to seal all the checkpoints." I heard him curse as he hung up on the call.

I knew what Vince was going to say even before I had the chance to ask him what was wrong.

"Jasper has escaped prison," he confessed calmly.

*　　*　　*

With the news of Jasper escaping prison, it was like havoc again. I thought life was going to be easier. With him gone, I thought Tyler and I could finally live without looking for a shadow. Vincent knew that the first place Jasper would show up to after escaping was the mansion, and he had made sure a lot of security guards were hiding in places around the mansion to ambush him if he decided to show up.

"Mommy, why is Daddy in prison?" Tyler suddenly asked me that night. Since Jasper had been taken to prison, I had completely stopped sleeping in our bedroom upstairs. Instead, I slept in Tyler's room. His bed was large enough to accommodate an adult.

"Who told you that, honey?"

I had tried to keep Tyler away from everything as much as I could, but it was obvious the child was going to hear something.

"I heard Lily say it to her friend. She said Daddy was in jail because he's not a good man. She said Daddy is crazy. She saw it on the news." His blue eyes peered at me. "Is it true, Mommy?"

I couldn't lie to him and say that his father had escaped, neither could I lie about Jasper being a good man because he was not.

"Yes. He is in prison."

He became teary-eyed. "Is it because he was always mean to you?"

When I didn't say anything, he asked me. "Will Daddy be okay?"

"I'm not sure, Tyler," I answered.

Tyler was too young to know that his father was a killer or the fact that he was a psychopath. I wondered what Tyler would think when he grew up and learned the truth. I needed my child to have a normal life, and in order to have that, I needed to find a way to get away from the mansion, find a job, and lay low. This was my chance to have the freedom I craved, and I wasn't going to let an opportunity like this slide. If it came down to the worst scenario, I could change my name, my identity and start over. With a little help from Vince, I knew that was possible.

Tyler peered at me with those innocent blue eyes, and I was dreading a few more questions about Jasper, but he surprised me when he reached towards his little bookshelf and pulled out a children's book that was mature for his age. Then again, I realized that Tyler was smarter than the average four-year-old kid—something I knew he had acquired from his father. I just hoped he wouldn't pick on any other traits like manipulation or Jasper's psychopathic behavior.

"Can you read this to me?" he asked innocently, yawning.

"Of course, honey." I was halfway through the book when Tyler's warm body snuggled close to mine. He picked up his favorite *Winnie the Pooh* stuffed toy and hugged it close.

I read him the story, and soon, I heard soft snores. It must be the fatigue from overthinking that brought me to the oblivion of sleep. Sometime past midnight, I heard a knock at the door. I thought I had imagined it so I closed my eyes again, but the rap on the door got louder.

"Who is it?" I called out.

"It's me, Vince," he said from the other side of the door.

I checked the Mickey bedside clock and it read 2:10 AM.

What did Vince want at this hour of the night?

"What is it?" I asked him.

"I've got some news," he said, and from the tone of his voice, he didn't sound cheerful. In fact, he sounded quite the opposite. "Can you open the door for a minute?"

I took a cautious step towards the door and opened it. Vince appeared stressed, the bags under his eyes more prominent than ever.

"I received a call from Blackford Correctional Center again."

My heart began to drum faster. "What . . . what did they say? Did they find Jasper?"

Vince's expression made my blood turn cold. "You're not going to like this, Kiara. Do you want to sit down while you listen to it?"

"Just tell me what's going on!" I was almost shaking.

And then my stomach knotted with what Vince confessed. "Jasper stole a car from a department store parking lot. It was a blue Toyota."

"I don't care what color or which car he was driving, Vincent. Please get to the point," I said, frustrated.

"I am getting to the point," Vince said. "He stayed at a motel for a few hours and was on his way somewhere. As usual, they suspected he was driving recklessly. The car had collided against a pole near a residential area. The car was in a blaze. When the police reached the area, they found the car and a body inside that was burned beyond recognition. There were only a few parts of the body remaining. I'll spare you the details."

I stared at him, dumbfounded.

"That means?"

"Jasper is dead."

CHAPTER THIRTY-SEVEN

It was funny how life threw a curveball at me when I learned that Jasper Lockhart was dead. At first, it was hard to come to terms with the fact that he wasn't in this world anymore, to control the reins of our lives. I had spent the better part of six months looking for a shadow until I realized that he really was no more.

True, Jasper was a psychopath, but he was also made of flesh and blood, like any other man, and it was impossible for any human being to walk out of a blazing fire alive.

After the entire incident with the bodies being found in our barn and Jasper's previous assault cases having been investigated by the police and FBI, the case had been closed. It was proven that the remnants of the burned chards in the car were that of Jasper's, and that left me as the widowed heiress of a multibillion-dollar conglomerate. Naturally, Vincent was appointed as the CEO of the Lockhart Enterprises.

I hadn't been interested in a romantic relationship with him, so Vince and I had remained friends and nothing had changed between us. I didn't think I needed a man in my life at that point. I had left the estate and moved into another town, Archmount Valley.

With its quaintness and smaller population, it was the perfect place to start over. We had bought a nice little villa by the lake. Tyler went to a private school that was just twenty minutes away. We weren't living a life full of luxury, the way we had when we lived at the Lockhart's mansion, but we were still happy and content.

In addition to that, I had written a book about my life—a memoir, *"True Accounts of Life with a Billionaire Psychopath"*, and within a month, it had turned into a *New York Times Best Seller*.

People wanted to know what it was like to be a billionaire's wife, being married to a man who had lived a double life, the story of a powerful businessman by the day and a ruthless killer by night. My editor had specifically told me to add gory details, and while I wasn't very keen on taking a walk down the memory lane, I had nothing better to do with my time, so I wrote the book in accordance to my knowledge and without sugar quoting the lies Jasper had led everybody to believe.

Within a few months, I had wealth of my own. While I still had access over Jasper's money, I had become such a successful author that I didn't really need his money. I was also a local celebrity.

A year later, and the house right next door had a new tenant. Mr. and Mrs. Rogers were a kind old couple in their sixties. I had enjoyed Mrs. Rogers's companionship while it lasted, and it was sad to see them leave, but people needed to eventually move forward in life.

I was nervous when I had seen a mover's van from my window. I watched curiously as the movers loaded new furniture into the house, and I hoped that it was a loving family like the old couple.

One afternoon, while I played with my little girl, Maya, a GMC had rolled into the neighborhood house and I secretly peeked out the window, curious to see my new neighbor.

A man climbed out of the car, wearing a white t-shirt over ripped jeans. His hair was honey colored which glimmered in the sun, and even from a distance, I could tell he had a nice body underneath those clothes.

My neighbor was an attractive man, and I almost low whistled when I realized how shameless I was being. I hadn't noticed how close to the window I had been standing or that I wasn't hiding behind the curtains anymore until Mr. Attractive-New-Neighbor caught my eye, smiled, and gave me a small wave.

I waved back awkwardly, feeling my face burning as I had been caught staring. I watched him go inside the house and I waited to see if he had a wife or perhaps a girlfriend follow him but no one did.

To welcome and get to know my new neighbor, I had given him baked cookies and found out his name was Liam Price. Liam was an orphan, unmarried, and planned to buy the *Archmount Lake Resort*. He had moved in here because he needed to be close to his work.

When I visited the local bars on weekends, I had seen Liam there and we'd talk. He'd then told me how much he liked my book, and how brave I was. He'd give me so much praise that I end up blushing the entire time. He told me he was a fan. Liam was so easy to get along with. We were like old friends who had lost touch through the years.

The town ladies were crazy for him, but Liam wouldn't give them the time of day. I noticed how he would politely decline all the advances of the single ladies. Sometimes, Liam would hang out in our home, he played video games with Tyler and read bedtime stories to Maya. Liam was like Tyler's best friend now, and all Tyler talked about was Liam. He was slowly making his way into our hearts.

One night, while Liam put Maya to bed, I watched as he talked to the baby and my heart broke. I often compared Liam with Jasper and wondered how nice life would have been if Jasper had been someone like Liam.

When the children had gone to bed, we mostly hung out in the living area. Liam knew about my ex-husband and what I had endured in my previous marriage, so it was nice to see how understanding the man was.

We sat together on the couch, watching a *Friends* episode when Liam scooted closer. I wasn't blind not to his advances, but I was a bit reluctant to jump into a new relationship. He was nice, but I felt like he deserved better and not become riddled with a widow and her two children.

His warm hand covered mine and when I looked at him, he smiled kindly.

"Your past doesn't matter to me, Kiara. I hope you know that I'll always be willing to hear you out."

"Thank you, Liam, that really means a lot," I said. He was so pure and sweet. His hazel brown eyes burned with compassion, kindness, and so much love.

"I would like to take you out sometime. Although I'd love to have the children accompany us, I want to do something just for the two of us. You and me."

I giggled. "That would be nice."

And just like that, when he leaned in, my eyes fluttered shut. He kissed me, openmouthed, and fiercely, like he had wanted to kiss me like that for ages.

It had been a long time since I kissed a man and this felt so good, especially when his tongue moved inside my mouth with such expertise. He threw a glance at the door joining the passage that led to the kid's bedroom and pulled me into his lap possessively. I went to him willingly.

He was lonely and so was I. His jawline was rough against my palm and I liked it. He raised my t-shirt, unbuckled my bra and palmed my breast, his hands were bold on my body. His mouth moved to my throat as he rained sloppy kisses there.

"Liam . . ."

I heard a low growl deep from his throat.

He pulled my dress up, unbuttoned his jeans and entered slowly inside me. There was something so naughty about having sex with the fear of having being caught, but I knew Tyler and Maya never woke up in the middle of the night.

It took me a while to accommodate Liam since he was thick and long. I felt a twinge of guilt as that reminded me of Jasper. His hazel-brown eyes looked so lovely, like golden Champagne. We moved together in rhythm. He drove into me with a severe passion like there was no other woman in this world other than me.

"My sweet, sweet Kiara."

EPILOGUE

It happened a year ago, and I could still remember how the car rammed into the pole, and the way it trigged the airbags which deflated into my face. My head pounded against the leather seat. The sounds of the roaring crash of the metal followed by the shattering of the windshield still rang in my ears to this day.

I had been lucky enough to survive such a bad accident, but the man on the driving seat, not so much. He lay back against the seat with his eyes and mouth wide open, blood trailing down his chin. I reached for the door handle and threw my body against the ground which is when I noticed the car engine catching fire.

I gathered all my energy and climbed to my feet, dragging my bad foot as far away from the car as I could get. I watched from the bushes as the car went into flames.

I had gotten out of there before the police could make it. Laying low was fairly easy, ditching my fancy lifestyle wasn't. Vince sealed most of the bank accounts, but he hadn't got a clue about the one account that I kept a secret plus a few other ones deposited overseas under an alias which made the transactions smooth. I had enough money that would sustain me for a lifetime—enough to live a billionaire life, but of course, I had to be careful.

Jasper Lockhart was dead to the world.

And I planned on keeping it that way.

"Mr. Liam Price?" The secretary peered into the waiting room at me with a smile. "Dr. Becker is waiting for you, sir."

*   *   *

The surgery took four hours to complete. A whole month was needed for my total recovery, and it had been a few months since then.

I looked at myself in the mirror and saw a different person. My jawline, although sharp, looked different than before. My nose was longer and my cheekbones were more prominent.

Anyone who knew Jasper Lockhart wouldn't be able to tell the similarities if they met Liam Price. While Jasper's hair was dark raven, Liam had honey blonde. The stormy-blue eyes used to be a dead giveaway. Liam had a solution for that too.

I pulled a tiny case of contact lenses from the glove compartment of the car and popped the hazel brown contacts into my eyes. Whenever I visited a bar, I still had women flocking around me like I were a Michelangelo's sculpture come to life.

While Jasper had brooding, dark looks, Liam was as good-looking, but had a friendlier air to him. He was fun and goofy, and of course, brutally honest to a fault.

I walked into the crowded bar. The weekend crowd was already here. Sweaty bodies were dancing on the floor, while the quiet ones sat near the bar, sipping their drinks while enjoying watching people.

"Liam, how are you doing, buddy?" Otis Green patted my back with his beefy hand. He was the owner of the bar and had been hounding me to invest in a lakeside resort.

"Never better," I said.

To the townies, Liam Price was a handsome single bachelor, orphaned when his parents died in a crash, never married and was now sole proprietor of the wealth his parents had left him. To them, Liam was also very kind, the one who helped old ladies cross roads and always spoke to everyone with respect. Town wives eyed Liam with obvious adoration, single women wanted him in bed, and old ones liked talking to him for hours.

Liam was a good man.

It was fun to sit alone in the little villa and laugh at the stupid people. No matter how many women threw themselves at Liam, he had sworn to love only one, and that made the ladies melt into a puddle and wish I was their husband. I hadn't moved into Archmount Valley just because I liked their secluded town or the scenery. I had moved for completely different reasons.

I was parked in the shadows. I watched from my binoculars as the woman entered the bar in a silk blue blouse and denims that hugged her curves deliciously. My cock sprang to life just thinking of her underneath me. I had watched her for days and nights on end. Since I had the money rolling in, I didn't have to worry about meetings and such.

The excitement was real.

The thrill was real.

It wasn't unknown to the townies how within a few months of moving into Archmount Valley that Liam had started to take notice of the widow, Mrs. Kiara Lockhart. He had known she had a son, Tyler who was five, and a daughter Maya, one, who was also a splitting image of her late husband.

Kiara enjoyed Liam's company. They were great friends. Liam visited them on the weekends, brought the children gifts, and played with her son.

Unlike Jasper, Liam was a patient man and that's what Kiara liked about him. She would also confide in him as friends and tell Liam everything she had endured in her previous marriage. Like a good friend, Liam always listened to her.

It was about time, but Liam could sense she had lost her heart to him. He had been inside her, and the way Kiara had reacted when he fucked her was proof enough. She was hungry for the cock as much as he was dying to taste that pussy.

317

I sighed. It was a wonderful story and a very convenient way to get back my family. I grinned.

I ran a hand through my hair, straightened my shirt, and doused myself in perfume before entering the bar. I spotted Kiara at once. She was as beautiful as ever. Her dark hair was longer than before. A literal goddess, her body was meant only for one person. Me.

I placed my hands over her eyes and heard her giggle as she caught my hands. "Liam."

I spun her around and kissed her full on her lips. I was making this official, and if it wasn't official, well, the people in the bar could certainly see it that way. She looked at me so lovingly. If I had the same old face, she would have been disgusted. Right now, her eyes shone only with admiration.

"I thought I was late for our date and made you wait," she said.

"For you, I'd wait a lifetime, Kiara," I said. My own voice sometimes sounded alien to me. My voice sounded deeper than before due to the voice-altering surgery I had gone through a few weeks back. I couldn't take the risk of Kiara recognizing the voice, and so even when the doctor had mentioned the risk I was taking, I still went ahead with it. Just to be on the safer side, I changed my accent a little bit too.

She passed me her genuine smile, one that reached her eyes. I made sure I didn't call her *precious*. It would have been a dead giveaway, not to mention the extra drama about how much that reminded her of her ex-husband.

She shook her head. My hand slid to her bottom as I passed her my boy-next-door-smile. I squeezed her ass gently, leaned in and whispered, "Can't wait to take you home and fuck you until I blow your mind, Mrs. Lockhart."

She laughed.

"Why are you laughing?"

She shook her head, the laughter still clear in her eyes. "I hope you don't mind me saying this, Liam, but sometimes your bluntness reminds me of *him.*"

I froze. "Does it?" I tried to play discreet. I needed to control the words that tumbled out of my mouth. Liam didn't fuck, he made love.

"But I know that you're not him. You're far better than any person I've ever met. I'm so lucky to have met you, Liam," she said, pulling me a friendly hug.

"Likewise, baby. Now that I have you, I will never let you go." I tightened my arms around her, burying my face in her hair and smelling the familiar scent of peaches and lime. I was home. "Not ever."

The End

Do you like billionaire
romance stories?
Here are samples of other stories
you might enjoy!

T. R. IYER

UNWANTED
Attraction

PROLOGUE

Sitting in the huge mansion, Ornelia was busy walking down memory lane. Within just a few months, her life had drastically changed—from being a shy twenty-one-year-old with big dreams to chase to becoming a namesake wife to a billionaire who had yet to grace her with his presence since the day he'd left for his business trip.

From the very day Ornelia had learned to walk and talk, her father had made sure to instill politeness and kindness in her. She had always been one to obey her parents, because what would anyone ever get from rebelling?

Surely, her father was proud of his obedient little daughter, striving to be perfect in all sense. In fact, any parent would have been. However, when he wished for her to become a doctor, she negotiated her way out and took psychology after promising him that she would get her doctorate sometime in her life.

She had never doubted her father's decisions, but marrying her off to a coldhearted bigot was a leap of faith he should not have taken.

The news had come as a shock to her—to be married off at twenty-one was not a part of her big dream—but out of respect for her parents and the man behind this arrangement, she agreed to get married. She tried to find a silver lining out of the whole situation, like the possibility of continuing her studies after the wedding.

Little did she know, her life was about to take a turn for the worse. This was only the calm before the storm; never had a calm ever felt so turbulent.

CHAPTER ONE

ALEXANDER

Alexander and Ana Dawson, two lovers in their forties, lived a very humble life in their little house in Fresno, California. They had a young daughter studying psychology at Fresno University, and they were immensely proud of her. She was the best thing that had ever happened to them.

But Lord knows, good things don't come easily.

Alexander was reminiscing the past of how he and his wife had met. He'd just graduated from college with a degree that landed him a job as an accountant in a small firm, thirty minutes away from where he was renting at that time. His parents lived far away and couldn't afford to move in with him; neither could he have managed to support them if they had indeed come in the city. Sending them money as regularly as possible was the best thing he coul do, and they were content with that. Their only complaint had been that he didn't visit them enough.

Alexander and Ana had met when they worked in the same firm. Alexander was an accountant, and Ana was a receptionist. It was love at first sight for Alexander. As for Ana, she was completely unsure about her feelings toward him, but Alexander was incredibly persistent about pursuing her.

Only then did her ice-cold heart melt when he went on his knees, begging her to be with him.

Eventually she fell in love with him, and that love only kept growing as time went by.

They'd dated for about four years before he put a ring on her finger. All those years of courtship had been worth it as their relationship became stronger than ever.

"Honey, something came in the mail for you," Ana called for her husband.

"Good morning, Papa." His daughter, Ornelia, gave him a kiss on the cheek as she made her way out of the door.

Today was the last day of her exams. His daughter was about to graduate soon.

"All the best, little girl. I know you are going to ace this one too." Alexander waved to her.

His wife came up to him to hand him the letter. "She didn't eat breakfast today. Your daughter is going to be the death of me," she complained.

"She'll eat something with Jake and Emily. Stop worrying too much about her," Alexander said. He ripped the envelope open and took the paper out of it.

"What is it about?" Ana asked in an anxious tone after seeing Alexander rocking to and fro on the couch.

"Harrold King, he . . . uh . . . He passed away. I have been invited to the will reading."

Ana gasped at the news. Harrold King's passing away meant the beginning of their doom.

"What if . . . you don't go? What if we just . . . pretend that we didn't get the letter in the mail? Oh, Alex, I don't like the sound of this will reading. Please, let's not go," she begged. Her heart knew it was bad news. As sad as the news of Harrold's death was, this will reading was going to be worse. Instinctively, she knew; she sensed it.

"It's a legal notice, Ana. And when you picked up the mail, you must have signed the receiving copy. Not going to the reading would only delay what is about to come, not eliminate it," he reasoned with his wife.

"When is it?" she asked, sounding disheartened.

"A week from now, but everything will be fine, Ana. I promise I will do whatever it takes to sort this out." He held her hand and gave it a little squeeze.

They had no other choice. This was inevitable. He had seen this day coming for a very long time. All he could do was wait for the reading and see what it actually stated.

Prayers were all he had.

If you enjoyed this sample, look for
Unwanted Attraction
on Amazon.

HER

PERFECT

REBOUND

BOOK ONE
LOVE AND LUST SERIES

E.R. KNIGHT

CHAPTER 1

Emily threw her phone on the covers of her bed. It bounced once and then lay still.

She was pissed.

Parker hadn't been answering her calls for the past hour. He was still monkeying around with the football team, hours after the end of their practice session.

Emily prided herself on not being the nagging and needy girlfriend, but this was taking things too far. Parker had promised to be early today because she really didn't want to be late for the musical this evening that was going to begin in exactly an hour.

Emily was a theatre buff. She had saved up for three entire months so that she could get not one but two tickets for the musical. She had wanted to spend time with Parker. With all the running about due to the midterm examinations, they hadn't gone out for a long time.

She had wanted today to be special, just the two of them, but it looked like Parker had other plans.

Emily turned to the mirror. She had taken efforts today. Her hair was curled up in a loose bun at the back of her head and showcased her slim neck. She had worn a sleeveless navy-blue dress with a sweetheart neckline that showed off her curves and completed the outfit with a pair of black sandals with high heels. Her makeup was minimal and consisted of a tinge of blush on her cheeks, eyeliner that highlighted her olive-green eyes, and a dab of lip gloss on her full lips.

She wrung her hands while she stared at her reflection.

This was the second time Parker had stood her up. The last time was when they had decided to go to his house to celebrate Thanksgiving with his family. More like with his uncle and guardian, Gage.

Parker was an only child. His parents owned their own company in Greece and lived there most of the time. Since they couldn't be around that much for Parker, they had sent him to America to live with his mom's younger brother.

He and Emily had met in college. She had been pursuing her medical degree at MSU and was in her second year while Parker was a third-year student.

She was an orphan and had grown under the care of her housekeeper who had chosen to look after her after she lost her dad due to cancer. Her mom hadn't survived after giving birth to her.

After six months of knowing each other, Parker asked her out, and they began dating.

They had been together for a year now. Emily still remembered her first kiss with him and also, the night she lost her virginity. It had been their eighth-month anniversary. Parker had taken her out for dinner that day and told her that he loved her. Emily had felt like the luckiest girl.

He dropped her off at home that evening. But when he kissed her goodnight, they had suddenly found themselves inside her dorm room, tearing each other's clothes off. They had slept together that night, and Emily couldn't help feeling that everything had turned out perfect for them.

The musical that she had bought the tickets for was based on a famous movie, *Mamma Mia*, and was going to be held at the Orpheum Theatre.

She glanced at her phone again, willing it to ring, but it didn't.

She couldn't believe Parker could be so inconsiderate. She had called him before she began to get ready to remind him to be there on time, but he told her off by saying that she was acting like his mom and was getting on his nerves. Emily had been hurt, but she excused him, thinking he was just tired and needed a bit of time to relax with the guys.

The clock ticked by, and Emily tried calling Parker a few more times. But he didn't answer.

The show would begin soon, and she was sure the theatre would be full today. She was starting to get frustrated when suddenly, her phone rang. Startled, she grabbed it, expecting Parker's face to flash on the screen, but it wasn't him.

Her hopes were shot down.

Trying to keep calm, she took a deep breath and answered the call. "Hello?"

"Emily?"

She had heard that voice before.

"Who's this?" she asked.

"It's Gage."

Emily stared at the floor in confusion. Why was Gage calling her? Where the hell was Parker?

If you enjoyed this sample, look for
Her Perfect Rebound
on Amazon.

MY POSSESSIVE
BODYGUARD

JAMI GALLARDO

CHAPTER 1

The freezing cold air hit me like a pile of bricks, sweeping my long brown hair all over my face. If it were any other girl, it would look like a shampoo commercial but I was pretty sure I just looked all dorky and stupid. I pulled my hair away, cringing when my icy cold fingers touched my cheeks.

This was exactly why I didn't like having my hair down, I hated having to take care of it. My hair was wavy but it was also frizzy and those two didn't make a good combination. I usually liked to put it up in a high ponytail but my hair kept me warm, and in this freezing New York weather, I constantly had to find ways to keep myself warm. I wasn't complaining; I loved this weather. I loved wearing cozy sweaters and scarfs and sitting close to the window somewhere with a hot cup of coffee.

I walked down the stairs as people rushed past me. I had just taken my last final of the semester and it sure felt great. Being a college student kept me really busy, but I didn't mind at all. I liked having something to do. Especially after going through the worst possible break-up ever…

Don't go there, Hannah.

"Ms. Collins," Robin, my bodyguard for the day, greeted me with a nod when I made it back to the car. All of my dad's bodyguards looked pretty much the same: tall, muscular, and always in black suits with white shirts and black ties. They also wore an earpiece so they could all be in communication in case something happened. Most people would drool over them and I probably would too, if they weren't with me *all the time*.

I didn't always have bodyguards.

My dad was a famous actor. He had been acting since he was a teenager but his big break-out movie came out about five years ago, making his popularity skyrocket. Around the same time, my mom was attacked in a restaurant parking lot. The men took her purse, jewelry, and her car but not before beating her. My dad's success had put a spotlight on my family and people now knew my family had a lot of money which put us in danger. So we moved to a house with much more security and my dad hired an army of bodyguards.

It wasn't just my dad's success that put us in danger. My oldest brother, Colton, was the owner of the most famous nightclub in New York. Nicholas, my second oldest brother, had started our family's clothing brand company and he ran it as the CEO. A year ago, my youngest brother had decided he wanted to pursue a modeling career. He was currently in Paris.

Who knew success came with a cost? It cost us our safety which was what the bodyguards were for.

Unlike my brothers, I had yet to start my career. I didn't have the same talent as Nick and Colton in running a business or the flawless looks to become a model like my brother Derek. I liked to draw.

I wanted to be a wedding gown designer. I loved designing dresses and had a lot of sketch books in my room where I had started drafting a lot of dresses. Some pages just had doodles, others had the silhouette of a dress; each page had a random design that only I understood. The problem was that I had yet to finish a single whole gown; I always just stopped in the middle of it and started a new one.

I got in the car and Robin shut the door. I watched as he went around it and got in the driver's seat. I looked out the window as he began to drive.

Good-bye school, I thought happily as I watched us pass by the school.

I loved school but finals week killed me mentally and drained me physically. It was enough to make me not want to set eyes on school for a while. I had a whole month to myself. I could lie around in my room, not doing anything *and* not feel guilty about it. It was official: I had nothing to do but draw all day if I wanted…or sleep.

Robin pulled up into the driveway and I watched as he input the six-digit code so the gates could open.

My favorite part of the house was outdoors: the green grass, the big trees, and the different flowers planted in strategic places to make up the garden. The house was beautiful, of course, but I always thought it was too big. I never understood my dad's logic in moving us into a much bigger house after my mom's attack. I thought it made it easier for intruders to break in because there were more windows and more doors to break into. Of course, I knew that it was my vain mother who had a lot to do in choosing the house.

The car stopped in front of the house and I opened the door before Robin had time to reach it. "I got it." I smiled at him.

He nodded but hurried to open the front door for me. I couldn't help but roll my eyes at him. I could open my own doors, thank you very much. I wasn't the famous actress or rich businessman. I wished they wouldn't treat me like I was royalty when the only reason I needed bodyguards was because of my family's success. I was no one.

Inside, the house was warm and spotless clean, like always. The living room was the first thing you saw when you walked in, with very expensive and elegant furniture. Everything in the house was so expensive and beautiful and new. The furniture, the decorative ornaments, the expensive floor almost made this house feel like an exhibit rather than a home.

Money had cost me my parents. Especially my mom.

"Honey? Is that you?" my mom called as she hurriedly made her way into the living room. Her face fell when she saw that it was just me. My mom was a very attractive woman. She was tall with perfect hips and short blond hair with piercing blue eyes. I looked nothing like her. She was always dressed up, as if ready to meet the President of the United States. I often thought how exhausting it must be to be her but she seemed to love being Christina Collins, Richard Collins's first and only wife.

Today, she was wearing a pale pink pencil dress with white high heels, her hair was straight and she had perfect make up on. She did not look forty-five.

"Dad isn't home yet?" I asked taking off my jacket.

"He'll be here soon," she said looking annoyed by my comment.

My dad was supposed to be here last week. He was out, doing interviews or something. He was currently not working in any movie and was supposed to be here by now.

"Okay," I said as I began to make my way up the stairs.

"Dinner is almost ready," Mom called behind me.

I just nodded.

I didn't have the best relationship with my mom. It wasn't always like this but money and fame had really gotten to her. Ever since my dad became famous, she began to worry about appearances more than anything. She wasn't that motherly either, she only cared about looking good in front of the cameras. It was stupid, but I couldn't change that. She also cared more about her sons with big businesses and careers. I think she began to be even more distant with me when I refused to let her open a business to start my own brand. She didn't understand that I wanted to graduate first. She didn't understand the fact that I wasn't ready—I didn't even have a full gown finished! She found it stupid that I didn't want to be successful because of my dad, just like everyone else. I wanted to be successful on my own.

My phone began to ring just as I reached my room and I smiled when I looked at the caller ID.

"Hey, Pat," I answered taking off my scarf.

"Hannah Banana, how are you?" he said on the other end.

I used to cringe when he started calling me 'Hannah Banana' back in middle school but I began to get used to it when I realized he wasn't going to stop calling me that. Apparently, he thought he invented that nickname.

I smiled. "Good."

"What are you up to?"

"Nothing," I said as I closed my bedroom door.

"Oh come on, anything interesting? I didn't call you to be bored to death."

I laughed. "I'm done with finals?" I offered.

"Mmm... that's something I guess."

Patrick and I had been best friends since we were in middle school. He was truly my other half. I never thought a guy would understand me better than a girl but it was true. He understood me better than anyone. After we graduated from high school, he moved to Miami for school and I haven't seen him since then.

"What are you doing?" I asked throwing myself on the bed.

"Getting ready for the club, baby!" he yelled in my ear. "Hold up—I'm going to FaceTime you because I need outfit advice."

"Okay," I said rolling my eyes. He hung up and FaceTimed me a few seconds later. He was in front of a mirror, trying on different jackets.

Patrick was a fuckboy. There was no other way to describe him, maybe manwhore? He liked to sleep around. It got worse when he moved over there, just like I knew it was going to happen. Which was why, before he left three years ago, I made him take a sexual education class since high school failed to give us any useful advice.

"Now you can whore around all you want," I had told him which made him laugh.

Sometimes, I wondered how we were still friends. It had been three years since he left and we lived in different states but somehow, we had made it work. He was all I had.

I talked with him for a while, he told me about his latest hook-up and I listened like the good friend I was. After we hung up, I got in the shower and it was when I was changing that there was a knock on the door.

"Yes?" I called as I threw a blouse over my head.

"Mrs. Collins would like me to tell you that dinner is ready," Katie, one of our maids, called from the other side of the door.

"I'll be right down!" I called back as I put on some jeans.

My dad must have gotten here after all. I was excited about seeing him. I missed him whenever he was gone. I finished combing my hair and then quickly made my way out. I ran down the stairs, feeling like a little girl.

"What have I told you about running down the stairs, Hannah?" my mom asked, looking annoyed when I walked into the dining room.

I ignored her and smiled when I saw my dad. My dad was a handsome man. He was tall with broad shoulders and short brown hair with brown eyes and fair skin. I looked like him and I loved it. His smile always took me back to when I was a little girl and he would read to me while I sat on his lap. All of that was gone. He was always flying somewhere nowadays.

"Dad!" I said walking to him.

He stood up as he smiled. "Hey, sweetie," he said as he put his arms around me.

I suddenly had the urge to cry. I missed him so much. "I missed you," I mumbled.

"Me too," he said as he stroked my hair.

"Hannah, your father wants to eat," my mom said sounding annoyed.

I let him go. "Sorry, Dad."

He shook his head. "You okay?" he asked with a frown. His brown eyes studied my face as if trying to read what I had been up to for the past few months.

Oh if only he knew.

I nodded as we took our seats. "Yeah, I just missed you."

He winked at me as he squeezed my hand. I hadn't realized that Nick and his wife, Rachel, were also at the table.

"Hey." Rachel smiled across the table from me.

I smiled at her. "Hey."

I really liked Rachel. She was tall, with long blond hair, hazel eyes, and fair skin. She was not only beautiful but also modest and perfect for my brother. They had been married for about a year and they made the perfect couple. *Literally,* they were always all over the magazines as the perfect couple. Rachel was a fashion designer which was perfect because she fit right in with Nick's business. I admired and wanted to be as good as her someday.

"How was school?" she asked as my mom and dad carried a conversation. I swear she cared more about me than my own mother.

"Good. I'm done for the semester," I said as one of the maids served me pasta. "Thank you," I told her. She smiled. My mom wasn't exactly nice to the housemaids or to anyone who helped keep the house beautiful so I always tried to make up for it.

"What are we talking about?" Nick said looking at Rachel and me. Nick was the spitting image of my mom. They had the same nose, same blond hair, and blue eyes. Nick always kept himself groomed and he was always wearing suits; he fit right in with the bodyguards like camouflage.

Rachel rolled her eyes at him. "So nosy."

He smiled as he leaned in and kissed her on the lips which earned him a glare from my mom who didn't miss anything. *No kissing at the table Nick!*

I smiled at them. They always made me think that true love existed. Up to a few months ago, I thought I had found my true love but all I got was heartbreak instead. Another one added to the list. I was still in the stage where thinking about it still hurt. Thinking about him and everything that happened still made me want to crawl up in a ball and cry.

I never had luck when it came to relationships.

I fell too hard, too fast…and they ended just as fast.

I was starting to believe that maybe love wasn't for me. Maybe I was meant to be alone.

At least I wouldn't hurt that way.

If you enjoyed this sample, look for
My Possessive Bodyguard
on Amazon.

ACKNOWLEDGEMENTS

I had a lot of fun writing this book, and I have so many people to be thankful for.

Firstly, to all my Wattpad readers, who have supported this book throughout my writing journey. You guys are the best and this wouldn't have happened without your support! I can't thank you guys enough.

My family, to Geetanjali and Santosh Kamat, for being amazing parents and personal cheerleaders and never letting me give up on my dreams.

To my cousin, Disha Bohra for her valuable input throughout the book. Thank you for listening to me ramble about Jasper and Kiara for hours without complaining.

To my other cousin, Shweta Kamat for her tremendous support.

To Sameer Goswami, for assuring me that it's an amazing book. Thanks for having the colossal trust in me ;)

To my gang Noushin Jamil, Akshata Shirodkar, Shazneen Sethna for being such fabulous friends and for always asking me when the book was going to be published. I'm so blessed to have you all.

I'm also thankful to all my other friends for their support.

Special thanks to my editor Precious Vidad, for giving me the guidance and advice that I needed the most for this book. (Her name has nothing to do with Jasper calling Kiara 'Precious', I swear it was a total co-incidence)

I'm grateful to my agent, Michelle Yanez, for everything that she's done for this book.

And last but not the least, Thank you from the bottom of my heart to the entire team of Typewriter Pub for giving me this amazing opportunity and for making my publishing dream come true.

Love,

Kashmira

AUTHOR'S NOTE

Thank you so much for reading *Psycho Billionaire*! I can't express how grateful I am for reading something that was once just a thought inside my head.

I'd love to hear your thoughts on the book. Please leave a review on Amazon or Goodreads because I just love reading your comments and getting to know you!

Can't wait to hear from you!

Kashmira Kamat

ABOUT THE AUTHOR

Kashmira Kamat is also known as KittyKash92 on popular reading apps. She had a passion for writing from a very early age. She writes stories with a kick of dark romance and thriller. Her books have garnered over ten million reads online. Apart from writing and reading, she's a horror enthusiast who loves binging on Anime shows in her free time and is a slave to her six cats.